"YOU HAVEN'T CHANGED A BIT."

Mariah stalked angrily toward the door. "You're just as cold and unfeeling as you were ten years ago."

Jake blocked the doorway. "You really don't know me, do you, *Doctor*?"

Mariah backed up a step as he advanced on her, but it was too late. He cupped her shoulders and brought her against his solid chest, then tipped up her chin to capture her lips. His kiss was deep, unyielding, and oh, so familiar that she ached inside. She remembered his clean, musky scent too well, felt the faint scratch of his beard against her face, and tasted his mouth, hot and sweet, making her yearn for more.

These old feelings couldn't be alive. They had no *right* to be alive.

Jake broke the kiss and stared down at her, his gaze so intense she had to look away. "Still think I'm unfeeling?"

LINDA O'BRIEN

His Forbidden Touch

AVON BOOKS
An Imprint of HarperCollinsPublishers

AVON BOOKS
An Imprint of HarperCollins*Publishers*
10 East 53rd Street
New York, New York 10022-5299

Copyright © 2000 by Linda Tsoutsouris
ISBN: 0-380-81343-2
www.avonromance.com

First Avon Books paperback printing: November 2000

Avon Trademark Reg. U.S. Pat. Off. and in Other Countries, Marca Registrada, Hecho en U.S.A.
HarperCollins® is a trademark of HarperCollins Publishers Inc.

Printed in the U.S.A.

OPM 10 9 8 7 6 5 4 3 2 1

To my husband Jim.
To Jason and Julia,
Cindy, Bonnie, and Barb,
my mother, my extended family,
and, of course, the Avon Ladies,
for all their support and care.

A special thanks to Mr. Terry Edgeworth
at the Victor Oolitic Stone Company,
Bloomington, Indiana,
Rose McIlveen and
the Bloomington *Daily Herald Telephone*,
Maxine Kruse
at the Bedford Indiana Chamber of Commerce,
and Mary Lou Rainford,
for her invaluable information.

Chapter 1

Coffee Creek, Indiana
July, 1898

A powerful explosion shattered the quiet summer afternoon. China cups rattled in Gertrude Johnson's cupboards, her dozing cat scurried for cover, and Mariah Lowe, who was bandaging Gertrude's sprained wrist, jumped.

In the eerie stillness that followed, Mariah held her breath and waited, praying silently, as the mantel clock ticked off the seconds.

The alarm sounded moments later, a high, mournful wail that turned her blood to ice. Quickly, Mariah finished wrapping the woman's wrist and closed her medical bag. "I'll check on you tomorrow, Mrs. Johnson."

Mariah joined other women pouring into the

1

street—wives and mothers—as they hurried toward the limestone quarry.

Explosions were common; the Jefferson quarry was mined with dynamite. The men who set the charges were experts, and serious injuries were rare. Yet two serious accidents had already occurred at the Jefferson in the past month. And now this explosion was much too loud. Something had gone wrong.

Mariah caught snippets of the women's conversation as they hurried along, some talking about her: "Thank the Lord she's come home." "She's a godsend." "A loyal daughter." "Just like her father." "She'll fight for us."

They didn't know how wrong they were.

Since coming home two weeks ago, Mariah had avoided the quarries—and the man who ran them. The thought of having to see Jake Sullivan again was too upsetting.

This time, however, she had no escape.

An image of Jake as he had looked ten years before flashed through her mind. Tall and broad-shouldered, with gleaming black hair and mischievous dark blue eyes, he'd been a bold, handsome daredevil with a passion for adventure. Nothing had been too risky for Jake Sullivan.

How she had loved him! At the age of sixteen, Mariah had never felt such a deep connection with anyone before. He was four years her senior, and she'd trusted him implicitly; she couldn't have imagined life without him. He'd been her confidant, her advocate, and her heart's true love.

He had also been her brother's best friend. And his murderer.

Mariah knew it was inevitable that they would meet again—as a doctor she could hardly avoid it—and the thought of seeing Jake now strained her already taut nerves. She steeled herself. She had work to do; nothing should distract her from that.

Mariah paused at the crest of the hill to survey the mine below. Half of the hillside had been cut away, exposing a sheer wall of limestone that fell twenty-five feet to the immense quarry floor. Wooden derricks jutted skyward at each end of the floor, and the horses that operated them pranced nervously nearby.

In a corner near the wall, three bodies lay amidst a huge rubble of stone. All that made them identifiable was their bloodied, torn clothing. Close by lay others who'd been injured by flying debris.

Mariah started down, a handkerchief pressed to her mouth to keep out the choking dust. Why had she come back? She'd been perfectly content working in the hospital in Chicago. There she'd been anonymous. Here she was Doc Lowe's daughter. Charles Lowe had devoted his life to caring for the stone workers and their families as well as fighting for their causes. Now the people assumed she would do the same.

It wasn't that Mariah didn't love the picturesque town, with its wooded hills, sparkling creek, and underground caverns. It just held too many painful memories for her. She was back for only one reason: her father had requested it on his deathbed. And being the dutiful daughter, she'd come home to step into his practice. It was his bag she carried now—but she was reluctant to take up his sword.

Mariah pushed through the frantic women searching for their loved ones and the men milling around in shock. She knelt beside a young boy of about ten years of age lying close to the dead miners. Blood oozed from his ears and eyes as he moaned in pain. He didn't respond when Mariah spoke to him.

She examined him quickly, then called over her shoulder, "I need bandages and water. Someone fetch a cart! Does anyone know this boy?"

One of the stone workers crouched beside her. "This is Willy Burton, our water boy. His pa is over there." He nodded toward one of the dead men.

A women dropped to the ground on Mariah's left, rocking back and forth as she sobbed hysterically beside another body. "It's my Clyde. I know it is. He was wearing that shirt this morning. Oh, Lordy, he's dead, he's dead!"

As women gathered around to comfort her, one came rushing up with an armload of cloth, followed by a man with a bucket of water.

"Is Willy all right?" the woman asked.

Mariah dipped a piece of cloth in the water. "He has a concussion."

"Poor little tyke," the woman said. "His ma died

two years back, and he ain't got no relatives here. Someone's gonna have to take him in now that his pa's gone."

Mariah had learned not to show emotion when she was doctoring, yet she could feel the sting of tears behind her eyelids as she wiped the blood from the child's face. Willy didn't know it, but he had just become an orphan. "I'll take him to the dispensary. Is someone bringing a cart?"

"Right here, Doc."

As Mariah rose to oversee the boy's move, a full-bearded, red-haired man on her right said in a low, gravelly voice, "This accident shouldn't have happened." He glanced over his shoulder, as though he feared being overheard. "They've been working us too hard to finish the road. It's greed, pure and simple, that caused this blast."

"Dr. Lowe!"

She turned as a foreman ran over. "Doc, one of the dead men is Edmund Watts. He was touring the quarry today as part of his campaign."

Mariah drew in a sharp breath. Edmund Watts was a candidate in the upcoming senate race. His opponent was Senator Hugh Coffman, one of the owners of the quarry.

"What caused the explosion?"

"All I know is that we were on the far end of the floor, loading stone on the wagons," the foreman told her. "Pickner, Burton, and Pullins were over here giving Mr. Watts a demonstration of how to set the charges, and the danged thing just blew.

But they wouldn't have used percussion caps or a detonator for a demonstration, and there's no way it can go off without 'em."

"But it did go off, didn't it?" Mariah snapped.

"Willy was standing by his pa when it happened. He might be able to say what caused it."

Mariah glanced down at the small, pale face. "If he lives."

The bearded man rumbled in her ear, "They're working us too hard, I tell you. You gotta do something, Doc."

Mariah stiffened. How many times had she heard someone tell her father that? And how many times had her father charged off to do battle for them? Had it ever changed anything?

"Inform the sheriff of Mr. Watts's death," she replied crisply. "He'll have to notify the family. Let's get Willy to the dispensary. Has someone sent for the undertaker?"

"Aren't you gonna talk to Jake?" the bearded man rasped.

At the mention of that name, a jolt went through Mariah's body. She hadn't seen Jake yet, but she knew he was there. Every fiber of her being sensed him. "No, I am not going to talk to Jake. I have work to do here."

"Doc, come quick! Sam's asking for you," someone called.

Sam Pullins, an old friend of Mariah's father, lay on the ground, covered by a blood-soaked blanket. Widowed years ago, Sam had worked his entire life as a stone man.

"Mariah," he croaked weakly, reaching out a trembling hand as she knelt beside him.

"Lie still, Sam. I'm going to help you." But when Mariah peeled away the covering and saw the gaping hole in his middle, she knew there was no help for Sam. Quickly, she opened her black bag, searching for the bottle of laudanum to ease his pain.

Sam clutched her sleeve, grimacing. "Mariah, gotta tell you something."

"It's all right, Sam. Take it easy."

"Explosion—" He licked his lips and tried to finish, but his words came out in a weak rasp. Mariah put her ear close to his mouth.

"Not an accident."

She lifted her head to stare at him. But before she could ask questions, his hand fell away and his head rolled to the side. Mariah immediately checked his pulse, then listened for a heartbeat. Slowly, she pulled the blanket over Sam's head. Her own bowed in silent prayer for the lost lives and the grieving families.

But as she prayed, Sam's words echoed in her head: *Not an accident.* Surely she had misunderstood him. The alternative was unthinkable.

Around her she heard the wails of mourning women, the frightened sobs of children, and the low, rumbling voices of concerned men. Then that haunting, gravelly voice whispered, "This shouldn't have happened. You gotta talk to Jake, Doc."

Mariah kept her head bowed and hands folded,

pretending not to hear. She had no desire to see Jake, let alone talk to him.

But when she opened her eyes and raised her head, he was standing not ten yards away, watching her. And despite everything, Mariah was shocked to discover he still had the ability to make her heart skip a beat.

Jake stood with his legs braced and arms folded, as though expecting an attack. He was as ruggedly attractive as she remembered, except for the stony set of his features. Her eyes narrowed, and her insides roiled in fury. That cold, dispassionate expression was the same one he'd worn the day of her brother's funeral—the last time she'd ever seen Jake.

It was that more than anything else that brought her to her feet.

Jake's whole body tensed as Mariah came toward him, her stride brisk and purposeful. He knew she'd come home, but he'd managed to avoid her, knowing she'd just as soon not see him. But the sure sway of her shapely hips was enough to remind him of the spunky, green-eyed, sixteen-year-old girl he'd vowed to marry come hell or high water.

As she drew closer, Jake wasn't surprised to see that she'd only grown more beautiful over time. A wide-brimmed straw hat shaded those eyes he remembered so well and covered her honey-blond hair except for stray wisps that brushed her neck. White powder from the blast dusted her cheeks and straight little nose and smudged her long navy skirt and shoes. She'd rolled back the long sleeves of her shirtwaist, exposing forearms streaked with blood. Her hands were balled into angry fists at her sides.

Jake unconsciously touched the scar across his right cheekbone. How ironic that an accident had brought them together again.

Mariah knew Jake was sizing her up as she walked toward him, but she was too incensed to care. She stopped directly in front of him and tilted her head up. "I'd like to know who's responsible for this explosion."

"I'm the boss, so that would be me."

"And the last two accidents, as well?"

"Me again."

"What do you intend to do about it?"

"Clean up the mess."

Jake had always been a man of few words, but now his clipped answers further infuriated her. "I'd think you'd want to try to find the cause, so you could prevent such tragedies from happening again. Or is finishing this road more important than your workers' lives?"

His eyes glittered dangerously. "You don't know what you're talking about."

"I do know a rash of serious accidents has occurred these past several weeks, and I also know you've been pushing your men to finish the road. It doesn't take a genius to tally those facts and see what the cause is."

"Go do your doctoring, Mariah," Jake ground out, "and let me run the company."

He started to turn away, but Mariah gripped his arm. "You can't just walk away from this tragedy." *As you did the other.* But this was not the time to bring up the past.

Jake froze at her touch and slowly turned his head to give her hand a pointed look. Mariah instantly drew it back. "I want your word you'll ease up on the men," she said.

Jake's hard gaze raked over her. "You're a chip off the old block, aren't you—Doctor?"

He stalked away, leaving Mariah to stare after him in stunned silence.

A chip off the old block.

She was *not* a chip off the old block; she was her own person, and anyone who thought otherwise had a lot to learn about her. Giving herself a hard mental shake, Mariah started back across the stone floor. She had wounded to tend. And she didn't have the time to fight anyone's battles but her own.

"Dan, I want answers," Jake said to his foreman. "Find out where we got the dynamite. Find out who drilled the holes. Find out every damn thing you can and let me know at once."

Jake slammed into his small office at the cutting mill and threw himself into his wooden swivel chair, his mind in turmoil. Mariah wouldn't believe anything but the worst about him, and he had only himself to blame.

Raking his fingers through his hair, he leaned

back and closed his eyes, remembering a time when Mariah, young and unburdened, had given him not only her love, but also her trust. He recalled in vivid detail the exact moment that had changed.

"My brother can't be dead," Mariah had cried hysterically, watching as Ben's lifeless body had been carried away from the cave. Jake had held her against him, letting her sob into his shoulder, wanting desperately to protect her from the pain of her loss. The brother she'd idolized had drowned; a drunken dare had turned tragic. He'd jumped into the underground lake despite Jake's pleas and had died despite Jake's attempts to rescue him.

"It was an accident, a stupid accident," he'd tried to explain, only to have Mariah's head snap up, her gaze angry and agonized.

"What was Ben doing in the water? He couldn't swim."

Jake hadn't wanted to tell her the truth and ruin her sterling image of her brother. All she had now were memories, and Jake wouldn't taint them. Instead, he'd said stoically, "It's my fault. I didn't stop him."

"Why?" she'd wept, tears streaming down her face. "Why didn't you stop him, Jake? You're the oldest. You were responsible."

The accusation in her gaze had cut him to the core, yet he'd merely pressed his lips together in grim determination and hardened his resolve.

Mariah had stared at him for what had seemed an eternity, waiting for an answer that would never come. Then she'd turned and run to catch up with her father and sister following after the wagon. The next time Jake saw her was at the funeral, and the harsh reproach in her eyes had kept him at a distance. The following day he'd left town.

With a heavy sigh, Jake sat up. He'd buried the past a long time ago, and he intended to leave it that way. He had enough to handle in the present. Burton, Pickner, Pullins—honest, hardworking stone men, fathers, husbands—all dead. And Edmund Watts, an innocent bystander, also dead.

Damn his partner! Hugh Coffman had made a campaign promise to have the road finished before the election in November, then had left it to Jake to see that it was done, even though he'd known how impossible that task was. But Coffman had always handled their business operations that way.

Jake clenched his jaw. He had to buy Coffman out. He was fed up with the man's dubious practices. He'd heard rumors that Coffman was considering selling his fifty-one percent, anyway. But even if Jake mortgaged his home, he'd fall far short of the sum he needed. He had to dramatically increase business so that he could add in his percentage of the profits to get enough capital.

Jake's main concern was that Coffman would sell out to their biggest competitor, Bernhardt Limestone, before he had acquired the necessary funds. Bernhardt had the worst safety record of any limestone company in the state. Reinhold

Bernhardt, the company's owner, worked his men until they dropped. Jake couldn't stand the thought of him taking over the C & S.

He had to make the business more profitable, even if it meant pushing his men harder. Instead of waiting for limestone orders to come in, C & S would have to go get them.

Jake wrote a brief message to Coffman and gave it to a clerk to send out. Then he called in his two salesmen and told them to take the next train to New York City, where construction was booming, to drum up new business. Underbid if necessary, Jake told them, but win the jobs at all costs.

He left his office, rolled up his shirtsleeves, and went down to the mill floor to oversee the activity there. Work always took his mind off his worries.

But it didn't take his mind off Mariah.

In his office in Washington, D.C., Senator Hugh Coffman received a telegram from his partner outlining the accident. As he read it, a smile spread across his face. Watts was dead, poor fellow. A laugh burst forth as he crumpled the wire. He'd have to send a congratulatory letter to his accomplice at the quarry for a job well done.

He called for his aide. "Make arrangements for my return to Indiana. Notify the press that I will be going home to console the unfortunate people of Coffee Creek. Oh, and express my deepest sympathy to the Watts family. This is indeed a sad day for us all."

Then he began to compose letters of condolence to the bereaved families. He knew people liked that personal touch, so Hugh gave them plenty of it. After all, he had his good reputation to maintain. And a senate seat to keep.

Hugh Coffman had started the C & S Indiana Limestone Company with the help of Michael Sullivan, a hardworking stone-cutter. Hugh had handled the business end, while Michael had done the physical labor. When Michael passed on, his son Jake had become co-owner.

The business had grown from a two-man operation to a huge company consisting of three quarries and a cutting mill, where large squares of limestone were cut and carved into decorative moldings for buildings. Hugh had grown comfortably wealthy off the limestone, but that hadn't been enough. He wanted power, too. He'd campaigned hard, made lots of promises, and won a senate seat by a narrow margin.

But his popularity had dropped when his constituents figured out that his promises were nothing but hot air. Now he was desperate to win back their favor, and one way was to build a good, solid road all the way to Bloomington, a road desperately needed. A road he had promised to build five years ago.

Now the other party would have to put in a last-minute substitute for the popular Edmund Watts. Hugh chuckled. There was no way in hell they'd find someone to beat him at this late date.

Once he was reelected, Hugh intended to cut

himself loose from the limestone company. Jake had first rights to buy him out, but Hugh knew that Reinhold Bernhardt would readily make an offer at a much greater sum than Jake could afford. Maybe he'd contact Bernhardt now and dangle the bait to see how high he could get him to bid.

At that same moment, a small group of weary, grit-covered stone men gathered around their foreman at the Jefferson quarry.

"We've suffered a terrible loss today," Dan Morgan told them sadly, doffing his hat. "You've put in extra time to get this area cleaned up, and I want you to know you'll be compensated for it. I know Jake appreciates your efforts, too. Now everyone go home and get some rest."

As the group of men broke up, the foreman fell into step beside one of the younger laborers, Luther Sinton. "Son, you shouldn't have been out here working. You need medical attention for that hand."

Luther shrugged sheepishly as he examined the gashes in his palm. He liked it when Dan called him son. Sometimes he even pretended Dan was his father. If his own father had been alive, the men would have been close to the same age. "It doesn't bother me, Dan. I wanted to help."

The foreman put his hand on Luther's shoulder. "Well, then, have your ma take care of it, you hear me?"

Luther grinned. "I'll sure do that. Thanks."

He left Dan, climbed to the top of the hill, and

stood looking down on the site of the explosion. If he squinted real hard, he could still see blood on the limestone walls. Luther inhaled deeply, smelling death in the air. His stomach tensed with excitement.

"Ka-boom," he whispered.

Chapter 2

Mariah removed her wire-rimmed spectacles, rubbed the back of her neck, and rolled her head from side to side. She had been sitting at her father's rolltop desk in the small parlor of her family home ever since dinner, laboriously recording information about the accident victims in her new black notebook and filling out death certificates. Her father's golden retriever, Lazarus, slept beside her chair.

It had been a long, difficult day. In addition to the four men who had died, another had lost an eye in the explosion, and one had been thrown so hard against a pile of stone that his shoulder had been dislocated and several ribs cracked. Five other men had hand and face lacerations from flying debris, and little Willy still lay unconscious from his head injury.

Mariah dipped her pen in the inkwell before filling in the last entry for her father's friend, Sam Pullins.

Poor Sam. He'd worked so hard and had saved so long for his retirement. How unfair to have his life end so tragically. Putting her pen to paper, she wrote, "Cause of death: internal injuries suffered in dynamite explosion."

Mariah reached across the desk to put the pen in its holder but paused as Sam's whispered words ran through her mind. On impulse, she added, "Not an accident," and drew two lines underneath. If Sam was correct, what was the reason for the explosion? Who might benefit from those men's deaths? Was it a coincidence that Edmund Watts had been there?

One name instantly came to mind: Hugh Coffman. Mariah had never cared much for the man, but did she believe he would kill to keep his senate seat?

Mariah shut the notebook and put the pen in its holder. She didn't want to think about Sam's cryptic statement, and it irritated her that she was doing it anyway.

She straightened the papers on her desk and closed the top with a firm thunk. Through the open window beside the desk, she saw the street lamps come on. Crickets chirped in unison in the shrubbery around the house, and a breeze billowed the gauzy curtains, bringing in the scent of pine and freshly cut grass.

Mariah rose and stretched her arms over her

head. The dog rose, too, gazing up at her with his soft, hopeful eyes. "Poor Laz," she crooned, bending to scratch him behind the ears. "You're lost without Papa, aren't you, boy?"

Her father had found the dog in the woods six years earlier, half starved and half frozen. Under the doctor's faithful ministrations the animal had survived and had been appropriately dubbed Lazarus.

Mariah turned to gaze at the big oak bookcase that stood near the desk. Besides a few of her father's favorite novels, a book on anatomy, and a thick, well-worn dictionary, the shelves were filled with his black notebooks. Lined up in chronological order, they ran from the first year of his practice to the year of his death. The last book was only half completed.

The notebooks held a wealth of information about the people of Coffee Creek, but she'd already decided she didn't need her father's records. She would make her own.

"Let's go check on Willy," Mariah told the dog.

A door in the kitchen provided private access to the dispensary built onto the side of the house. Like her home, the dispensary also had an entrance on Center Street, the small town's main thoroughfare. The house and dispensary stood three blocks up from the shops and businesses of the town. A brown shingle above the dispensary door read **DOCTOR** in heavy black letters, with the words CHARLES LOWE in smaller letters underneath.

The house itself was a small, blue clapboard one-story, with a parlor, kitchen, and pantry on one side and two bedrooms on the other. A small herb garden, a doghouse for Lazarus, and an out-house occupied three corners of the narrow, deep backyard. The whitewashed picket fence surrounding the yard had been put there many years ago by Mariah's mother to keep hungry animals out of the garden. At the back of the yard, a creaky wooden gate opened up to a hilly, thickly wooded area.

Entering the dispensary, Mariah stepped into the supply room and scrubbed her hands at the sink with a bar of strong lye soap. Charles Lowe had been an early supporter of Dr. Lister, who believed germs were spread by unwashed hands.

The other end of the narrow storage room had been partitioned off by a curtain to provide a bedroom for the occasional overnight patient with a chair for a visitor. The room was painted a cheerful light green, with a green and yellow plaid curtain framing the window and a colorful rag rug on the wooden floor beside the bed.

At the front of the building, a small waiting area held an oak desk and five ladder-back chairs. A bell over the door announced visitors. The room was simply decorated, with a scuffed hardwood floor and light green walls, broken only by a pair of windows framed by matching green and yellow plaid curtains.

At the far end of the waiting area was the surgery, where patients were examined and treated. It

held a long, metal examining table and two wood-
en chairs. Against one wall stood a locked, glass-
fronted cabinet full of tonics, ointments, lotions,
and bandages.

Mariah stepped through the curtained doorway.
In the narrow bed, the comatose child lay still, his
head swathed in bandages. Annie Applegate sat in
the chair beside him, quietly reading passages
from her worn black Bible. Annie was fifty-five
years old and had run the dispensary for as long as
Mariah could remember. She wasn't trained as a
nurse, but she'd assisted Mariah's father long
enough to know what she was doing.

Annie had faded strawberry-blond hair that she
wore in a loose knot on top of her head, a pink-
cheeked, round face, and lively brown eyes nearly
hidden behind her wire-rimmed spectacles. Short
and plump, she always smelled of cinnamon and
cloves. She lived alone in a small cottage at the
other side of the building and had practically
raised the three Lowe children after their mother
died. To Mariah, she was not only her substitute
mother, but also her friend.

As Mariah approached, Annie closed her Bible
and got to her feet. "No change," she reported,
keeping her voice low.

Holding a lantern above the child's face, Mariah
lifted his eyelids, but there was no response. She
checked his pulse and found it strong. Peeling
back the quilt, she saw that Annie had washed him
and put on fresh clothing. A small, worn satchel
sat beneath the bed.

"A neighbor brought his things," Annie told her.

"It's after eight o'clock. Why don't you go home now?" Mariah suggested quietly. "Laz and I will stay the night."

"No need for that. I've got shifts of women coming in to care for Willy around the clock. First one's due any minute."

"Then I'll make up a strengthening drink for him," Mariah said, referring to her mixture of angelica root, water, brandy, and lemon.

"I've already made a batch, and I'll instruct the women how much to give him."

Mariah put her arm around Annie's shoulders and gave her a hug. "I don't know what I'd do without you."

"You don't have to do without me. I'm just glad you're home, honey."

"Yes, well, the less said about that the better."

Annie pulled back to gaze at her. "I know you're not happy to be here, but just remember one thing: these people need you."

"You know as well as I do that any doctor could have taken over from my father. Come on, Laz. Let's go outside."

"But they trust you," Annie reminded her. "You're a—"

"Don't you dare say 'a chip off the old block,' " Mariah cautioned.

"I was going to say a fine doctor."

Noting Mariah's contrite expression, Annie said, "Honey, I know you well enough to see that something's gnawing at you. Is it because you saw Jake today?"

Mariah sighed resignedly. "There are no secrets in this town."

"Grace Holmes told me you and Jake had words. It must have been painful to see him again."

Mariah didn't want to think about Jake. She couldn't look at him or see the scar on his face without remembering that horrible day her brother died. "I'm going for a walk, Annie. I'll see you in the morning."

Annie followed her to the front door. "Grace also said there was some talk about you knowing something about the cause of the explosion."

"All I know is what the foreman told me."

"Did Sam Pullins tell you something before he died?"

Mariah paused, her hand on the doorknob. She'd had her ear next to Sam's mouth; no one could have overheard. "Why do you ask?"

"Because Grace and others saw him talking to you. He didn't want to talk to anyone but you."

"It was nothing, Annie. Take my word for it. The men have been pushed too hard to finish the road, and that causes accidents."

Mariah walked down Center Street with Lazarus running ahead then circling back, trying to get her to play. The encounter with Jake *had* bothered her, but not for the reason Annie thought.

The powerful attraction she'd felt to Jake ten years ago hadn't gone away. Despite time, despite tragedy, that appeal was still very much alive. The whole time she'd argued with him, she'd been acutely aware of his clean, musky scent, his virility, his handsomeness, and that soul-deep connection they'd once had.

She had to fight the attraction with all she had. She didn't want any emotional connection to Jake Sullivan, now or ever.

And she'd have to see him again tomorrow at the memorial service. Mariah knew just how he'd look, too—remote, uncaring, and bored.

She turned around and started back, whistling for the dog to follow. He came loping up alongside her, his tongue hanging out. Lazarus rarely left her side now; the poor fellow couldn't understand what had happened to his master.

Mariah had a sudden vision of what would happen when Willy learned he had no father. He'd feel just as abandoned as Lazarus.

Damn that explosion! Damn the greed that had caused it! Indignant fury began to build inside Mariah, forcing her to take slow, calming breaths. She had to distance herself from the situation to concentrate on her medical practice. The workers could handle their own problems.

So why hadn't she told Annie what Sam had whispered to her?

Jake was on the floor of the Jefferson quarry at daybreak, inspecting the site of the explosion. He'd had men cleaning up after the accident until sunset the evening before. Today he was going to implement the revised safety rules he'd stayed up half the night composing.

Jake took a hard stance against any worker whose carelessness caused an accident, even a small one. He hated taking risks, which was why he battled his conscience over the rapid completion of the road. The rigorous labor and long hours exhausted his men, but they had miles and miles to go before the roadbed was finished and only two months to do it in.

Ease up on them, Mariah had insisted. Ha! If only he could.

But Mariah didn't know him anymore. Perhaps she never really had. He'd loved her deeply and thought she'd loved him, too, but clearly she'd been too young. It mattered little now. Her bitterness had destroyed any hopes he had of marrying her.

He thought of Willy Burton lying unconscious, with no parents to care for him. Jake knew he should go see him, but he wasn't eager for another confrontation with Mariah.

With her still in his thoughts, Jake walked the two blocks to the cutting mill, where his office was located. He skirted the dust-covered floor of the huge structure and climbed the wooden steps. His office was situated in a corner overlooking the mill, with a window where he could watch the operations below. The mill was still empty at this early hour; it was his favorite time of day.

Jake reached for the coffeepot and found it cold. Obviously his brother hadn't come in yet. He was probably sleeping off a hangover; the accident yesterday would have given him a new excuse to drink. With a muttered curse, Jake lit a fire in the small stove and put on a pot to perk.

When Owen stumbled in an hour later, a sluggish look on his young, wasted face, Jake thrust a cup of coffee into his hands. "Drink up," he barked. "I don't want the men to see you pie-eyed."

"I'm sorry, Jake," Owen mumbled. When he didn't slouch, he was nearly as tall as Jake but had softer features, brown hair, and a body gone to flab.

"There's a memorial service today. You're going to have to go home and put on a suit."

Owen's eyes widened. "You know I can't go to that, Jake. I heard about their terrible injuries. . . ." With a shudder, Owen buried his face in his hands.

Jake couldn't help but pity him. Owen was weak; he'd always been weak. But he'd gotten worse after Ben Lowe had drowned. Owen had been at the cave that day, too, and for a year afterward he'd pulled away from family and friends, spending all his time alone in his room, sleeping and drinking. Gradually he'd rejoined the world, but his drinking hadn't stopped.

Jake had given him an easy job at the quarry, hoping it would keep him busy and away from alcohol. But it hadn't worked. Owen always found an excuse to drink.

"They won't show the bodies," Jake assured him. "This is just a memorial service for the town. The funerals will be held privately."

Owen winced as the hot brew burned his

tongue. Jake watched him for a moment then returned to his work with a frustrated shake of his head.

A tent had been erected in the churchyard cemetery to shield the mourners from the sun. The minister waited patiently at the front while a large group of townspeople gathered on the left. Jake's family was on the right with Hugh Coffman and his wife Bess, who'd returned that day for the service. Jake noticed how neatly the townsfolk had separated themselves from the two partners and their families.

He stood beside Owen, who still reeked of whiskey and looked as though he'd slept in his suit. Their nineteen-year-old sister, Emeline, stood next to Owen, while her myopic fiancé, Percival Whiteside, shifted from foot to foot behind her, like an eager puppy waiting to be scratched behind the ears.

Jake almost felt sorry for Percy. Emeline was a beauty but so spoiled it took the patience of Job to live with her. Vivid blue eyes, dimpled, cherubic cheeks, and auburn curls drew men like flies, but few could handle her. She'd been spoiled by their parents, and at their death, Jake had continued supporting her in the lifestyle to which she had grown accustomed.

Jake tried to shrug off his concern. At the advanced age of thirty-five, sixteen years older than Emeline, Percy should know what he was getting himself into.

As the minister spoke, Jake covertly scanned the crowd, stopping suddenly when he came to Mariah. In a dark gray dress with short, leg-of-mutton sleeves and a white collar, Mariah was a study of intriguing curves. Wisps of dark blond hair showed beneath her black hat, and even at that distance he could make out her arresting green eyes. She was alone save for the dog sitting at her feet.

Jake couldn't take his eyes off her. He knew there was no future with Mariah, yet that didn't prevent him from wanting her. His blood thickened with desire as he recalled what it had felt like to hold her in his arms, to feel that lithe, supple body against his.

Suddenly, as though she felt his perusal, Mariah glanced his way. As their gazes met, all sounds seemed to cease—the minister's preaching, the birds chirping, the flies buzzing—and everyone else faded away. Only he and Mariah existed.

Mariah instantly looked away, pink coloring her cheeks. She sat stiffly in her seat, her features tense, as though she was affronted by his attention.

Jake understood Mariah's feelings and accepted her hatred. But life moved on: he'd learned how to tuck his guilt deep inside, where it couldn't hurt him.

Mariah was still hurting though. She'd have to find a way to bury those bitter feelings, or they would bury her.

Chapter 3

❧

Mariah kept her eyes focused on the minister, aware that Jake was watching her. She tried to listen to the soothing words without remembering her brother's funeral, but it was impossible.

When the service was over, Senator Coffman begin to work the crowd, shaking hands and soliciting votes as though he were at a campaign rally. His silver hair and mustache were perfectly groomed, his skin pink and smooth, belying his fifty-odd years. His expensive suit and shoes looked out of place among the stone men, as did his wife, who remained aloof beneath the extra-wide brim of her black hat.

Mariah heard Jake's voice and turned to see him speaking to Abner Pickens's widow and children. His stilted words sounded insincere, and his emotionless expression irritated her. Didn't he feel anything?

After conveying her condolences to the families, Mariah called to the dog and headed for home. A dinner was being held at the church for the mourners, but Mariah didn't have time to attend. She cut across the churchyard to the woods that encircled the town, taking a shortcut along Coffee Creek.

As Lazarus splashed along the water's edge, Mariah let her thoughts return to happier times. She and Jake had often walked that path to the creek. He'd given Mariah her first kiss there, standing barefooted in the ankle-deep water.

She smiled wistfully, remembering how she'd stood on tiptoe, the hem of her skirt tucked in her waistband, her arms over his shoulders, her fingers entwined in his hair, pressing her lips to his in a very inexperienced fashion.

"Tilt your head," he'd told her. "Now close your eyes and don't clamp your lips so tightly together. You look like a prune." And then he'd kissed her slowly, sensually, until she'd grown as limp as a wet noodle.

"Kiss me again!" she'd ordered

"That's enough for your first time."

"You beast!"

"Brat!" Laughing, he'd swept her into his arms and swung her around, splashing the cool water with his bare feet. "I have to leave you hungering for more."

But two months later, her brother was dead, and Jake was no longer welcome in her life. For a long time afterward Mariah had been inconsolable, feeling as though her heart had been ripped from her chest. She'd lost two people she loved. She'd been betrayed by her own naivete. How could she have loved Jake and not understood his true character?

Mariah shook those unhappy memories from her thoughts, determined not to let them haunt her. "Come on, Laz," she called, and, lifting her skirts, began to run. The dog joined in the romp, and soon Mariah was laughing so hard she had to stop to catch her breath. How good it felt to smile again.

Back home, Mariah faced the unpleasant task of visiting Joe Krall, the man who had lost an eye in the explosion. She picked up her medical bag and walked to his house, Lazarus tagging along behind. Joe's wife, Myrtle, met Mariah at the door and took her to the bedroom. Laz posted himself outside the door.

"How are you, Mr. Krall?" Mariah asked, placing her bag on the bed.

Joe watched her with one bloodshot eye. "I'm all right," he answered stoically.

Mariah put on her spectacles and unwrapped the gauze around his face to check the damage. He would have to wear an eye patch for the rest of his life.

Mariah's outrage once again reared its head, but she immediately tamped it down.

"Have you talked to Jake about the explosion?" Myrtle asked.

"Yes, I did, not that it did any good," Mariah

replied as she closed her bag. She couldn't help but see the disappointment on the woman's face.

When she returned to the dispensary, Annie was sitting on the stoop having a cup of tea.

"How's Willy?" Mariah asked.

"No better," Annie rose and opened the door for her. "You have two patients in the waiting room."

"Would you tell them I'll be right there?"

Mariah washed her hands, put on her long white apron, and stopped to check Willy's vital signs before seeing her first patient.

June Roberts sat on the end of the table with her shoulders slumped forward, her skin pale, and her eyes lifeless. "I'm just so run down, Doc. I don't have any energy."

Suspecting the woman was simply overworked from caring for eight children, Mariah felt the glands in her neck, checked her eyes, took her pulse, and listened to her heart. Everything seemed fine. "How are your children?"

"Ornery as ever."

"Your husband?"

"Working too hard. He's going to drop dead one of these days, and do you think anyone cares?"

Mariah didn't follow up on that subject, but the woman persisted anyway. "Your father cared. He was a good man, Mariah. He got the stone men a raise and made sure they got paid when they were laid up from an accident. But that last one, that explosion, it shouldn't have happened. Mr. Roberts told me the dynamite shouldn't have had caps. Why would those men have used caps?"

"Could you be with child, Mrs. Roberts?" Mariah asked, pressing on her abdomen.

"Huh-uh. What do you think caused that blast, Doc?"

"I don't know," Mariah replied, helping her patient down from the table. "What do you think?"

"I think someone fussed with the dynamite."

Mariah turned to stare at her. "Who—and why?"

"The why is the easy part. For the who, I guess you'd have to ask yourself which of those men had an enemy that wanted him out of the way. I know those stone men. They were all decent men."

It seemed Mariah wasn't the only one who suspected a connection between the explosion and Candidate Watts. She was tempted to mention her own suspicions, but without proof of the senator's involvement, she couldn't make any accusations.

"Here's what I want you to do, Mrs. Roberts: get some meat in your diet—especially liver—and eggs, nuts, and beans. I believe your problem is that your blood is iron-poor."

"Meat's expensive. Can't I just take some medicine? I saw an advertisement in the newspaper for Dr. Powers' Essence of Life and Invigorating Elixir. Couldn't I try that?"

"That's sheer quackery, Mrs. Roberts. Try this diet for a week and let me know if you feel better."

Mariah saw three other female patients that afternoon. All of them complained about the explosion; all of them wanted her to do something about it. And Mariah knew they wouldn't be the last.

There was only one way to put a stop to it: she'd have to see Jake again.

Luther Sinton stepped quietly across the threshold of the tiny house where he lived with his mother, Dolly, hoping she wouldn't hear him come in.

"Who's there? Is that you, Luther?" a harsh, raspy voice called out.

"Sure it is, Mama," Luther replied with forced cheer. "I brought you a plate of food from the memorial service dinner. Let me get a spoon for you, and I'll be right there."

"It's about time you got home," she snapped. "The dinner ended hours ago. I could have starved to death in the meantime, not that you'd care."

In the kitchen, Luther picked through a bowl of utensils, looking for a clean spoon. He found one and stuck it on the plate, then carried it to his mother's room.

The three-room house was cramped and meagerly furnished, the furniture old and worn. His mother complained about the house constantly, but Luther had always been comfortable there, even though he slept on a makeshift bed in the pantry. His mother occupied the only bedroom.

"Here you are, Mama."

Dolly Sinton sat propped against pillows in her

bed, her graying brown hair pulled in a tight bun on the top of her head, causing her ears to stick out like handles on an urn. Luther remembered a time when she'd been considered a pretty woman. But now her narrow, thin-lipped face wore a perpetual scowl that had made deep groves between nose and chin and had put permanent pucker lines around her mouth. Her eyes were never more than thin, angry slits.

Luther tried hard to be a good son, but his mother was a difficult woman to please. As she always reminded him, she'd given up the best years of her life to raise him, so he owed it to her to take care of her.

"Mrs. Bailey stopped by after the service," his mother said, spooning a mound of potatoes into her mouth. "She says there's talk about the blast being jimmied. She says it wasn't just bad luck that put Mr. Watts there."

Luther's heart began to race. "You told her she was wrong, didn't you?"

"I didn't tell her nothin'."

"What I want to know," Luther said, pacing nervously from the door to the bed, "is where she heard that baloney."

Dolly stopped eating to glare at him. "Who cares where she heard it? Would you stand still? You're giving me a headache."

"Well, is it the women who are talking? Or is it the sheriff, or who?"

Dolly shoved the plate away. "Oh, for heaven's

sake, Luther. You drive a body to the grave, you know that? Take away this food. You've made me lose my appetite."

"Mrs. Bailey's talking nonsense, that's what she's doing," Luther said, scooping up her nearly empty plate. "It was an accident. There's nothing that can prove otherwise."

Dolly threw him a disgruntled frown. "Well, Mrs. Bailey told me that Sam Pullins knew something about the blast and told it to Doc Lowe's daughter just before he died. The word is that Mariah Lowe's got her suspicions. You mark my words, Luther. If she's anything at all like her daddy, she'll get to the bottom of it."

"There's nothing to get to the bottom of," Luther insisted. "I've got to get back to the quarry, Mama. The senator's going to be there." He leaned down to give her a peck on the cheek, only to have her jerk her head away. But that was all right. He knew she loved him; she just didn't know how to show it.

Luther took the plate back to the kitchen and placed it on the stack of dishes. Let Mariah Lowe have her suspicions. She couldn't hurt him.

But what about the senator? If that gossip spread, people might think he had something to do with the explosion and not vote for him. If he lost the election, he'd be devastated. Luther couldn't let that happen; he owed the man too much.

Luther dug in his pocket for his switchblade, letting the soothing feel of cold metal calm his nerves and clear his mind.

Mariah would have to be watched. If she got nosy, it would be very bad for her indeed.

Chapter 4

～◯◯～

Jake washed his hands and arms at the pump outside the mill and splashed water onto his face, relieved that the day was over. He'd had the difficult task of giving tough talks to men still mourning the death of their coworkers, men who were already tired of working twelve- and thirteen-hour days. He wasn't at all pleased when he walked into his office and found his partner sitting in his chair, the account ledgers open on the desk before him.

Coffman looked up and smiled. "Looks like business is doing well, Jake."

"It is."

"I haven't been out to see how the road is coming, but I trust it will be done by September first."

Jake stopped short. "That's less than a month away. You told me November first."

"The thing is, Jake," Coffman said, with a concil-iatory smile, "I want to have a ribbon cutting cere-mony and let the people enjoy the road before the election."

"I can't get the road finished that quickly."

"Jake, do you know how important this senate seat is? It's the only thing that matters to me. Your father understood that." Coffman paused, his eyes growing misty. "I don't know what I'll do if I lose this election. I need your help, Jake. Don't let me down."

For a moment Jake debated telling his partner to go to hell. Finally, his mouth in a hard line, he strode to the door and opened it, saying over his shoulder, "It'll be done—but you'll have to settle for October first."

From the window, Coffman watched Jake descend to the mill floor. "Not a bad performance, if I do say so myself." He shut the office door and started down the stairs. What he needed now was a good meal at the hotel restaurant.

On the mill floor, Coffman stopped to shake hands with the men, calling those he remembered by name. "Hello, Jeb. Good to see you. How are you, Frank? Tragic about that accident, Robert. What a waste of good lives."

"Senator Coffman, can I get you anything to drink?" the foreman offered.

"I'd appreciate it, thanks, Dan. Got any coffee?"

A voice from behind said, "I'd be pleased to get it for you, Senator."

Coffman swung around and smiled at the

earnest-faced young man standing before him, shyly holding his cap against his chest. "Why, hello, Luther. Good to see you again, boy."

"Thank you, Senator."

Hugh put his arm around Luther's thin shoulders. "I knew this boy's daddy," he told the foreman. "Sinton was one of my first employees. The best charge man of his day, wasn't he, son?"

"Yes, sir, he sure was."

"I want to hear how your mama's doing, Luther. Say, Dan, can you spare Luther for a few moments? Perhaps he'd be good enough to get my coffee for me."

"Sure, Senator. Take your time."

Coffman followed Luther to a small room built into one corner of the mill. The room held a cast-iron stove, shelves filled with tins of coffee and sugar, a small wooden table, and several chairs.

Luther poured coffee from a tin pot and handed the senator a mug.

"Is everything going all right?" Coffman asked quietly.

Nervously, Luther rubbed a hand over his hair. "There's a rumor going around that someone wanted Watts out of the way."

"That was bound to happen. You leave that pesky rumor to me, Luther. I know how to sway public opinion—it's what I do best. You're sure there's no trail leading to me?"

"I know what I'm doing." Luther never doubted his abilities. He was smart; he knew how the charge men set their explosives.

Coffman drained his mug. "You know what's riding on this, Luther. Don't let me down."

Luther's grin dissolved. Let him down? How could Coffman even think such a thing? He worshiped the senator. "I wouldn't do that," he answered. "You know I wouldn't. Not after what you did for me."

"That's what I like to hear," Coffman said, handing him the mug. "Don't forget to tell your mama that Hugh was asking about her."

The sun was setting as Luther walked through town, heading for home. The only person about at that time of the day was a man named Oscar Drubb, who shuffled along, head down, as though the sidewalk's wooden planks held some fascination for him.

Luther considered Oscar the town fool. He had the brains of a child—a very slow child at that—and the annoying habit of always being underfoot, mumbling and drooling and smiling inanely. With his brown hair jutting out at odd angles, a flat nose, and missing teeth, Oscar even looked like a fool.

As Oscar approached, Luther glanced around to make sure they were alone, then he snapped, "Mad dog," and barked sharply.

Oscar's head jerked up, and his eyes grew wide. He drew back with a strangled gasp, as though Luther had raised a hand to him. Whirling around, Oscar loped away, muttering unintelligibly in a high-pitched whine.

Luther chuckled. He felt no pity for Oscar or

anyone else, for that matter. Why should he have any concern for others when he'd never had an easy road in life himself? As far as he was concerned, pity was wasted energy.

Although Mariah dreaded her forthcoming meeting with Jake, she kept a positive frame of mind as she made her house calls the next morning. Helping others always took her mind off her own problems and buoyed her spirits.

But as she and Lazarus trekked the half-mile from town to the stone mill, her optimism disappeared and she braced herself for the confrontation. It was something that had to be done, if for no other reason than to tell people she'd done all she could.

Standing in the huge open doorway, Mariah glanced around the immense mill, squinting through the haze of dust. Everywhere she looked, there were stacks of limestone blocks, some waiting to be cut, others in the process of being carved. Noisy planers, gang saws, and lathes spewed more dust into air that smelled of wet stone.

She finally saw Jake crouched beside an intricately carved column of limestone, inspecting it. The sleeves of his white shirt had been rolled up, exposing muscular, tanned arms. Slim, brown canvas pants enclosed his long legs, and brown leather boots covered with limestone dust protected his feet.

For an instant, the years dropped away; she was sixteen again and madly in love with this daring young rogue who had captured her heart.

Hey, green eyes, come for a ride with me. I have a surprise for you.

Those words, spoken a decade ago, triggered the memory of a morning she'd never forget.

Jake had appeared at her doorstep on horseback, with the mischievous gleam in his eyes that always signaled adventure.

She'd taken his hand and let him hoist her onto his lap. With his arms securely encircling her, they'd galloped away over hills, through a meadow, and into the woods, finally stopping near the creek. He'd swung down, then lifted her off the saddle and pulled her into his arms to kiss her.

"Was that the surprise?" she'd asked breathlessly.

At that, he'd dropped down on his knee and gazed up at her with such a serious expression that she had been startled. "I'd like you to marry me, Mariah. I know you're too young now. But someday, when you're ready to settle down, I want you to be my wife. I want to take care of you forever."

She'd gazed down into those intense blue eyes and known she and Jake were destined to be together. "Yes," she cried, flinging her arms around his neck. "Oh, yes, Jake. I'll marry you."

"I love you, Mariah."

She'd thought her heart would burst from happiness. Surely she had to be the luckiest girl alive.

She had a beau who adored her and who would never let her down.

How could she have known he wasn't the person he seemed?

Mariah took a slow breath and let it out, willing those painful memories away. She shouldn't lose sight of her reason for coming.

As Mariah started across the mill, someone must have told Jake she was there, for he suddenly looked around and got to his feet. As he strode to meet her, his blue gaze locked with hers, sending her heart into a tailspin that instantly slowed when she saw the forbidding look on his face.

Mariah squared her shoulders. "I'd like to speak to you," she said crisply.

He pointed toward a set of wooden steps. "My office is up there."

As Mariah gathered her skirt and started up the stairs, she saw Jake glance back at his men, who had all stopped to watch. At his scowl, they resumed their work.

Mariah allowed Jake to open the door for her, then she stepped into his office, surprised by its austerity. Other than a scarred pine desk, there was only a chair, a simple table with a coffeepot and cup on it, and a pine cabinet. The aroma of stale coffee and stone dust filled the air. Mariah turned to face Jake as he closed the door and leaned against it.

"Would you like to sit?" he asked, indicating his chair.

"Thank you, but I'd rather stand."

Jake shrugged. "What are you going to lecture me about today?"

Ignoring his sarcasm, Mariah stated matter-of-factly, "You need to investigate the explosion."

"The site has been cleaned. There's nothing to investigate."

"Apparently you haven't heard the rumor that someone tampered with the dynamite."

"No one would tamper with the dynamite, Mariah. Those men look out for each other."

"What if someone wanted Edmund Watts out of the way?"

Jake eyed her skeptically. "Is that part of the rumor, or is that your conjecture?"

"It would certainly be one way to beat an opponent, wouldn't it?"

Jake pushed away from the door and walked over to his desk, shaking his head as though her idea was absurd. "You think Hugh Coffman would commit murder to keep his seat?"

"Who else would have benefitted from Watts's death?"

He perched on a corner of the desk. "If you're hunting for suspects, then you'd better include me."

"You?" Mariah asked in surprise. "What would you have to gain?"

"If my partner keeps his senate seat, he stays in Washington and out of my hair. Or have you stopped believing I'm capable of murder?"

An angry pulse throbbed in Mariah's neck. But before she could reply, he said, "I don't think you realize, Mariah, that if your hunch about the explosion is correct, you're putting yourself in danger by investigating it."

"What do you mean?"

"If you believe someone purposely killed those men, then we have a murderer in town—a person who wouldn't want you stirring up trouble." He leaned closer, his eyes locking with hers. "Who do you think it could be, Mariah?"

For a moment, all she could do was stare at him—until she realized he was only trying to frighten her. "I knew I shouldn't have come here. It's useless to talk to you."

"Then why did you come?"

To satisfy a group of complaining women, Mariah wanted to answer. But was that the only reason? Or had she been lured by that strong attraction between them? "It doesn't matter why. Would you just consider what I said?"

"About the explosion being jimmied? No."

Somehow she had to convince him her idea was sound. "Explain something to me, if you will," she said. "How is dynamite used?"

Jake gave an impatient sigh. "Holes are drilled in the stone. Sticks of dynamite are placed in them. The fuse is lit. It blows up."

"But it can't blow up unless there are percussion caps on the dynamite, is that right?"

"Essentially."

"So why did it?"

"Accidents happen, Mariah. Sometimes we don't know why. Use your head. Which one of my men would deliberately rig the dynamite, knowing he or his friends would be killed?"

For that Mariah had no answer. Jake seemed satisfied that the explosion was an accident, and surely he knew more about dynamite than she did. She was wasting her time trying to convince him, anyway. "Then let me restate my original request: ease up on the men so there won't be so many accidents."

"And let me restate mine: go do your doctoring and let me run the company."

Mariah fumed at his callous reply. "You haven't changed a bit," she muttered angrily, stalking toward the door. "You're just as cold and unfeeling as you were ten years ago."

Jake lunged forward, blocking the doorway. "You really don't know me, do you, *Doctor?*"

Mariah backed up a step as he advanced on her, but it wasn't far enough. He cupped her shoulders and brought her against his solid chest, then tipped up her chin, holding it steady as he captured her lips with his own. His kiss was intense, unyielding, and oh, so familiar that she ached inside. She inhaled his clean, musky scent, a scent she remembered too well; she felt the faint scratch of his beard against her face; and she tasted his mouth, hot and sweet, making her yearn for more.

As his kiss deepened, Mariah's head began to swim. Those old feelings couldn't be alive. They had no right to be alive. They should be dead, just like her brother.

Jake broke the kiss and stared down at her, his gaze so intense she had to look away. "Still think I'm unfeeling?"

Mariah turned her back on him and walked out.

Jake watched her walk down the stairs and through the mill, her head erect, her back straight and proud, her bearing reminding him so much of her father. What Mariah had claimed just didn't make sense. He knew his men. There wasn't one among them who would deliberately rig a blast to take a life—anyone's life. When the sheriff's report came in, Jake was confident that it would prove him correct.

But something else bothered him: if Mariah knew it was useless to talk to him, why had she come? She'd said it didn't matter, but suddenly it did. Very much.

Jake poured himself a cup of stale coffee and drank it down. He realized he hadn't avoided Mariah to spare her from seeing him; he'd avoided her to keep from reawakening his own futile desire. He'd actually found himself hoping she would faint so he could hold her in his arms again.

You haven't changed a bit, she'd told him.

She was right about that: he still wanted her.

Mariah hurried across the floor of the cutting mill, her emotions in a whirl. His kiss had proven that her attraction to Jake was not only alive, but seemed stronger than her determination to fight it. He had only to gaze at her to make her heart thump wildly.

Was it possible Jake could have set up the explosion? Had he warned her about possible danger to keep her from investigating? Mariah pursed her lips, remembering Jake's pointed question: *Have you stopped believing I'm capable of murder?*

She had nothing to prove his innocence. But deep down, Mariah knew that Jake could not have murdered those workers. That realization, along with her own feelings for him, surprised—and confused—her.

Luther jumped down from the stool in the storage room beneath Jake's office. By standing close to the ceiling, he could hear every word said in the room above.

Just as his mother had warned him, Mariah Lowe had suspicions about the blast. But suspicions weren't dangerous; evidence was. And there was no evidence. Still, the senator didn't want *any* attention given to the matter.

"Need any help, Luther?" one of the workers called, poking his head into the room.

Luther pretended to search the shelves. "I found it," he said, pulling out a freshly sharpened chisel. "Thanks, anyway."

Luther walked out of the room and deliberately crossed Mariah's path. "Beg pardon, Doc," he said, quickly doffing his cap as he stepped out of her way.

Mariah barely glanced at him as she nodded and hurried on. Luther knew she was pretending not to know him. She'd been a year ahead of him in school, one of those prissy, nose-in-the-book types that didn't have time for the likes of him. But she knew him, all right.

Luther's eyes narrowed as he ran his finger over the sharp edge of the chisel. He had to make sure Mariah curbed that nosy tendency of hers.

Chapter 5

⌒⌒◯◯⌒⌒

As Mariah crossed the street toward the dispensary, she saw a young farmer waiting on the stoop, twisting his hat in his strong brown hands. When he spotted Mariah, he jumped up. "Doc, my Sue's time has come."

"I'll get my bag and ride with you."

Mariah hurried inside to fetch her medical equipment and found Gertrude Johnson in the waiting room. "You didn't come back to check my wrist yesterday, Mariah," she scolded.

Gertrude had been the town schoolteacher for many years. Now retired, she had devoted herself to charity work. Kind-hearted and caring, she had nevertheless retained her strict, no-nonsense ways.

"I'm sorry, Mrs. Johnson. I don't have time to look at it right now, either—there's a baby on its way—but I'll come see you this afternoon."

Annie came out of the surgery carrying Mariah's black bag. "Here you go, Doctor," she said, her pride in Mariah radiating from her eyes.

"Thanks, Annie." Mariah started outside, then noticed that Lazarus was following her. "Stay, Laz," she ordered. She stepped out once again, only to find the dog on her heels. She planted her hands on her hips and scowled at him. "You have to stay!"

Lazarus sat on his haunches, tilted his head, and gave her a mournful stare. Mariah softened. "All right, come with me. But you'll have to wait outside the house."

She hurried across the street and climbed up onto the bench seat of Ned Grady's buckboard. She needed to keep her mind off her encounter with Jake. Too many dangerous feelings had surfaced.

Three hours later, Mariah handed the young farmer his firstborn child, a son, bundled in a clean blanket. It wasn't Mariah's first delivery, but it was the first time she'd been the only doctor present. She left the farm beaming.

After checking on Gertrude Johnson's sprained wrist, Mariah returned to the dispensary, still in a cheerful mood. With tail wagging, Lazarus ran up to Annie, who was seated at the desk, for a scratch behind the ears.

"The Gradys have a baby boy," Mariah announced proudly.

"Honey, that's wonderful news! Next time you

go out there, you'll have to take them one of my pecan pies."

"How's Willy?" Mariah asked, starting for the back room.

"He's the same. But Mariah, wait. There's something you should know first."

Mariah turned to give her a puzzled look.

"Jake is here. He came to see Willy."

Mariah's good mood vanished. She wasn't ready to see Jake again. Bracing herself, she donned her apron, then parted the curtain and stepped into the room. But as soon as she saw him, her heart did a flip, as though it had a mind of its own.

Jake had been sitting in the chair beside the boy's bed, and he instantly got to his feet. "Hello, Mariah."

"I'm surprised to see you here," she said coolly, as she perched on the edge of the bed.

He studied her as she reached over to smooth back Willy's unruly brown hair. The long white apron she wore over her prim navy dress and the traditional pompadour style of her hair gave Mariah a professional air. Yet the silken blond wisps that had escaped their pins to curl at her nape and temples reminded him of the sensual woman beneath, the woman he had tasted that morning—and wanted more of.

"How's he doing?" Jake asked, nodding at the child.

"He still hasn't regained consciousness."

Jake watched as Mariah took Willy's pulse and

checked his eyes. A strange warmth spread in his gut as she bent over the boy and pressed a light kiss on his forehead. "You'll be fine, won't you, Willy?" she murmured soothingly.

"Any idea when he'll come out of it?"

Mariah motioned for him to follow her outside the curtain. "I hope in another day or two," she said in a whisper. "The longer it goes on, the more there is to worry about."

"What kind of worries?"

"Damage to the brain."

Frowning, Jake stuck his hands in his pockets. "Are there any treatments? Could they do better for him in Bloomington?"

"I wish there *was* something more that could be done," Mariah said as she washed her hands. "For now, we'll have to wait and see. But I'm optimistic that he'll come out of it."

She took the towel from the ring and turned to look at him, her breath catching at the sight of his handsome face. Her gaze dropped to his mouth, and her animosity vanished as she recalled the feel of those lips on hers.

For a reason Mariah couldn't explain, she suddenly found herself asking, "Would you like to come into the kitchen and have some tea? I was just about to make a pot."

Jake stood just inside the kitchen doorway, arms folded, watching, as Mariah put a kettle of water on the stove to heat. He hadn't intended to follow her, and now he knew why. It was all he could do to keep from taking her in his arms and crushing her lips with another hungry kiss, from carrying her off to the bedroom and making love to her. Sweet blazes, how he wanted her.

Jake brooded silently as she measured out the sweet-smelling tea leaves, put them in a pot, opened a cabinet, and removed two cups—actions so domestic that he knotted up inside. If not for that day ten years ago, Mariah would be making tea in *their* kitchen, using *their* cups.

Why had she asked him to come? Had his kiss rekindled something in her? It suddenly seemed important that he know.

"Mariah," he said huskily, "I have to know—"

Something in his voice must have alerted her. She turned suddenly and gazed at him with wary green eyes.

Jake broke off, swallowing hard. A clock in a distant room ticked softly, the only sound other than the wild thumping of his heart. *Ask her.*

He unfolded his arms and straightened. "I have to know—"

As though she sensed what he was thinking, Mariah stammered, "I-I don't like to talk too much in front of Willy. I'm always concerned he can hear what's being said."

Jake's heart slowed to a heavy thud. Why had he allowed himself such ridiculous hopes? She'd only asked him into the kitchen to discuss Willy. To cover his disappointment, he walked to the door and peered out. "What will happen to Willy when he recovers?"

"Someone will have to take him in. I was told he has relatives, but I wouldn't have any idea how to find them."

"I'll find them," he said quietly, turning to face her. At least it was something he could do to help.

Mariah's brows rose. "That's very generous of you."

For a moment she continued to gaze at him, as though trying to figure him out, then she turned to the steaming kettle. "You don't use sugar, do you?"

"No."

Jake took the cup and drank the tea as quickly as possible, wanting to escape the torment of being near her. "I have to get back," he said, handing her the cup. "Thanks for your hospitality." He opened the door and walked out.

"Jake," Mariah called, following him outside into the bright sunshine. "Thank you for coming to see Willy."

He didn't look back at her. He couldn't.

Mariah made a cup of tea for Annie and took it to her, still mulling over Jake's visit.

"Did you and Jake get along all right?" Annie asked, as if they were two battling children.

Mariah paused, remembering the way Jake had gazed at her so intensely. He'd tried to ask her a question, but she'd sidetracked him, fearing what he'd wanted to know. Now she had to ask herself what it was she'd suspected he was going to ask her. And why had she been afraid to hear it?

"We got along fine," she told Annie, as she checked the supplies in her medical bag, "although I have to admit I was surprised he thought of the child."

"I imagine you were."

"What does that mean?" Mariah asked.

"You won't like my answer."

"Then don't tell me. I'll be back after I see some patients." With Lazarus leading the way, Mariah left before Annie could say more.

Her first call that afternoon was on Joe Krall. As before, Myrtle met her at the door and took her to the bedroom.

"How are you, Mr. Krall?" Mariah asked, placing her bag on the bed.

"Not too bad."

Putting on her spectacles, Mariah removed the bandage around his head and inspected the eye socket. "Looks like it's healing just fine."

Myrtle stood at the foot of the bed, nervously plucking her apron. "Ask Joe about the blast, Doc."

"Myrtle, hush!" Joe said irritably.

"Well, it ain't right to keep it quiet. Doc, Joe says that dynamite had to have been fiddled with."

Mariah studied him closely. "Why do you think that?"

"I don't want to get nobody in trouble," he said, clamping his lips together.

"Well, I ain't afeared," Myrtle said, though her nervous gestures indicated otherwise. "Go talk to one of the charge men, Doc. You'll understand then."

"Should I, Mr. Krall?"

He looked away. "I can't stop you."

"What will this man be able to tell me?" Mariah persisted.

His wife answered for him. "He'll tell you how it ain't possible for the dynamite to go off with no cap."

"Are you sure there wasn't a cap on the dynamite, Joe?"

"Willy'd know," Myrtle insisted. "He was standin' near his pa afore the blast."

Mariah replaced Joe's bandages in silence. It was becoming apparent that talk about the explosion wasn't going to go away until everyone was satisfied it had indeed been an accident.

Myrtle walked her to the door, where Lazarus waited patiently on their stoop. "You'll go talk to one of the charge men, won't you, Doc?"

"To be honest, Mrs. Krall, I don't see what good it would do."

"At least you'd know what you were talkin' 'bout next time you met with Jake."

"Why don't the men talk to Jake themselves?"

The woman's eyes bulged as if Mariah had just asked her to kiss a frog. "Why, they couldn't do that. It would be disrespectful. He's their boss, after all. You've got to do it for them. Please, Doc!"

There was no arguing her logic. "I'll talk to one of the charge men."

*   *   *

Early the next morning, Mariah started down the incline into the Jefferson quarry. Below her, groups of men shoveled loose stone into wagons to be hauled to the surface by teams of oxen. Spotting the foreman who had talked to her after the explosion, Mariah set off in his direction. The men around him stopped working as she approached.

"Good morning," she said to the foreman, with a smile.

"Morning, Doc."

"Is your charge man here?"

The foreman pointed to a small group of men drilling holes in a stone ledge. "That'd be Earl. He's the one with the red kerchief around his neck."

Mariah felt their curious stares as she walked across the quarry floor. "Earl?"

The man swung around, staring at her warily. "Yes, ma'am?"

"I'd like a word with you, if I may."

Looking ill at ease, he doffed his battered hat and glanced around at the other men before following her a few feet away.

Mariah launched right into it. "Do you know if the sticks of dynamite used the day of the accident had caps?"

"Can't rightly say, ma'am. I wasn't there."

"Should they have had caps?"

"No, ma'am, they shouldn't have. It was only a demonstration."

"Could the charge man have made a mistake?"

"No, ma'am!" Earl exclaimed. "Abner was the

best charge man in the area. He knew his business."

"Then what could have caused the explosion? Could someone have tampered with the dynamite?"

Earl cleared his throat and again glanced at his fellow workers, as though he hoped someone would help him out. "I'm sorry, ma'am. I just don't know."

Mariah wasn't convinced he was telling the truth. But before she could ask more, she saw his gaze shift to something behind her. Instantly he clapped his hat on his head and returned to his work.

Mariah swung around and scowled frostily as Jake strode closer. She'd never get the men to talk with their boss around. She started toward him, wanting to be well out of earshot, and met him in the middle of the quarry floor.

"What are you doing out here?" he asked.

"Talking to your charge man."

Jake took her arm to lead her away. "I don't want you here. It's too dangerous."

"I'm being careful," Mariah retorted, pulling her arm out of his grasp.

"Not good enough."

"Why? Are you expecting *another* accident?"

"Why were you talking to Earl?"

"It's a personal matter."

"Then do it on personal time." He started to stride away, but stopped and came back. "This is about the explosion, isn't it?"

"Of course it is," Mariah said evenly. "You don't want to investigate, so it looks like I'll have to."

"Mariah, you do try a man's patience." Jake started to take her arm again, but she dodged his grasp. "Will you please come with me?" he asked in exasperation. "The men are watching."

Throwing him a disdainful glance, Mariah gathered her skirt and followed him up the incline to the grassy hilltop. When Jake faced her, she could see he was exerting a great deal of effort to stay calm.

He crossed his arms over his chest, the muscles of his upper arms bulging through the cotton material. "I thought we had settled this matter."

"Perhaps in *your* mind it was settled, but I had a few more questions."

"And what were they?"

"I wanted to know if the charge man would have used caps for a demonstration."

"What did Earl tell you?"

"That he shouldn't have."

"What else?"

"Nothing else. At that moment, you came stalking toward us, looking as though someone had tied a knot in your—"

"Look, Mariah, either caps were used or the dynamite was unstable."

"Wasn't Abner Pickens the best charge man around?"

She could hear the mounting frustration in Jake's voice when he answered. "Yes, he was, but that doesn't mean he couldn't have made a mistake. I know it's difficult for you to understand, but people do make mistakes, Mariah."

"But wouldn't his partner have caught it?"

"He should have, but that doesn't mean—"

"That he couldn't have made a mistake—I know. But two mistakes Jake? By two qualified men? Do you see now why I'm asking questions?"

"No, I don't. You're a doctor, Mariah, not the sheriff."

Mariah threw up her hands in disgust. "Then why isn't the sheriff investigating?"

"He did investigate," Jake ground out. "He came to the same conclusion everyone else did: it was a tragic mistake. If you don't believe me, ask him. Now go home."

Mariah bristled at his command. "Don't order me around, Jake. I'm not sixteen anymore."

His jaw tensed, making the scar on his cheek stand out against his tanned face. "I didn't order you around when you were sixteen, Mariah." With that, he turned and strode away.

Guilt stabbed her like tiny pinpricks around the heart. Jake had always treated her like a lady. Why had she said that? Was it frustration because he wasn't taking the matter seriously? Or had she just wanted to hurt him?

Standing beside the wooden derrick, Luther Sinton watched Jake stalk away from Mariah. "I wonder what that was about," he said to the man working with him.

"Let's go find out," the man said.

They walked over to the men drilling holes in a ledge. "What was the doc doing here?" Luther asked. "One of you get sick or something?"

"Nah! She was asking Earl questions about the blast."

"What'd she want to know?" Luther asked.

"If the caps had been on the dynamite."

"What'd you tell her, Earl?"

"What could I tell her? They shouldn't have been."

Luther shook his head, sighing sadly. "I sure wish we knew what happened."

"Son, I don't think we'll ever know for certain."

The men went back to their work, and Luther and his partner returned to the derrick. As Luther snapped open his switchblade and began to cut off the frayed end of one of the ropes, he pondered what to do about Mariah. She could poke that pretty nose of hers into the explosion as much as she liked, but she'd never find anything to point to him or Hugh Coffman. He prided himself on being much too clever for that.

Still, he had a duty to protect the senator. It would be best if Mariah wasn't around to poke at all.

Luther considered various ways to get rid of her. He couldn't leave threatening notes; they would only confirm her suspicions—and give her something to show the sheriff. A murder in Coffee Creek wouldn't be wise, either. The smartest thing would be to make it look like she had gone back to Chicago.

A delicious thrill ran through him as he formulated his plan. He drew his thumb down the sharp edge of the knife, watching, transfixed, as a thin line of blood appeared.

First he'd persuade Mariah to get on that train. Then he'd make sure she never got off.

"Castor oil. That'd take care of her problem. Your daddy always recommended castor oil for the bowels."

Mariah silently counted to ten before replying. The Hodges were the last patients of the day, and she was tired. "Perhaps he did, Mrs. Hodges, but I'm sure your daughter would much rather eat something tasty."

"I don't want that stinky oil!" Jane Hodges whined. Sitting on the steel table, swinging her legs, the eight-year-old screwed up her freckled nose and folded her arms defiantly. "I won't take it!"

Her mother leaned over her, shaking a finger in her face. "You'll take it if Doc tells you to!"

"Let's try something else instead," Mariah offered. "Feed her a diet of boiled cabbage, greens, oatmeal, wheat bread, and apples, Mrs. Hodges, and at least four tall glasses of water or cider a day."

"I still say a dose of castor oil will cure what ails her."

"Just try those foods, Mrs. Hodges," Mariah said, escorting the pair from her surgery. "I promise Jane will feel better in two days."

She walked out into the waiting room and saw Annie scowling from her desk. As Mrs. Hodges and Jane left the building, Annie motioned Mariah over.

"That snoopy John Grimes from the newspaper is here to talk to you. I made him wait outside."

Mariah stepped outside onto the stoop, where a heavy, perspiring man in a boiled white shirt and brown pants waited in the hot sun.

"Dr. Lowe? Name's John Grimes," he said, lifting his gray hat. "I spoke with your father many times but haven't had the pleasure of making your acquaintance. I'm writing a story about the explosion at the quarry, and I was told you had some interesting information."

Mariah studied him warily. "I don't know what you mean."

"I was talking to some of the women who were at the scene." He lifted an eyebrow, as if they shared a secret. "They said I should see you."

"All I know is what I've been told by Jake Sullivan, Mr. Grimes. He's trying to get Tower Road finished before the election, and as a result, the men are tired and overworked. Mistakes are made that way."

"Huh!" he said, blinking at her as though he couldn't see how that information was so interesting. He opened a notepad. "So you believe the blast occurred because of careless men?"

"Not careless, exhausted," Mariah corrected him. "The men work strenuous twelve-hour days, six days a week, in every kind of weather. That would put a strain on anyone." Alluding to the lack of caps on the dynamite would just get her more involved than she was ready to be.

"Exhausted men wouldn't be thinking about their safety," the reporter muttered to himself, scribbling notes. "And the owner is pushing them to get the road finished." He stopped writing and looked up. "This quarry is owned by Senator Coffman, isn't it?"

"Yes and by Jake Sullivan. He handles the daily operations."

"Huh." He wrote some more, then flipped the notepad closed. "Thanks for your time, Doctor."

The article came out the next day.

"I think you'd better see this," Annie told Mariah, handing her the paper before lunch, after the last patient had gone.

Mariah scanned the article, growing angrier by the moment. John Grimes had exaggerated what she'd told him, strongly accusing Jake of abusing his men and ignoring safety precautions to help the senator win the election. And Mariah had been credited as Grimes's source of information.

"Jake's not going to like it," Annie cautioned.

Mariah knew how furious Jake would be. "There's not much I can do about it now," she said grimly. "I certainly won't talk to that reporter again. Do I have any more patients to see?"

"Not until two o'clock, honey. You've got a two-hour break. Go have something to eat. I'll keep Lazarus here with me."

Mariah took advantage of the respite to make herself a light lunch. She had just sat down at her kitchen table to eat it when there was a hard knock on her back door. She opened it to find Jake holding the newspaper in his hands, a thunderous look on his face.

"You've gone too far this time, Mariah."

Chapter 6

Mariah stepped back as Jake barreled inside. He slammed the newspaper on the table and swung to face her. "Lax safety measures? Mistreated workers? What in blazes are you trying to do to me?"

Already upset by the reporter's blatant exaggerations, Mariah bristled at Jake's attack. "Then tell me how I was wrong," she said defiantly.

Jake's insides twisted with anger and outrage. Clearly, she hated him so much that she wanted to ruin him. He paced to the door and back, trying to control his emotions. "There's no point in trying to explain to you, Mariah, because you're never wrong. I wish like hell you had stayed in Chicago."

"I wanted to stay in Chicago," she retorted icily.

He stopped to glare at her. "Then why did you

come back? To torture me? To make my life miserable?"

Mariah's fingers curled into her palms. "You have the arrogance to think I came back just to make your life miserable? At least you have a life, Jake. Ben never had that chance, did he?"

Her words hit him hard. He wheeled around, flung open the door, and strode blindly toward the woods.

Ben never had a chance to live. That pain was with him always, waiting to spring forth. Mariah's return had unleashed it and he had to quell it, to shove it back in its place.

Before he realized where he was headed, Jake came out of the woods into a clearing. In front of him the mouth of a cavern yawned wide, beckoning him into its damp, musty-smelling interior. He dropped to his knees and doubled over, wrapping his arms tightly about himself.

It was the cave where Ben had died.

In the course of her training, Mariah had seen many people in pain, but she'd never seen such raw agony on anyone's face as she had on Jake's. She tried to assuage her conscience by reminding herself that what she'd told him was true. Jake knew he was responsible; that was no surprise. He'd lived with it for ten years.

Then why had his reaction been so severe?

His words echoed in her ears: *Why did you come back? To torture me? To make my life miserable?*

She had never considered that her return might

be difficult for Jake. But of course it would be—she was a reminder of Ben's death.

Mariah's hands shook as she picked up the rolled newspaper. She opened the stove and shoved it inside, then walked back to the table and sat down. She tried to eat her lunch, but her stomach churned and her throat was too dry to be able to swallow. She washed the bite down with cold tea, then stood at the window above her sink and stared outside.

She wanted to believe she had just cause for being so blunt, but no matter how bitter she felt about her brother's death, she shouldn't have used it as a weapon against Jake. Her battle with him was in the present, not the past.

She still had over an hour before her next patient; enough time to find Jake and apologize.

Mariah put on her skimmer and headed for the woods behind her house. She followed the path that led to Coffee Creek and beyond that, to the outskirts of town and the limestone quarries. She kept to the trail until she saw signs that someone had veered off to the left, disturbing the undergrowth. Following the new lead, she went deeper into the woods, where the sunlight only barely filtered through the denseness of the treetops and the air was redolent with decaying leaves.

She came to a sudden stop a few feet before the clearing, staring at the cave not ten yards in front of her. Gooseflesh covered her suddenly clammy skin and her stomach heaved as she realized where she was.

It was called Devil's Cave, so named because of its deep underground lake and maze of tunnels that led the unwary to certain death. Mariah hadn't seen it since her brother died; now the sight of it chilled her to the marrow. She backed away, her mind spinning with images of that fateful summer afternoon. In her frantic rush to leave that terrible place, she stumbled over a limb and went down on her hands and knees.

With a groan, Mariah picked herself up and brushed off her skirt. She heard the snap of twigs behind her and swung around. Although she saw no one, the hair on the nape of her neck prickled. She sensed a presence.

As soon as Mariah started walking again, she heard movement in the brush, as though someone was following her. Yet each time she glanced around, she was alone. Logic told her it was only an animal, yet some instinctive feeling said otherwise.

Mariah picked up her pace; whoever was out there did likewise. Her stomach tensed. She tried reciting a poem to calm herself down.

A loud crash sounded in the brush right behind her. Gasping, Mariah began to run. A branch scratched her cheek and snagged her hair, nearly yanking her to a stop. With a panicked whimper, Mariah jerked free, knocking the hat from her head. She stumbled on, her breath loud in her ears, fearing even a glance over her shoulder would slow her down.

Suddenly the ground dropped off in front of her, and Mariah slid feet first down a steep, muddy embankment. She screamed for help, not knowing if anyone other than her pursuer was within hearing range. Her legs crumpled beneath her as she hit bottom, and then all was quiet.

Jake sat with his back against a large rock, his knees bent, his eyes closed, his forehead resting on folded arms. He tried to tamp down the memories Mariah's words had stirred but they had cut too deep.

With a heavy sigh, Jake got to his feet. He needed to get back to the mill, where he could throw himself into his work. He had to forget about Mariah and the tragedy of ten years ago.

And then he heard her scream.

With a racing heart, Jake dove into the woods, heedless of the branches that scraped him. When he saw the straw skimmer, his heart slammed to a halt. He snatched the hat and raced on, coming to a stop at the top of the embankment. Below, Mariah lay deathly still.

"No," he whispered as he slid down. "God, no. Mariah!" he choked out, dropping down beside her. At once, she opened her eyes and blinked in surprise. Jake picked up her hand and pressed it to his cheek, then rubbed it gently. "Are you hurt?"

Mariah gazed up at him, stunned by the fear in his eyes. She raised herself on her elbows and glanced down at her disheveled clothes. "Just bruised, I think."

Jake's body seemed to sag in relief. He brushed back her hair to examine the scratches on her face, his tenderness taking her aback. Discomfited, Mariah rolled to a sitting position and looked around. "Did you see anyone out there?"

"No. What happened?"

"Someone or something was following me, and I panicked. I didn't realize the embankment was so close." She leaned forward to examine her right leg. "I think I may have twisted my ankle. Would you lend me your arm so I can get up?"

Before Mariah realized what he was about, Jake had scooped her off the ground, one arm beneath her legs, the other around her back. "You can't walk all the way home on that ankle," he told her.

Mariah wanted to protest, but Jake was right. She'd only do more damage to the injured limb. "My hat," she said, pointing to where he'd dropped the skimmer.

Jake dipped down so she could pick it up, then he started up the embankment. Held close to his warm body, Mariah shut her eyes and breathed in his clean, masculine scent. Her nerve endings tingled from the feel of his firm arms around her, and the ironlike hardness of his chest against her breast raised a disturbing awareness of his potent virility.

Mariah wanted to blot out the sensations by holding herself stiffly away, but she was too weak from the fall, and her ankle hurt like the dickens.

She finally laid her head against his shoulder, giving in to the pleasure of the moment.

From his hiding spot, Luther watched Jake carry Mariah away. Jake's arrival had been a surprise, but Luther was still pleased. He loved terrorizing his prey.

With a chuckle, he headed back to the quarry. He'd wait a day or so until she felt safe, then he'd strike again. She'd be buying that ticket to Chicago in no time flat.

When Jake carried Mariah into the dispensary's waiting room, Annie jumped up with a gasp, causing Lazarus to bark in alarm. "Hush, Laz," Annie ordered. "What happened, Jake? Land sakes, she's covered in mud."

Mariah opened her mouth to answer, but Jake beat her to it. "She fell and twisted her ankle."

"Put her here on this chair," Annie directed. "I'm going to draw a bath for her."

"I hate to interrupt," Mariah said testily, trying to hoist herself up, "but I'm not an invalid and I'm certainly not deaf."

"What can I do, Annie?" Jake asked, as though she hadn't even spoken.

"She keeps a pair of wooden crutches in the tall cabinet in the surgery."

They were both off before Mariah could voice an objection. Now she understood how some of her patients felt when people answered for them.

Jake returned bearing the crutches, which he

helped her fit under her arms. Then he stood by, hands outstretched, ready to catch her, as Mariah took her first tentative steps.

"They're too tall for you," he said, watching her cross the room. "I'll have another set made this afternoon."

Once again his concern surprised her—and made her feel all the more guilty for the hurtful things she had said to him. "Truly, Jake, there's no need for that. I'm sure I won't be using these long."

"Long enough to need a pair that fits properly," he said, starting for the door.

Mariah's conscience jabbed her sharply. "Jake," she said, stopping him before he could leave, "you didn't ask me what I was doing out in the woods."

He paused, one hand on the doorknob. When he looked around, his expression was remote and his eyes were hard. "It's none of my business."

"I was on my way to apologize to you," she said quietly.

"You have no reason to apologize." He opened the door and walked out.

Jake took the shortcut through the woods to get to the quarry. Holding Mariah in his arms had been at once pleasurable and torturous. He'd thought of nothing but laying her down in a soft bed of leaves and kissing her sweet mouth until her desire matched his, until she cried out in passion and need. But the words that had sent him hurtling out of her house were words that could never be taken back. They were a powerful reminder that there was no future with Mariah.

At least you have a life, Jake. Ben never had that chance, did he?

She was correct—so why had she wanted to apologize?

When Jake reached the embankment, his step slowed. He glanced around for signs that someone had been there but found none.

Jake continued on until he came upon the creek, where he paused to watch the clear, babbling water run downstream. He remembered how Mariah had liked to go there to read or to just sit and contemplate the mysteries of life. She'd take off her shoes and stockings and wade into the cool stream, laughing and squealing when something brushed against her toes. Sometimes she'd even come down to fish with him. Of course, she'd never baited her own hook. She couldn't stand hurting the worms. Jake had always done it for her.

He turned away from the creek and from those bittersweet memories. Dangerous desires simmered just below the surface. He had to drive them down to a place where they couldn't hurt him. He'd promised Mariah a pair of crutches, but as soon as he delivered them, he'd stay away from her—for both their sakes.

Hugh Coffman finished reading the piece by John Grimes in the *Coffee Creek Gazette*, then leaned back and lit a cigar. That kind of publicity could permanently damage his chance of reelection. He had to disassociate himself from the accident and do it quickly. The only way was to keep the blame squarely on Jake's head, then sell the company and be done with it.

He sat forward and reached for his pen. This would take masterful strategy—but he was a master strategist. He knew just how to bend a story to put himself in the best light. Of course, Jake was bound to give him trouble over the sale; he wouldn't be pleased to learn his partner had turned on him.

If Jake proved a threat, though, he'd just have Luther step in.

Though her ankle throbbed and she felt out of sorts, Mariah saw all of her patients that afternoon. At supper, she sat at Willy's bedside with Annie.

"Want to tell me what's on your mind?" Annie asked.

Mariah sighed and looked away. "My ankle's bothering me, that's all."

"You never did say how Jake happened to find you in the woods today."

Mariah's gaze drifted to the window as she remembered the painful scene in her kitchen. She was too ashamed to confess her outburst to Annie.

"Oh, my!" Annie said suddenly, staring at the child's face.

Mariah glanced at Willy and saw his eyelids twitch and the eyes move beneath the lids. "Willy?" she called gently.

"I heard him moaning some this afternoon," Annie reported.

"He may be coming out of it." Mariah lifted one of his eyelids, then called his name again, but there was no further response.

Annie sighed. "Poor little tyke is getting so painfully thin. I hope he wakes soon."

Lazarus came up to Mariah and nudged her hand. She rubbed his golden head, then reached for the crutches. "I'd better let Laz out."

"Honey, you stay where you are; I'll let him out."

"I'm not helpless, Annie. I'll take care of Laz." Mariah winced as she placed the oversized crutches under her arms and made her way to the dispensary door. As Lazarus ran to a nearby tree and began to sniff, Mariah carefully lowered herself to the stoop and laid the crutches beside her.

Down the street, someone was striding her way. As he came into view, Mariah's heart began to race giddily. It was Jake, carrying a new pair of crutches, just as he'd promised.

Chapter 7

‿‿◦◦◦‿‿

The tingly thrill that ran through Mariah vexed her no end, but Jake looked so handsome, so potently male, that she couldn't take her eyes off him.

Jake propped the crutches against the wall beside her, gazing at her with his intense blue eyes. "Give these a try."

Annoyed further by the blush that stole across her cheeks, Mariah took the new crutches, hoisted herself to her feet, and tried them out. "They work fine. Thank you."

"You're welcome." As though he didn't know what to say next, Jake turned and whistled for the dog. Lazarus lifted his head and stared at Jake for a moment, then ran up to him for a scratch behind the ears.

Mariah sat down, placing the new crutches at her side. Her thoughts were shooting in so many directions that her head ached. She was thrilled to see Jake, yet she didn't want him there. She was grateful for his assistance, yet she resented it.

Mariah rubbed her temples. Why couldn't she simply accept his help as an act of kindness and let it go at that?

Her mind supplied her with an answer she wasn't prepared to hear: she didn't want to believe Jake capable of such consideration, and she couldn't let his kindness sway her from the truth. No matter how considerate Jake was, he could never take away what he did.

Jake saw Mariah rise and quickly stood to help her with the new crutches.

"Thank you again," she said, giving him a forced smile. "I'm sure these will come in handy. Come, Laz. It's time to turn in."

Jake waited until she had gone inside, then he headed for home. He hadn't missed Mariah's sudden change of attitude, but it hadn't really surprised him. It was only when she was kind that he was caught by surprise.

As Jake walked up the path to the big limestone house, he heard strains of "Wait for the Wagon." He stepped inside and closed the door as Emeline rose from the piano and hurried out of the parlor, her silk skirts rustling.

"Hello, Jake!" she called too cheerily. "I was just playing for Percy." She leaned close to whisper,

"You'd better go see to Owen. He's outside at the gazebo."

Jake let out his breath. After his tumultuous day, the last thing he wanted was a skirmish with Owen.

The octogonal white building sat on the lawn in the spacious backyard. Jake climbed the two steps into the airy structure and found Owen lying on one of the cushioned benches that ringed the gazebo, his arm over his eyes, one knee bent.

"Are you ill?" Jake asked.

Owen lowered his arm to fix his bleary gaze on Jake's face. "Just got a li'l pain in the gut."

"Then go see the doctor."

"They're all quacks." He covered his eyes once again.

"How long have you had the pain?"

"Since yesterday."

"You've been drinking again, haven't you?"

"There's a silly question." With effort, Owen got to his feet and walked unsteadily across the wooden floor and out one of the arched openings, nearly stumbling on the steps. Jake caught him.

"Leave me be!" Owen snapped. "I can manage."

"I want you to go see Dr. Lowe and let her check you over."

Owen swung around, then had to grab Jake's arm to steady himself. "I don't want to see her. I'll be fine. I won't touch another drop of liquor. I promise."

Jake stared at him, feeling helpless and

ashamed. *He'd* done this to Owen. "Fine. Stay off the booze, and I won't call her."

Mariah stifled a yawn as she listened to her patient's litany of complaints. Mrs. Detweiller had shown up in the middle of the afternoon, demanding immediate attention. By the looks of things, it was going to be a long visit.

Mrs. Detweiller ran the Presbyterian church's women's group and seemed to believe every word she uttered should be recorded for posterity. In her late fifties, she was a bulldog of a woman, short, stout, and uncompromising. She knew exactly what was ailing her and even the treatment she needed. Mariah wondered why she'd even bothered to come.

"Excuse me," Annie said, sticking her head around the door. "Could I see you for a moment, Doctor?"

Using her crutches, Mariah followed her friend to the back room.

"Willy opened his eyes and looked at me," Annie said excitedly. Leading the way to the boy's bed, she picked up his hand and rubbed it. "Willy? Can you open your eyes again for Auntie Annie?"

Mariah lifted his eyelid and saw the pupil contract. She ran her hand along the boy's cheek. "Willy, open your eyes."

The child's legs moved, and his hands twitched, as though he had heard and was trying to respond. "Annie, would you get some sugar water, please?"

Using a cloth dipped in the sweet liquid, Mariah

opened Willy's mouth and let the moisture coat his tongue. His head turned and his breathing quickened.

"If you can hear me, Willy, open your eyes."

Both women watched as the child's eyelids fluttered, then slowly opened. He looked dazed as he tried to focus on Mariah's face.

"I'm Dr. Lowe, Willy. You're here at the dispensary. Do you remember Annie?"

His gaze slowly shifted to his left, and he nodded ever so slightly.

Mariah smiled in relief. "Are you hungry?"

He shook his head, his eyes shut, and he seemed to fall back to sleep.

"Is he all right?" Annie asked in concern.

"I think this is a normal sleep now. He's just made a giant stride, Annie."

"I'll keep watch over him," Annie offered.

"Did Willy wake up?" Mrs. Detweiller bellowed from the doorway.

Mariah headed her off before she could march into the room. "Yes, for just a moment," she said, leading her patient back to the surgery.

"Well," the woman said with a huff, "maybe now we can finally find out what happened at that quarry!"

The news of Willy's awakening spread quickly. By the next morning, Mariah found herself guarding the dispensary against a horde of well-wishers.

The child had opened his eyes once again, and the neighbor who had taken the earliest shift had roused Mariah from her bed to tell her. Willy had then spent the morning dozing on and off, and eating bread and vegetable soup.

"You'll all have a chance to visit Willy when he makes a full recovery," Mariah announced to a crowd in the street outside the building.

"When will that be, Doc?" someone called.

"In a week or so."

"Did he say anything about the explosion?"

"He doesn't remember it."

There was a collective disappointed murmur.

"I trust you will all use good judgment in what you say to him," Mariah told the crowd. "I don't want anything to shock him. His memory will return gradually. When that happens, I'll be able to ask him about the explosion. We'll have to be patient until then."

Annie stepped out onto the stoop next to Mariah and shooed them away. "Go on with you, now. The doctor's got patients to see."

Mariah hobbled inside on her crutches and found Willy propped up on pillows, staring out the back window. She sat down beside him. "How do you feel?"

"M'head aches," he told her, placing his small hand on his bandaged forehead.

"You suffered quite a blow. Do you remember what happened?"

He shook his head, looking very confused. Mariah patted his hand. "It will come back in due time. Are you hungry?"

"Annie fed me some pudding."

"Did I hear my name?" Annie called cheerfully. "Now, what are you telling the doctor about me? It had better be something nice, or no more pudding for you."

Her teasing coaxed a tiny smile from the boy. Mariah gazed down sorrowfully on his pixieish face and bandaged head. After his mother died, Willy had left school to work alongside his father, fearing even a day's separation. Mariah dreaded the moment when he found out his father was gone, too.

Luther Sinton moved away from the dispensary with the rest of the crowd, who speculated as to what Willy would tell them about the explosion when his memory returned. Luther smiled to himself. Willy wouldn't tell them anything.

"Hello, there, Luther," Mrs. Krall called.

Luther turned and politely removed his hat. "Morning, ma'am. How's Mr. Krall?"

"Gettin' used to his condition. Good news about Willy, ain't it? I was thinking about payin' him a visit when he's better. You know, Luther, considerin' that you lost your pa in an accident, too, Willy might appreciate a visit from you once he gets his memory back."

"That's a good idea, Mrs. Krall. In fact, I was thinking of doing just that."

Chapter 8

"Honey, I have a suggestion," Annie said, when Mariah returned from visiting the Gradys' new baby that afternoon. "I think we should limit Willy's visitors to just children and their mothers."

"Why? Did something happen?"

"One of the quarry men stopped by today. When I told Willy who his visitor was, he got all upset and wouldn't let me bring him in."

Mariah pondered the situation as she headed for the supply room. "I suspect Willy doesn't want to be reminded of the explosion. By all means, let's limit his visitors. I don't want anything to upset him."

"There's one more thing," Annie said. "You should go talk to Oscar Drubb. His mother says he's been acting odd ever since the day of the accident. She thinks he may know something."

Mariah gave her a skeptical look as she washed her hands and put on her white apron. Since the swelling and pain in her ankle had subsided, she'd put away the crutches. "Oscar *is* odd, Annie."

Oscar had been born with the umbilical cord twisted around his neck and as a result had suffered brain damage. He was thirty-one years old but functioned as a seven-year-old. His days were spent roaming the town, chatting with the storekeepers, washing windows, and sweeping sidewalks in return for sweets. He lived in a small cottage with his elderly mother and father. His brothers and sisters had grown up and moved away years ago.

"But what if he knows something about the explosion?" Annie persisted.

"What could Oscar possibly know? He doesn't work at the quarry, and he wasn't even in the area when the blast occurred. I'd have noticed him if he'd been there."

"I'd think you'd want to at least talk to the man, in case he knows something that can help you find out what caused the blast."

"We have a sheriff who is supposed to be handling this investigation," Mariah said impatiently. "Tell him to talk to Oscar. Do I have any patients to see?"

"Not right away."

Ignoring Annie's perturbed look, Mariah untied

her apron, yanked it over her head, and tossed it aside. "I'm going for a walk."

Despite the slight twinge in her ankle, Mariah headed for the woods. She felt bad about taking out her frustration on her friend. But what she'd said was true: Oscar couldn't possibly know anything about the explosion. And even if he did, it was the sheriff's responsibility to question him, as Jake had so rudely pointed out.

Yet her conscience told her otherwise. The townspeople needed answers, they deserved answers, and they weren't getting any from either the sheriff or Jake. Like it or not, they were counting on her to find the cause of the explosion.

A snap of a twig brought her around with a gasp. Seeing a squirrel digging for a nut, Mariah let out her breath, realizing she still hadn't recovered fully from her fright. She scanned the trees, but saw nothing to alarm her.

Arriving at the creek, Mariah pulled off her shoes and stockings, hitched up her skirt, and stepped into the cool water. With legs braced and eyes closed, Mariah tilted her head back, spread her arms wide, and let the sun hit her full on the face. The fragrance of pine filled the air, birds chirped gaily above, and the water frothed and gurgled over the smooth pebbles beneath her feet. The sensations washed over her—hot and cool, wet and dry—calming her thoughts and renewing her energy.

A tiny fish tickled her foot and Mariah crouched down to watch it. Across the creek, a squat green frog jumped onto a rock and observed her like a grumpy ogre. Mariah smiled, remembering how her sister Eliza had once tried to make a pet out of a frog. She'd taken it home in her pocket, determined to keep it hidden from Annie, but she'd been found out. Annie wouldn't hear of keeping the "poor little critter" penned up and had ordered her to return it at once. Eliza had been so heartbroken that Ben had offered to take it back to the creek for her.

Mariah sighed wistfully. Ben had been such a good brother. Her father had always hoped his son would follow in his footsteps so they could work together, but it was Mariah who'd had to undertake that responsibility, Mariah who'd had to fill the empty spot created by her brother's death.

Now she was filling the empty spot left by her father's death.

Mariah waded out of the water and went to sit on a large, flat rock, letting her bare legs dry in the warm sunshine. It seemed everyone in town wanted her to be a duplicate of her father. Why couldn't she just be valued for herself?

Hearing a bark, Mariah looked around to see Lazarus loping along the creek, tongue hanging from his mouth. "Where did you come from?" she asked, laughing, when he licked her cheek.

"I brought him."

Mariah's heart lurched as Jake walked toward her, ever handsome in his white cotton shirt and slim brown pants. She quickly covered her bare ankles with her skirt.

"I stopped by the dispensary to see Willy," Jake told her, finding a seat on another rock. "Annie wouldn't let me in and the dog wanted out, so I thought I'd take him for a walk."

"Annie wouldn't let you in?"

"Not so much as a foot. She said Willy needed his rest."

"That's not exactly the truth," Mariah confessed. "Willy won't see anyone from the quarry. It appears he doesn't want to be reminded of the explosion."

"Makes sense." Jake paused to scrutinize her from head to toe. "Annie also mentioned that you were feeling out of sorts."

"I'm perfectly fine." Irritated but not sure why, Mariah rose and brushed off her skirt.

Jake got up, too. "Didn't mean to disturb you. I know you've always liked to come here when you're troubled. Come on, Laz."

The dog sniffed at the water's edge, then bounded after Jake. Mariah watched the pair, amazed that Jake had remembered that about her.

"Jake," she called, snatching up her shoes and stockings and hurrying after him. "If you want to visit Willy, I'll see what I can do."

He gave her a cautious glance as she fell into step beside him. "Are you sure?"

"I know the boss."

A hint of a grin crossed his solemn features. "Tell the boss I appreciate it. And tell the boss she's going to hurt her feet and have to be carried back unless she puts on her shoes."

With the dog bounding ahead, stopping occasionally to sniff at a curiosity, Jake walked silently beside Mariah, enjoying the tranquil moment alone with her. He didn't tell her that he'd come out that way hoping to find her there.

He'd broken his vow to stay away, but he didn't regret it. Watching her standing in the water, her straight little nose pointed toward the sun, her arms outstretched, her calves bare, was worth the price. He could have gone on watching her all afternoon, but Lazarus wouldn't cooperate.

Jake glanced at Mariah covertly, his gaze traveling the length of her slim body, taking in the tiny pulse beating in her throat, the curve of her bosom beneath the fitted pink-and-white-checkered dress, the sensual sway of her hips. Sweet blazes, how she stirred his ardor. If he didn't look at her eyes, he could almost pretend ten years hadn't passed. But if he did look, the bitterness in them told him otherwise.

"How's your ankle?" he asked, noticing a slight limp.

"Almost healed."

"Are you sure you can make it all the way back?"

"I can make it."

Not knowing what else to say, Jake fell silent. Mariah was in some kind of turmoil, but clearly she didn't want to share it with him.

Then again, maybe *he* was her turmoil.

Willy surprised Mariah by allowing Jake to see him the very next day, although he still refused other male visitors. After that first visit, Jake came every day during the noon hour to play checkers, with Lazarus lying contentedly at his feet.

Mariah found it difficult to give Jake any credit for his kindness, preferring to think he had an ulterior motive. However, Jake never asked anything of her other than inquiring as to her health. After a few days of keeping her distance, she found herself making up excuses for being nearby.

Willy still had no memory of the blast and never asked any questions about it. If he wondered why his father never visited, he didn't mention it. Mariah wondered if perhaps he was afraid to find out what had happened.

"Honey, will you take Willy his lunch?" Annie asked her one day. "I've got an errand to run."

Mariah carried the tray into the back room, where Jake was sitting at Willy's bedside.

"Hello, Willy," she said cheerily. "Hello, Jake." She tried to ignore the sudden flush of heat on her cheeks and the rapid beat of her heart.

"Mariah." He rose politely and took the tray from her while she settled comfortably on the edge of the bed. She perched the tray on the child's lap and tucked a linen napkin into his shirt.

"Where's Annie?" the child asked cautiously.

"She had some errands to run," Mariah answered.

At that Willy burst into tears. "She's cross with me, ain't she?" he cried, scrubbing his eyes with his fists as huge tears rolled down his cheeks. "She ain't comin' back. I spilled my milk 'smornin' and she's cross."

"No, Willy, that's not it at all," Mariah quickly assured him, glancing in bewilderment at Jake.

"My pa's mad, too. That's why he ain't been to see me, ain't it? I done somethin' wrong that mornin'."

Mariah's heart felt as though it were being squeezed in a vise, and her own eyes welled with tears. The poor boy thought he had caused his abandonment. Her stomach knotted. The time had come to tell Willy the truth.

She picked up the child's hands and held them. "Willy, your father was never angry with you. You were hurt in a dynamite explosion."

Sniffling, he glanced up at her. "Then why ain't my pa been here?"

Jake put a hand on the boy's shoulder. "Your father was in the explosion, too. He was hurt very badly."

"Why ain't he here at the 'spensary with me?"

Jake gazed down at the child, a muscle in his jaw working, then he said quietly, his voice catching, "He passed on, son."

As the words sank in, Willy snatched his hands away from Mariah, glaring at Jake. "That ain't so! He's down at the quarry. He just hasn't come to see me, is all."

"Willy," Mariah said, waiting until he looked at her, "your father would have come if he could. But he's in heaven now with your mother."

The child's eyes filled with fresh tears as he

looked from Mariah to Jake. "My pa wouldn't leave me. He promised he wouldn't. I don't have no one else but him." Willy folded his arms across his face and wept.

As deep, racking sobs shook the boy, Jake pulled him into his strong embrace. Pressing her fingers against her lips to stop their trembling, Mariah rose and walked to the far end of the room. The child's grief fueled that voice inside her that cried out for answers.

When she returned to Willy's bedside a few moments later, Jake was still holding the hiccuping child, but his gaze was on her. His features were once again set in an expressionless mask, yet Mariah saw a glimmer of pain in his eyes.

"I'll take over now," she said quietly.

Jake seemed relieved. He held the boy at arm's length and looked him in the eye. "You'll be taken care of, Willy. We'll all see to that." Then he got up and left.

Willy quickly became the object of every mother's attention. He received endless baked treats, homemade candy, knitted sweaters and socks, paper puzzles, books and toys, and accepted his sudden popularity with equanimity. He wouldn't talk about his father, and he didn't want visits from any of the stone workers, yet he seemed not to remember the explosion.

Mariah wasn't surprised when Jake stopped coming to visit—the surprise had been that he'd come at all. Yet after three days, Mariah began to grow angry. Willy had asked about Jake several times, and each time she'd made up an excuse as to why he hadn't come. But there was no good excuse for ignoring the child, especially since he was alone now.

On the fourth day, Mariah decided she'd had enough.

Chapter 9

❦

Mariah stormed around the corner of the cutting mill, ready to do battle, but stopped in surprise at the sight of Lazarus frolicking outside the building with Jake. She was even more astounded to hear Jake laugh as he wrestled with the dog. She hadn't heard that laugh in a decade.

A sudden, painful longing for the handsome, daring boy he had once been filled her with incredible sadness. Mariah yearned to put her arms around that boy and gaze into his eyes, to see the warmth, the vitality, and the courage she remembered so well. But she was longing for someone who didn't exist. Now there was only a hard man who would ignore an abandoned child.

Mariah marched up to Jake. "Willy has been asking about you. He wants to know why you haven't come to visit. What shall I tell him?"

Jake got to his feet, a muscle in his jaw twitching. "Tell him the truth: I've been busy."

"Too busy to see a boy who's just lost his father?"

"I can't be a substitute for the man."

"Tarnation!" Mariah exclaimed in annoyance. "Willy doesn't want a substitute. No one can take his father's place. You've become his friend, Jake. He's been orphaned, and now you've abandoned him, too. Has life toughened you so much that you can't feel anything anymore?"

Jake's gaze locked with hers, hard and relentless. "Do you really care?"

Stunned, Mariah had no honest answer to give him. She didn't want to admit even to herself that she still had powerful feelings for Jake.

Calling for the dog, she walked away, her thoughts in a wild spin as Jake's question played over and over in her mind. *Did* she really care?

Dear God, she did.

Jake was out on the floor of the Franklin quarry when he heard that Hugh Coffman had arrived. Cussing under his breath, he headed for the office.

"Hello, Jake," the senator boomed, rising to shake his hand.

"How are you, Hugh?" Jake asked perfunctorily.

"Encouraged. I hear the road is coming along. I'm going to go ahead and schedule a ribbon-cutting ceremony for mid-September."

"That's not what we agreed on."

"Now, Jake, I told you I needed the road done by September first."

"And I told you it'd be October."

Coffman shook his head slowly, as though he were dealing with a dolt. "Jake, don't you remember our conversation?"

"Clearly. I told you October first. I'm pushing the men as hard as I can. It just can't be done any sooner."

"How many hours are they working?"

"Twelve, thirteen."

"Pshaw! They're strong men. They can handle more than that. Why, your daddy worked from sunrise to sunset every day."

"Maybe that's why he died so young."

"Jake, let's not argue. My senate seat is at risk, as you well know. And as for this company . . . Well, it's in everyone's best interests to keep it profitable." Coffman walked around the desk and put his arm around Jake's shoulders. "It's for the best, Jake. Explain it to your men. Line them up behind you. I have every confidence in you."

Jake's hands squeezed into fists. It was all he could do not to tell his partner to go ahead and put the damned company on the market. Ten years, ago he would have told the senator to go to the devil. Now he couldn't take that chance. Men's jobs were at risk.

Hugh Coffman walked the mill grounds with Luther, talking quietly. "No hint of trouble about the explosion?"

"Just Doc Lowe asking some nosy questions, but

she's backed off." Luther didn't mention the water boy's recovery. He'd been frustrated because he hadn't been able to get in to see the brat. Still, he'd already put the fear of God in him. There wasn't a chance the kid would talk.

"Is that Charles Lowe's daughter?"

"The same."

"If she's like her father, she won't back off for long. Are you sure there's nothing for her to find?"

"I'm sure."

Coffman shook his head doubtfully. "I can't have any more attention brought to this matter, Luther, especially after that newspaper article. It's bad for my image."

"I've got a plan to keep the doc from getting any nosier," Luther quickly assured him.

The senator held up his hands. "You know how I feel, Luther. I don't want to know anything about it. That's your job. That's what I count on you for."

Luther swelled with pride. This great man was counting on him. "Does Jake know you're selling the company?"

"I want to get that road completed first; it wouldn't do any good to get him up in arms now. However, I do have a meeting lined up with that *Gazette* reporter to give him my opinion on the cause of the explosion; Jake won't like that."

"But the deal with Bernhardt has been made?" Luther asked.

"A very good deal, my boy. We're going to make a lot of money, you and I. Then you can build your mama a fancy house. She'll like that, won't she, Luther?"

"She sure will."

The senator put his arm around Luther's shoulders. "I knew from the time you were fourteen, when I steered you away from that bit of trouble, that I'd be able to count on you. We're a team, Luther. Don't ever forget it."

Those were the words Luther craved to hear. A team. He and the senator together, like father and son. He smiled, thinking back to the day when their unbreakable bond had been formed.

Luther had sought revenge against a little bitch named Doris who'd snubbed him one time too many. He'd stolen a fuse from the supply shed at the quarry and some kerosene from home, and had been about to set fire to her house. But Coffman had caught him. That was when the senator had promised to keep it a secret between them, as long as Luther behaved. The senator had saved him from going to prison. He'd cared about Luther, just like a father would.

"You be sure and give your mama my regards," the senator said. "I always had a soft spot in my heart for her."

Luther beamed. "She'll be mighty pleased to hear that."

At dawn, Jake stood before the men gathered at the Jefferson quarry. He'd explained the new work schedule to them, and he knew they were angry.

Working from dawn to dusk would rile any man. "Do you have any questions?" he asked.

A voice from the back of the crowd: "What happens if you decide the road needs to be done in August? Do we give up sleeping, too?"

Jake ignored the sarcasm. "Our deadline is September, no sooner. And I'll be working right alongside you. Keep in mind this is only temporary, and you'll be well paid."

"At least it'll cover the cost of our funerals," someone else grumbled.

"Maybe so," another added, "but who'll take care of our children?"

Jake decided he had to be frank with them, or lose their support entirely. "I don't like this any more than you do. In fact, I intend to change things before the year is over. But I can't make a move until I have the capital, and part of that will come from completing the road." He paused to scan their wary faces. "Are you with me?"

For a moment, no one answered. Then a man at the front said, "You've always been square with us. Yeah, I guess I'm with you."

He nudged the man beside him, who said, "Yeah, me, too."

"I'm with you, Jake," Luther called.

Around them, more began to answer, until Jake finally gave them a nod. "I appreciate your support. I won't let you down. Now, let's get to work."

* * *

Mariah learned about the workers' new hours when she paid a house call on the Kralls. As usual, Myrtle stood like a sentry in the bedroom while Mariah examined her husband's wounds and changed his dressings.

"Did you hear about the new policy down at the quarry?" Myrtle asked.

"No, I haven't heard anything." Mariah closed her black bag and rose.

"Myrtle, let her be. She's got others to see," her husband warned.

"They have to start at daybreak now," Myrtle offered anyway, "and they don't go home 'til dark. Working 'em to death is what Jake's doing. Hmpf!"

"Why have the hours been lengthened?"

"Got to get that gol-darned road done, that's why!" Myrtle replied.

Mariah felt her ire rise. She was sure there were monetary gains in it for both the senator and Jake.

"We heard you talked to the charge man," Myrtle continued, following Mariah to the door. "What'd Jake have to say about that?"

"He wasn't pleased."

"You gotta keep at him, Doc. It's the only way to get things changed. That's what yer pa always did: he'd give anyone what for."

Mariah struggled to temper her exasperation at being measured against her father. Placing her hat on her head, she said, "I'll be back tomorrow to check on your husband. Good day, Mrs. Krall."

As Mariah walked down Center Street, she

noticed Oscar Drubb sweeping the sidewalk in front of the general store. "Hello, Oscar," she said.

Hearing his name, the man turned, his mouth gaping open, then smiled crookedly. "Ma'am," he said, bobbing his big head.

"Oscar, do you remember the explosion at the quarry?"

"Don't 'member. Don't 'member." He turned and swept furiously.

"Oscar." Mariah touched his arm, and he jumped. "You're not bothered by it?"

"Don't 'member!" he shouted, and ducked into the store.

Mariah frowned as she continued down the street. It almost seemed as though he was afraid to admit he knew anything about the explosion. She made a mental note to speak to his mother. Perhaps she could coax her son to talk.

That afternoon, three stone men showed up at the dispensary with burns suffered on the job. Mariah could tell by their sullen expressions that they hadn't wanted to come. She guessed their foreman had insisted.

"What are you here for, Mr. Wade?" she asked the first patient, a tall, lanky man in his forties.

"Aw, just a little burn on the arm," he muttered.

"Take off your shirt, please, and I'll have a look."

"Can't you just give me something for it?" he asked grumpily, glaring at her.

"Mr. Wade, you've been coming here to see my

father for years. Don't you trust me to do a good job for you, too?"

"I ain't never took my clothes off in front of no female before, 'cept m'wife."

"Just think of me as a doctor, Mr. Wade, not a female."

"That's hard to do, ma'am. No disrespect intended. I wouldn't be here 'tall 'cept the foreman made me."

"Then I'm sure you don't want to go back and report that you didn't get treatment because you wouldn't cooperate."

Wade eyed her for a moment, weighing her words, then grudgingly began to unbutton his shirt. The skin over one shoulder and down his arm was an ugly red and already starting to blister. Mariah put on her wire-rimmed spectacles to take a closer look, then turned to douse a pad of cotton with vinegar.

"How did you get this burn?" she asked, as she gently swabbed the area.

He shrugged as though the matter wasn't even worth mentioning. "We got what's called a channeling machine down at the quarry—steam-operated. We're having problems with it."

"When did you get this machine?"

"This mornin'."

"And three of you have already suffered burns from it?"

He shrugged again. "We were told to use it."

Mariah simmered inwardly as she covered the

burned area with a poultice made from comfrey root and honey. Why would Jake make his men use a dangerous machine they didn't know how to operate? She asked that very question of her next patient—after first convincing him it was all right to take off his shirt.

"It's a matter of speed, Doc," Wayne Sutter told her. He was younger than the first man and not as skeptical of her ability. "This machine can cut the stone faster and straighter than a man can."

"And with a lot more peril, it seems to me," Mariah said as she dressed the burns on his stomach and ribs. "In which quarry do you work?"

"The Franklin. That's where we're testing the machine."

"Is it true you're working from sunup to sundown?"

"No, ma'am. I'm not on the road crew."

"What do you think caused the explosion, Mr. Sutter?"

The man shifted uncomfortably and looked down. "I can't say."

"Can't or won't?" Mariah waited for him to answer. When he said nothing, she explained, "Everyone I've talked to insists the two charge men who gave the demonstration were the best around. Then how is it possible that both of them made the same mistake?"

Sutter shook his head slowly, keeping his gaze fixed on the floor. "You don't understand, Doc. If we say it ain't possible, then we're saying that one of us is a murderer." He raised his eyes to hers—honest, sincere eyes. "None of the men I work with is a murderer. I'd bet my last nickel on it."

Mariah searched his face for a moment, then turned away. "Thank you, Mr. Sutter. You can put your shirt on now. I'll see you back here tomorrow to check on that burn."

By the time she had treated the third stone man for a serious burn, Mariah was outraged by Jake's treatment of his employees. His concern was profit, his workers' lives be damned; and no one had the courage to hold him accountable.

As soon as the last patient had gone, Mariah put on her hat, told Annie she had an errand to run, and made straight for the quarry.

Luther finished harnessing the workhorse to the derrick and gave the animal a slap on the rump to start him moving. Over the animal's back he caught sight of Mariah coming down the incline, and he quickly pulled the mare to a stop, pretending to adjust the harness.

Dang it! She was headed straight for Jake. What had she come about this time? Luther wiped his mouth with the back of his hand. He had to think of a reason to follow her. He had to know what she was up to. Mariah was becoming quite a nuisance—a nuisance he could do without. He'd given her way too long to get comfortable after that last scare. It was time for her to buy that one-way ticket to Chicago.

Chapter 10

The Franklin quarry was the newest of the three sites, its stone used primarily for building. Mariah scanned the area and spotted a group of men gathered around an object that resembled a small locomotive. It had pipes protruding at odd angles from a central boiler and sat on wheels that rode on rails across the quarry floor.

"So this is the new machine," she said, cutting through the men and stopping opposite Jake.

Hearing Mariah's voice, Jake's head came up, and his gaze hardened as he focused on her. "What the blazes are you doing here?"

"I'd like to speak to you, please."

Jake limped away from her, leaving Mariah no choice but to follow. He knew why she'd come, so he made straight for the toolshed, where Lazarus lay napping in the shade beside the small building. The dog had shown up after the lunch hour and had tagged along with Jake all afternoon.

"You pick the most damnable times to come here," he called over his shoulder.

"Jake, will you please stop and let me talk?"

He swung to face her, not realizing Mariah was so close behind. He had to grab her shoulders to keep her from running into him. She immediately stepped back, as though she couldn't bear his touch.

"I know what you think, Mariah, but I had nothing to do with it."

She tilted her head to glare up at him from beneath the brim of her straw skimmer. "You give the orders. If you're not to blame, who is?"

"I did not *order* him to come here."

"Him?" she asked in obvious confusion.

Jake nodded at the shed. "Your dog."

Mariah swung around to look, then planted her hands on her hips. "Lazarus!" she called sharply. The dog raised his head, got up, and moseyed toward her, tail at a half-droop.

She turned back to Jake. "That's not why I came to see you. I've just treated three of your men for serious burns. I think that requires some investigation."

Jake exhaled sharply. "*Another* investigation?" Exasperated, he pivoted and started back. He was in no mood for Mariah's lectures, his thigh hurt like blue blazes.

"Why are you using a machine you know causes injuries?" she called, following behind.

"I enjoy inflicting pain on the men."

"That explains why you have them working those ungodly hours."

"I'm sure you think so."

"Do you want to tell me why you're limping?"

"No."

Frustrated, Mariah came to a stop, while Jake returned to the machine. It was clear she wasn't going to get any answers from him. She saw a worker heading for one of the derricks and stopped him to ask him about Jake's injury.

"He got himself burned good this morning," the man told her.

Mariah swung to stare at Jake, who was crouched in front of the machine's boiler, examining one of its pipes. "Has he done anything to treat the burn?"

"Doc, you don't know Jake very well, do you? He wouldn't take time to fuss over it." The man leaned closer. "I tell you, though, I saw them burns on Wade and Sutter, and I know Jake's has got to be a humdinger. A big blast of steam hit him right on the thigh. That's worse than getting a scalding." The worker shook his head. "But just try and get him to have it looked after."

Mariah studied Jake thoughtfully. He wouldn't be limping unless it hurt. Burns were horribly painful and often led to serious infections, or even gangrene. She clearly couldn't treat his injury at the quarry. She'd catch him at home, where he couldn't hide behind his work.

Luther nodded to Kennard Johnson, who stood a few feet from the group of men working on the channeling machine. "Howdy, Ken. What did the doc come here for now?"

"To see Jake."

"She say why?"

"Not to me, but my guess is she's all riled up about the injuries caused by the channeler."

"Yeah, that's too bad about Sutter and the others." Luther glanced up at the hill. "I saw the doc talking to you. What was she asking?"

"Why, Luther, she was asking about you."

Luther grew still. "About me? What's she asking about me for?"

"Maybe she's got tender feelings for you," the man replied with a good-natured wink.

Luther's pulse slowed. "That ain't funny, Ken."

"Sorry, Luth. I was just joshing you. Don't get yourself in a stew."

"I knew you were joshing. Sure I did. I gotta get back to the derrick. See ya later, Ken."

Bastard. Simmering with rage, Luther led the horse away. He hated it when people ridiculed him. *You keep on joshing me, Ken, and you'll get yours someday.*

He didn't need Kennard to tell him, anyway. There were other means of finding out what Mariah was up to.

* * *

Mariah had walked all the way across the quarry floor and was ready to start up the incline when she heard Jake call out, "Dr. Lowe!"

She turned to find him standing in front of the group of men, looking down at a big furry object at his feet. "You forgot something."

"Lazarus, come here!" Mariah called. Slowly, the dog got up and ambled toward her, head lowered guiltily, tail between his legs. "You stay with me," she scolded, as they headed home. "You shouldn't be here. It's too dangerous."

As though he understood, the dog moped all the way to the dispensary.

As soon as she got back, Mariah put her medical bag away and went to wash her hands. Some children had come by to put on a puppet show for Willy, with their mothers looking on. Lazarus stuck his head around the corner, saw the children, and quickly retreated to the shelter of Annie's desk.

"We have to keep a close eye on Laz," Mariah told Annie. "I found him at the quarry with Jake again."

"That dog sure has taken a shine to Jake. The only other man he's ever taken a liking to was your father. Isn't that something?"

"I find it downright irritating," Mariah replied. Annie shot her a curious look, which she ignored.

"Did you talk to Jake about the steam machine?" Annie asked.

"I didn't have a chance, but I'll be seeing him soon." She nodded toward the back room. "Willy seems to be enjoying himself."

"His spirits have improved somewhat," Annie reported. "I asked him again about the day of the explosion, but he still doesn't remember."

"Or doesn't want to. Who's staying with him tonight?"

"Gertrude."

"Good. She and Willy seem to have hit it off well. I'll see you in the morning, Annie. Come on, Laz. Time to go home."

The dog came slinking out from beneath the desk, then skittered past the back room and through the doorway into the kitchen. He'd always had an unreasonable fear of children, and Mariah suspected he'd been mistreated as a pup.

After feeding Laz, Mariah ladled out the peppery beef stew Annie had left simmering on her stove. As she ate, she thought about her forthcoming confrontation with Jake and was tempted to forget the whole matter. She didn't understand what was prompting that strong urge in her to defend the workers. Was it an inherited trait?

But she still needed to treat Jake's burn. And as long as she had to see him, she'd bring up the subject of the machine and the men's hours.

Mariah changed into a fresh blouse, a crisp, celery-green and white stripe with a white bow that tied at the neck. With it she wore a dark green skirt, narrow at the waist and flaring at the hem. She topped the outfit with her straw skimmer and stopped at the hall mirror to pinch her cheeks for color. With Lazarus at her heel, she made a quick stop at the dispensary to pick up her medical bag, then started up Center Street.

The sun had been shining when she left, but as Mariah trudged up the long drive to the stately limestone house, storm clouds began to roll in. She'd left her umbrella at home and hoped the rain would hold off until night.

At the top of the wide stone steps, Mariah paused to admire the shady porch that wrapped around the front and sides of the house. Large pots of fragrant petunias in pink, purple, and white stood at each side of the steps. Dark green wicker chairs decorated with plump, colorful cushions made the area an inviting spot to sit and relax.

Mariah had never been to Jake's house, but she remembered when the handsome, two-story structure had been built. Not as elaborate or as big as Senator Coffman's residence, still, the Sullivan house reportedly had five bedrooms and three indoor baths.

She rang the buzzer and waited, her toe tapping nervously. The door was answered by Jake's sister dressed in an evening toilette of deep rose silk.

"Good evening, Emeline. Is Jake at home?"

The young woman's mouth fell open in surprise. "Why, Mariah, I never expected to see you here—that is, how good to see you here—or anywhere, for that matter—not that it matters." She giggled self-consciously, winding one of her banana curls around her finger. "Do come in."

Mariah glanced back at the dog, who sat on his

haunches, his head tilted, watching her. "Laz, you'll have to wait here. I'll be out shortly."

The dog sat down and put his head on his paws.

Emeline had been one of Mariah's sister's closest friends. There had been three friends in their circle: Eliza, Emeline, and a third friend, Eileen. They had called themselves The Three Es and had been inseparable until Eliza left for Chicago to study voice. Then Eileen had eloped with a slick fellow who'd billed himself as a man of medicine but in truth was nothing more than a snake oil salesman. That had left only Emeline who, unfortunately, had a habit of frightening away all the eligible young men in town with her tantrums.

She'd finally snared Percival Whiteside, a prosperous merchant from the neighboring town of Oolitic. Percy had made it to the ripe old age of thirty-five without ever having been engaged until the apple-cheeked, eyelash-fluttering Emeline had come into his life.

Mariah had always thought Emeline to be a spoiled brat, as did most of their schoolmates, although that had never bothered Eliza.

"I'll go fetch Jake," Emeline told her. "He's working in the study."

She sailed up the hallway, leaving the scent of roses in her wake, and disappeared into a doorway on the left. Mariah glanced around the spacious foyer as she placed her bag at her feet and removed her white gloves. Large squares of black and white marble made a checkerboard pattern on the floor, leading the eye up a long hall with an arched doorway at the back. Through the arched opening Mariah could see a roomy kitchen, with copper pots and pans hanging from a rack over a worktable and tall windows framed by pretty floral-print curtains.

On the left side of the front hall, a maroon and white carpet runner ran up the curving staircase. In front of the staircase was a wide arched doorway that led to a formal drawing room. A matching doorway on the right led to the dining room. All was tastefully decorated.

Emeline came sailing toward her, followed in short order by Jake, who seemed to be trying to downplay his limp. His expression was guarded, his face etched with exhaustion and pain.

"Here he is, Mariah," Emeline said breathlessly. "Percy and I will be in the parlor, if you'd care to join us for coffee."

"That's very kind, but actually I've come on a medical matter."

Emeline looked around at Jake. "Is Owen worse?"

Jake silenced his sister with a scowl. "What medical matter, Mariah?"

"The burn on your leg," Mariah replied evenly.

Emeline's eyes grew wide. "Did you burn your leg, Jake? Is it bad?"

"Who burned a leg?" Emeline's fiancé asked, peering at them from the parlor doorway.

"It's nothing, Percy," Jake said, with obvious vexation. "Emie, don't worry about me. Go back to the parlor."

"I don't believe I've had the pleasure of your acquaintance," Percy said to Mariah, strolling toward her.

Mariah was finding the whole scene quite amusing, but she knew by the tic in his cheek that Jake wasn't. "Mariah Lowe." She held out her hand and Percy took it.

"Percival Whiteside. Pleased to meet you, Miss Lowe."

"Mariah's a doctor," Emeline corrected, looping her arm through Percy's. "She's Eliza's sister."

"I do beg your pardon, Dr. Lowe. I don't believe I've ever met a female doctor. Is it difficult treating male patients?"

"Some more than others," Mariah answered, casting a pointed look in Jake's direction.

Jake pinned his sister with an icy look. "Emeline?"

She wrinkled her nose at her brother. "Come, Percy. Let's go finish our coffee. Mariah, please do join us later if you'd like."

"Thank you, Emeline." Mariah glanced at Jake. "Is your brother ill?"

"No more than usual," Emeline called over her shoulder. At Jake's warning glance, she gave a huff and disappeared into the parlor.

Mariah wondered what that warning glance meant. She remembered that Owen had been drinking heavily before she went away to college. Was he still suffering from that addiction?

"As long as I'm here," she said, removing her hat, "would you like me to see your brother?"

"Owen is fine," Jake said curtly. "So am I."

Mariah picked up the black bag. "I'd like to judge your leg for myself, thank you. Now, where may I set up my equipment?"

"The burn doesn't need attention, Mariah," he insisted.

"Then why have you been limping?" Mariah started up the hall, determined not to let him deter her. "Your study is back here?"

She rounded the corner and stepped into a cozy, mahogany-paneled room replete with built-in bookcases crammed full of books. A cold hearth snuggled into the bookcases on one wall, lending the room the pleasant odor of burned wood. A simple oak desk sat between two tall windows, its plain lines in stark contrast to the rest of the room.

Mariah headed for the desk, where a lamp was lit. As she opened her bag and took out her ointment and swabs, she heard Jake come in behind her.

"What do you think you're doing?"

Mariah kept her back to him. "I'm setting out my supplies so I can treat that burn properly."

"Like hell."

"There's no need to curse." She turned to face him. "If you want to get rid of me, then let me do my business and be off. I've had a long day, and I'm just as tired as you are."

For a moment Jake simply stared at her, as though unsure what to do. Then his face reddened, and he said quietly, "And just how do you intend to do your business? The burn is"—he glanced over his shoulder, as though afraid to be over-heard—"on my—uh—limb."

"I understand."

He shook his head, as though she was daft. "My upper leg."

Mariah put her hands on her waist and studied him. "You needn't be embarrassed. I've seen many thighs, upper and otherwise."

Jake winced at her use of the word *thigh*. "You haven't seen mine," he groused.

"Then we'll remedy that. Drop your pants."

Chapter 11

❧ ᴏ⧸⧹ᴏ ❧

At Jake's shocked expression, Mariah exclaimed, "For heaven's sake. I can't treat you with your pants on."

Jake glared at her as though he couldn't decide whether to throw her out or go along with her. Mariah crossed her arms and calmly held her ground.

Finally, giving her a disgruntled look, Jake limped to the door and shut it. With his back to her, he unfastened the buttons down the front of his pants, carefully eased the pants down over his injured leg, and stripped to his knee-length underdrawers.

He turned to face her, his features set stubbornly. "Don't ask me to take these off."

Mariah wouldn't have, anyway, although the idea momentarily quickened her pulse. She knelt down in front of him and gently lifted the left side of the drawers. His upper leg was swollen, and on the front and inside of his thigh, a large red patch of skin had blistered so badly that it was oozing, causing fibers from his clothing to stick to it.

Mariah glanced up at him, amazed that he had continued to work all day with such an injury. "This is terrible, Jake. Why didn't you let me look at it this afternoon?"

"It didn't hurt that much."

"You just didn't want the men to know how badly that idiotic machine burned you!"

"Did you come here to lecture or to help?"

Ungrateful wretch! With a huff of exasperation, Mariah removed a pad of cotton, vinegar, a comfrey poultice, and a pair of small pincers from the bag, lining them up on the desk.

"I'm going to wash the burn with vinegar first, then I'll have to remove those cloth fibers. It'll be easier if you sit down." She spread a towel on his chair and gave it an inviting pat.

Jake hesitated a moment, then limped around his desk and carefully lowered himself onto the seat.

"Do you want something to help dull the pain?" Mariah asked.

"Don't need it."

Mariah put on her spectacles, poured the vinegar onto the cotton, and again knelt in front of him. He sprawled in the chair, his legs spread wide apart, his head turned away. Mariah raised the leg of his drawers once again and gently soaked the burned area. She glanced at his face, knowing he had to be in pain, but his expression didn't change. Then she used the slender metal pincers to remove fibers and dead skin. Halfway through, Mariah glanced up to see how he was faring, only to find Jake studying her curiously.

"I've never seen you wear spectacles," he commented.

"I wear them for close work."

"Studious."

Mariah paused to look up. "I beg your pardon?"

"You look studious."

The thoughtful, almost tender expression on his face was so reminiscent of the old Jake that Mariah could only blink up at him, her heart filling with that almost forgotten passion of first love. But he wasn't the old Jake. She had to stop torturing herself with those memories.

Giving herself a hard mental shake, Mariah went back to picking out fibers. But something had subtly altered between them. Now Mariah was keenly aware of their close proximity, of his penetrating gaze on her, and of Jake's bare leg and muscular thigh. She found her curious gaze darting upward. The higher it rose, the more her imagination took over, until her pulse raced madly and her insides quivered like jelly.

What am I thinking? She'd seen many examples of the male anatomy. Why was this one sparking such a disturbing reaction?

Putting her mind to it, Mariah finished the

tedious task and began to apply the comfrey poultice. "You'll have to keep your leg elevated until the swelling goes down. And I'll need to check this again tomorrow. I fear an infection may set in since you let it go so long."

"I don't have time to fool with it."

"You must take the time, Jake. This is serious. You could develop gangrene and lose the leg."

As she gently spread the poultice with her fingertips, Jake gritted his teeth and looked away. Having Mariah kneel between his legs so close to his manhood, stroking his bare thigh, was more than a man should have to bear. He was grateful for the searing pain; it kept him from getting aroused. "That's good enough, Mariah."

"Be patient. I'm nearly finished. I still have to bandage it."

"I'll do it myself."

He should have known Mariah wouldn't be deterred. She took the roll of gauze and began to measure out a length. "Would you hand me the scissors, please?"

Releasing his breath, Jake handed her the scissors, then settled back against the chair, willing his mind to think of anything but Mariah.

"There!" she said, rising. "That wasn't so bad, was it?"

"You have no idea." With a wince, Jake got to his feet, then stepped into his pants and slowly eased them up over the burned area, fastening the buttons as she put away her supplies.

"I'll see you tomorrow," she told him as she started out of the room.

Jake limped after her. "I told you, I don't have time."

"Oh, that's right," she said over her shoulder as she sailed along the hallway. "You're busy. You stopped coming to see Willy because you don't have time for him, either. I guess all you have time for is making money."

Swearing silently, Jake yanked open the front door for her just as a light rain started to fall. He'd known there would be a lecture.

From across the porch, Mariah saw a ball of golden fur hurl itself at Jake. Quickly, he took a step back as Lazarus leaped up and tried to lick his face.

Mariah gasped, fearing the dog would hurt Jake's injured thigh. "Laz! Get down!"

The dog dropped down to all fours, his tail wagging excitedly as Jake bent to scratch him. Slightly annoyed by the dog's devotion, Mariah put on her hat and stepped around them onto the porch as thunder crashed overhead.

"I'll get the buggy," Jake offered.

"It's only a light rain. I'm sure I can make it home before the storm hits. Come, Laz." But as soon as she walked down the stone steps to the path, the sky opened up.

"Tarnation!" Mariah lifted the hem of her skirt and dashed up the steps to the shelter of the porch. The dog, she noticed, hadn't moved from Jake's side.

"Now will you let me get the buggy?" Jake asked.

"Thank you, but I'll wait it out," she said. "The clouds are moving quickly, so it should be a short rain. Besides, you should stay off your feet so you don't irritate your burn."

Jake indicated one of the green wicker chairs on the porch. "You might as well have a seat."

Mariah took the offered chair, put her bag on the floor, and leaned back against a plump cushion. "You needn't feel obligated to wait with me," she said, knowing he would anyway.

His answering grunt as he eased himself into the chair beside hers told her she was right. Lazarus immediately curled up at his feet.

"Well?" he said.

She turned her head to glance at him curiously. "Well what?"

"Go ahead."

"Go ahead with what?"

"What you came for. The lecture about my men."

"That's not what I came for," she said. "But since you brought up the subject, I think you're over-working them."

"Anything else?"

"Jake, surely you don't think working sunup to sundown is reasonable."

He shrugged. "Right now it's necessary. It won't go on forever."

"Do I have your word on that?"

He gave her a long, pointed look. "Would you take my word on anything?"

Mariah blushed hotly and looked away.

"What else?" he asked. "I know there's more."

"I'm still not satisfied that the explosion was an accident." Seeing the stormy look on Jake's face, Mariah rushed on. "I've talked to a number of men, Jake, and all of them have told me the two charge men who died would not have made such a grievous mistake."

"So they believe one of those two purposely killed himself and others."

"I didn't say that, and neither did your employees. My point is, we think there's more to this than just an accident."

Jake rubbed his temples. "How do you expect to prove it, Mariah? Do you have evidence? Do you have a suspect?"

"I have nothing," she conceded. "It's just a feeling."

"I know the men who work for me. They're not killers." He sat forward, his expression registering his impatience. "Is there anything else?"

"Just one more thing. Are you going to continue to use that steam-operated machine?"

"If I don't, I've wasted two thousand six hundred dollars."

Mariah nearly gasped out loud at the huge price he'd paid. It figured money was behind his decision. "And if you do use it, more men are going to get burned."

"Not if we use it right."

"Can't they just cut the stone by hand?"

Jake clasped his hands behind his head and stared out at the rain. "It's rock, Mariah. There's no easy way to cut it."

"There has to be a safer way than that dangerous machine."

"The machine *is* the safer way," he told her. "The other way is with dynamite, and you've seen those results. Once the men learn how to use the channeler, I guarantee there will be fewer accidents."

Mariah considered his reasoning. "What caused the men's burns?"

"The piping."

"Then you will fix the piping before any more men get burned, won't you?"

Jake got to his feet, signaling the end of the discussion and probably his patience. "The rain is slowing. Would you like me to bring around the buggy?"

"I'll just borrow an umbrella, if you don't mind."

"I'll get one right now."

"Stay here, Laz," Mariah commanded, when the dog started to follow him. She pondered the information Jake had given her. The channeling machine did make a lot of sense—if it could be made safe. The question was whether Jake would take the time to do it.

But there was no arguing with the stubborn man. She opened the umbrella he'd brought her and walked down the steps.

"Doctor," Jake called.

Pressing her lips together, she swung around. It always sounded as though he was mocking her when he used her title. "What?"

He looked down at his feet. Lazarus stood beside him, panting happily, as though he belonged there.

"Laz, come on!" Mariah said crossly. She waited until the dog plodded down the stairs, then she turned and marched away.

Jake went back to the chair and eased himself into it, watching the two until they were no longer visible. When she'd knelt between his legs, he'd had to lock his fingers together to keep himself from pulling her into his arms—and she hadn't even been aware of it.

He didn't dare let her touch his thigh again. It would be more than his self-control could stand. Just the thought of her fingers stroking him that intimately made him so tight inside that he had to walk down onto the lawn and tilt his head back to let the cool rain douse his passion.

His lips were on her throat, pressing searing kisses against her flesh, traveling down her neck to her bare shoulder. He pushed the straps of her chemise down over one arm, letting the thin material slide down until her breast was bared. She moaned in pleasure as his seeking mouth found her nipple and gently tugged on it, his tongue circling and stroking enticingly. More, she thought. I want more.

A loud pounding jolted Mariah out of the depths of sleep. She came awake reluctantly and lay still for a moment, wondering if she had imagined the knock. Then she heard it again.

Lazarus barked furiously in the backyard as Mariah climbed out of bed. Her black notebook slid to the floor, and she stooped to pick it up, realizing she had fallen asleep while updating her records. Half awake, she stumbled toward the kitchen, still warm and drowsy from her dream. And what a dream it had been.

Mariah stopped suddenly, coming fully awake. Dear God, she had been dreaming about Jake!

"Mariah, are you there?"

Mariah opened the back door to find Annie in her wrapper and curlpapers, holding a kerosene lamp. "Honey, is everything all right?"

"I was about to ask you the same question."

Annie stepped inside. "Lazarus's barking woke me. I checked on Willy, then I saw your light through the back window and thought I'd better make sure you were all right."

"I'm fine. I fell asleep and left the lamp burning." Mariah glanced out the back door and saw Lazarus standing at the fence, looking toward the street. His barking had subsided into an occasional yap.

"Hush, Laz!" Mariah ordered. The dog gave a few more warning barks, then returned to his doghouse and lay down.

"Something must have spooked him," Annie said. "He doesn't usually carry on so for a critter unless it's a human critter."

"Or a female dog," Mariah suggested with a yawn.

"I'll let you get back to sleep. I'm glad you're all right."

Mariah returned to bed, doused her lamp, and tried to doze, but bits of her dream kept floating through her thoughts. She tossed from one side to the other, trying to ignore the delicious stirrings those provocative images had kindled, but the feel of Jake's lips on her bare flesh was so vivid that she couldn't push it aside.

"Damn him," she muttered. There was no way she could sleep now. She relit the lamp, opened the black notebook and resumed where she'd left off.

Luther pressed himself against the front wall of the dispensary, waiting until the dog was quiet before slinking away. He'd discovered something interesting: Mariah kept records. He'd seen an open journal on her bed but hadn't dared enter her bedroom with the lamp lit. He'd check it out later. He was a stickler about loose ends.

Luther chuckled to himself as he opened the door of his mother's house and slipped inside. He wished he could be there when Mariah discovered the little surprise he'd left earlier. She'd know someone had been there, but she wouldn't be able to prove it. He'd been careful; he couldn't leave any evidence that she could take to the sheriff.

Maybe it would spook her enough to make her buy that train ticket.

In the darkness of the tiny kitchen, Luther covered his mouth to muffle his snicker, so he wouldn't wake his mother.

The sounds of birds chirping outside her window woke Mariah. She stretched leisurely, then glanced at the clock and saw that she had overslept. Grumbling to herself, she slid out of bed, dressed hurriedly, and carried the notebook to the parlor.

She'd taken only two steps into the room when the hairs on the nape of her neck suddenly prickled. Mariah came to an abrupt stop, hugging the notebook to her breast, as a shudder raced up her spine. Her gaze fell on the desk, and her stomach gave a lurch. She had closed the top before she'd gone to bed; now it stood open. The personal letters she had stacked neatly in the upper right-hand corner were scattered, as though someone had rifled through them.

Someone had been in her house. Maybe still was.

Mariah grabbed the heavy poker from the hearth and moved stealthily from room to room until she was satisfied no one was there. She returned to the parlor and straightened her desk, tucking the notebook in a corner and closing the top. She knew she hadn't left it in disarray. But why would anyone want to look through her papers?

Mariah ate a quick breakfast and fed Lazarus, all with the eerie feeling that someone was watching her.

"Good morning," Annie called cheerily, walking up to the sink, where Mariah was vigorously scrubbing her hands. "Slept in, I see. Good for you, honey. You needed it."

"Annie, you didn't by any chance go through the papers on my desk last night, did you?"

"Not on your life. Did you lose something?"

"No." Mariah dried her hands on the towel. "I found my desk open this morning and a stack of letters strewn over the top."

"Are you sure you didn't forget to close it last night?"

Was she sure? Mariah frowned thoughtfully as she went over the events of the previous evening. "I'm sure. Besides, I wouldn't have left my letters scattered."

"If you're worried, honey, report it to the sheriff."

"I've thought of that, but what would I tell him? That my desk was open? Since nothing was stolen, I'm not sure what he could do." Mariah took her white apron from the hook behind the door. "How many patients do I have this morning?"

"Two in the waiting room."

"Would you take the first one into the surgery?" Mariah slipped the apron over her head and tied the strings at her waist. The more she thought about it, the more probable it seemed that she had left her desk open. It wasn't like her, yet it made more sense than to think someone had rifled through it. There was certainly nothing of importance in her letters. The only other thing she kept there was the notebook, but she'd had that with her all night.

For some reason, Jake's warning flashed through her mind. *If your hunch about the explosion is correct, you're putting yourself in danger by investigating it.*

Tarnation! She wasn't in danger. Yet a tiny voice in her head told her she should take Jake's warning seriously. There had now been two unnerving incidents. She hoped they were coincidental.

After an early emergency with a sick baby, Mariah spent the rest of the morning making house calls on her patients. By the time she returned to the dispensary at half past noon, she had nearly forgotten about her scare.

She slipped on her apron and walked through the curtain into the back room. "Where's Willy?"

"Maude Pullins and her kids came to take him out for the afternoon. I warned them that he had to take it easy."

"I'm sure the outing will do him good."

Annie parted the curtain and followed her in. "He asked me today if he was going to live here forever."

"Poor child," Mariah said sadly.

"What are we going to do about him, honey? I'll be glad to keep him, but he needs young parents and a family."

"Jake said he would try to find Willy's relatives.

In the meantime, I'll ask Reverend Ekin. He might know of a family for Willy."

"Have you talked to the sheriff about last night?"

Mariah shook her head. The matter wasn't significant enough to report.

As Mariah saw patients that afternoon, she found herself foolishly looking forward to her next visit with Jake. She ate dinner with Annie and Willy, put Lazarus in the backyard, then walked to the cutting mill, timing her arrival for sundown.

She had just removed her hat and set her medicine out on Jake's desk when he walked in. He stopped abruptly, his whole body tensing.

"You don't need to scowl at me," Mariah told him. "I'll clean and bandage your burn and be on my way."

He looked as if he were going to argue, but he didn't. "I'm covered in stone dust," he said irritably. "Would you mind if I at least wash up?"

"Not at all."

Cursing to himself, Jake limped down the stairs and through the mill to the pump behind the building. It wouldn't do any good to try to dissuade Mariah. She'd only catch up with him somewhere else. But now that the pain had lessened, how in blue blazes was he going to hide the fact that her touch aroused him?

Pumping cool water into a bucket, Jake cupped his hands and splashed his face. If Mariah knew what went through his mind when she knelt before him, she'd be shocked senseless. Indeed, she'd avoid him like the plague.

His hands stopped in midair, water trickling down his arms.

That was exactly what he wanted.

Smiling to himself, Jake unbuttoned his shirt and stripped it off, tossing it next to the pump. After dousing his head and neck with water, he raked his hair back from his face and started for his office. There was no need to hide the passion he felt for Mariah. Let her see it and take heed.

Chapter 12

~~~◯◯~~~

When Jake appeared in the office doorway, Mariah's eyes widened in astonishment. He was freshly scrubbed, his jaw was shadowed by his dark beard, his wet hair was pushed back. But that wasn't what caused her to gape. Neither was it the tiny beads of water wending their way down his bare torso, nor the droplets glistening in his curly black chest hair.

It was the predatory look in his eyes.

Mariah watched warily as Jake shut the door and pulled a curtain across the window, the muscles across his back rippling with the motion. Pivoting, he came toward her, his thumbs hooked in his waistband, his mesmerizing gaze never leaving her face. Only a slight limp gave any indication of his injury. Mariah clasped her hands together to steady her suddenly taut nerves, but she was unable to quell the rapid beating of her heart.

He stopped directly in front of her, almost touching her knees. Mariah swallowed hard as Jake began to work the row of buttons down the front of his pants, opening them slowly, deliberately, until the fly was unfastened. This time he didn't turn his back; instead, he slipped his thumbs under the waistband and eased the pants down.

Fearing he was about to reveal all, Mariah scrunched her eyes shut, then opened them to mere slits, only to find Jake still wore his underdrawers. Giving herself no time to focus on the obvious, she quickly lifted her gaze to his hard-muscled chest. A drip traveled leisurely down his rib cage, raising a curious urge to trace it with her fingertip.

She glanced up to find Jake watching her closely, an inscrutable smile on his face. He gazed at her through heavy-lidded eyes, bringing a sudden throbbing between her thighs and an erratic fluttering of her pulse. What was the man up to?

She rose carefully, trying not to brush against him. Jake gave her no leeway, making her back the chair to the wall.

Trying to maintain a professional demeanor, she frowned in concentration as she put on her spectacles, knelt down, and raised the leg of his drawers. But she couldn't prevent her gaze from sliding up to the enormous bulge at his groin.

Good heavens! Inhaling sharply, Mariah averted her gaze, fighting the urge to bolt.

"Is something wrong, Mariah?" he asked quietly.

She quickly shook her head. "No," she answered, her voice coming out in an embarrassing squeak, "nothing's wrong." She was a doctor, for heaven's sake. She had come to treat an injury. She couldn't let his male reaction affect her.

Mariah's hands were slippery with perspiration as she peeled off the gauze. Yellow pus had formed several small pockets of infection in the burned area. She was almost relieved to find them—it gave her a much-needed point of concentration.

"I feared this would happen," she told him in her most professional manner, shaking her head ruefully. "You haven't kept it elevated, either, have you?"

"No lectures, Mariah."

The huskiness in his voice brought her head up. She searched his gaze, finding in it what she had feared to see: desire, hot, intense—and contagious.

Pressing her lips together, Mariah cleaned out the infection, put more of the comfrey poultice on it, and covered it again. "There," she said crisply, avoiding his gaze as she rose to her feet. She immediately turned her back on him and began putting away her supplies.

"Let me help you," he said, his lips so close to her ear that she felt them brush against it, sending a delicious shiver through her.

"I-I really don't need"—she drew in her breath as he reached around her—"any help."

His turgid manhood pressed against her derriere as his body molded itself to hers. Mariah's breath came in short, quick bursts, her imagination running wild.

What if he turned her around, leaned her backward over his desk, raised her skirts, and . . .

"I've been thinking," he said in a soft, animal-like growl. "It might be better tomorrow if I took off everything."

Mariah closed her eyes and swallowed hard at the image forming in her mind. She'd seen nude bodies, but never that of an aroused male. Judging by what she'd witnessed just now, she had no doubt it would be an impressive and highly stimulating sight.

You're a doctor, for heaven's sake. And he's your patient.

But she was also a woman. And Jake was indisputably a man.

"Th-that won't be necessary," she managed to say.

He lifted a wisp of hair beside her ear and toyed with it. "I didn't say it was necessary," he murmured. "Only better."

Trying to shut out the desire sweeping through her, Mariah hurriedly stuffed the last of her equipment into her bag and closed it. "There," she said breathlessly, keeping a smile in her voice, "that's done." She nearly sagged in relief when he stepped back.

Yet the desire that raged within her was terribly disappointed.

"Same time tomorrow?" he asked, as he fastened his pants, his voice rich with the promise of untold pleasures.

Turning, Mariah instantly regretted it. His eyes were still hooded, his face sublimely secretive. Her gaze drifted down to that firm, sensual mouth that had taught her how to kiss, and her body throbbed anew. She swayed toward him, her lips parting, her eyes drifting shut, already tasting his lusty kisses. With a startled gasp, she caught herself.

"Same time," she said hoarsely, and fled.

Mariah hurried home in the growing dusk, nodding distractedly to people calling greetings. Her thoughts spun in a crazed whirl. The desire Jake had ignited shook her to the core. She'd actually yearned for him to kiss her, to touch her intimately. Had she not escaped, she feared where her passion might have led.

She just wouldn't go back, that was all. She couldn't risk those dangerous emotions, that powerful attraction. She'd simply send some of her poultice and let him take care of the burn himself.

But she knew Jake would ignore his injury, and her conscience wouldn't allow her to let that happen.

The more Mariah thought about Jake's behavior—the way he'd sauntered into that office with his sly smile and bare chest—the more certain she was that he'd been testing her. She had no doubt about the kind of feelings he had for her; he'd wanted to know if she had those same feelings for him.

She had to go back—not only to treat the burn, but also to show Jake her only feelings were those of professional duty. And to prove to herself she could keep her emotions out of it.

Ahead, Mariah saw Sheriff Logan step out of his office and adjust his hat. Bill Logan was a tall, lanky man with the leathery skin and bleached brown hair of a man who'd spent too much time in the sun.

He saw her and lifted his hat. "Evenin', Doc."

"Good evening, Sheriff."

She passed him, then paused. "Sheriff," she called, as he headed down the sidewalk in the opposite direction. He stopped and turned, waiting for her to continue. Suddenly she felt foolish. What would she say? The dog had barked? Her desk had been opened?

"Is this about the explosion?" he asked, walking toward her.

"I beg your pardon?"

"Jake said you'd probably be wanting to know about my investigation."

"Yes, of course. What did you find out?"

"It was an accident, Doc. Pure and simple. Not one of the workers I talked to could give me any reason to think otherwise."

"Did you check their dynamite supply?"

"Yes, ma'am. They'd received a new shipment just a few weeks before."

Mariah knew she should be relieved. If the sheriff had deemed it an accident, then that was the end of it. She didn't have to worry about it anymore.

Yet some things still nagged at her: Sam's voice whispering, *Not an accident;* her strange conversation with Oscar Drubb; the disturbance at her house. She had no solid proof, just a troubled feeling.

Luther sauntered down the opposite sidewalk of Center Street, hands in his pockets, whistling casually and nodding to people as he passed. He kept a safe distance between him and Mariah, making sure it didn't appear that he was trailing her. He knew she'd been to see Jake again. He'd seen her come out of the office with her medical bag.

Luther couldn't stand the personal attention she was giving Jake. What had that bastard done to deserve it? Luther slowed to look at the display in the general store window, waiting until Mariah moved on, then he started walking again.

"Evening, Sheriff," he called with a big smile.

"How're you doing there, Luther?"

"All right, I s'pose."

"How's your mama?"

"Just fine. Thanks for asking."

The sheriff nodded and moved on down the street.

Luther slowed as Mariah unlocked the door to her house. He watched with satisfaction as she paused to glance over her shoulder before stepping inside. Oh, yes, he'd spooked her all right. He now had her fearing someone was following her. *You didn't do that in Chicago, did you, Mariah?*

Luther waited a few minutes, then crossed the

street and slowly approached her house. When he saw the glow of lamplight, he glanced around to be sure no one was nearby, then hid behind the shrub beneath her window, rising just enough to peer through the glass.

In a moment, Mariah came into view. He ducked down as she raised the sash, then listened as she pulled out her chair and rolled back the desk top. Soon he heard the scratching of her pen and the turning of a page.

Easing himself up, he peered in again. She was writing in that black notebook. He'd have to sneak in tonight and take a look at it. For now, he'd just enjoy watching her work, relishing their secret intimacy.

Suddenly, he heard the rapid patter of feet inside coming toward the window. Stifling a furious curse, Luther took off running just as Mariah's dog jumped up and sniffed the air. There would be no getting into the house with that mongrel around.

Lazarus's frenzied barking startled Mariah. The dog ran to the door and scratched the wood, then dashed back to the window, barking and whining, nearly frantic to get out. Gooseflesh prickled Mariah's neck as she turned down the lamp and knelt at the window, peering out onto the street illuminated by a streetlamp several houses down. She felt a presence, yet she saw nothing.

"What is it, Laz?" she whispered.

The dog ran to the door, stood on his hind legs, and pawed at the knob. Cracking the door open an inch, Mariah peered outside, then opened it the rest of the way. Lazarus dashed past her, ran a few yards, then stopped to look around and sniff. Lowering his head, he sniffed his way to the shrubs beneath the window.

Rubbing her arms to chase away the gooseflesh, Mariah glanced up and down the deserted street. Other than the chirping of crickets and the occasional croak of a frog, everything was quiet. She waited until Lazarus was satisfied that the area was safe, then she called him in and threw the bolt on the door, something she couldn't ever remember anyone in her family doing. After lowering the window sash and pulling the curtain, she returned to her work, but found herself listening for noises outside. She began to wish there were bars at the windows.

Lazarus was now curled up on the rug near the hearth. She'd never seen him carry on so. "Laz, you're staying indoors with me tonight," she told him.

He lifted his head to look at her, then lowered it again. Whatever had spooked him was gone—for good, Mariah hoped.

The late afternoon sun filtered through the towering maples as Jake returned from checking the progress of the road the following day. His temper was short; he'd had to forego riding horseback and take a buggy because of the burn, so the journey was taking longer than he'd planned.

He found himself urging the horse ever faster,

eager to get to the mill by sundown in case Mariah decided to pay him a visit. Once he arrived, Jake paced his office, checking the window every five minutes. If she showed up, how would he act? Bored? Cross? Should he try to frighten her away again or pretend to ignore her?

When Mariah finally came across the mill floor, wearing a straw skimmer and a yellow dress, Jake had to blink several times to make sure she was real. He pulled the curtain, strode to his desk, and sat down, pretending to study a paper before him.

He had to frighten her off. He couldn't go on behaving like a schoolboy with a bad crush. How much longer could he stand being near her and not touching her?

When Mariah knocked and walked in, Jake glanced up at her indifferently, though his heart was doing flips. He leaned back in his chair and folded his arms. "What will it be today: a lecture or a treatment—or both?"

"Just a treatment," she said coolly.

Jake could see the unease in Mariah's gaze. Given his previous behavior, he could hardly fault her. And wasn't that what he'd wanted?

"How is your leg?" she asked, keeping her tone brisk and businesslike, as she removed her gloves and hat and set her bag on his desk.

"You can see for yourself." He rose and began to unfasten the buttons of his pants.

"Just the trousers," she said quickly.

His hands halted their movements, and he slowly lifted his gaze to hers. "Are you sure?" he asked huskily.

Her frosty glance was answer enough.

As soon as he'd lowered his trousers, Mariah knelt before him, keeping more space between them this time.

"Would you mind lifting the material?" she asked, putting on her spectacles.

Jake raised the leg of his drawers, his heart melting at the sight of Mariah peering through her glasses, her mouth pursed thoughtfully, trying to maintain a cool composure as if yesterday hadn't happened. Had she come back simply out of professional duty or because of something more powerful?

He chided himself for wishing the impossible.

"It's healing," she said, with obvious relief.

"Well, then, you won't need to come back." He watched her anxiously, waiting for her answer. If she agreed, so much the better for him. Or so he tried to tell himself.

"I think one more visit would be in order."

Jake tried not to watch as Mariah poured some of her poultice in her palm and smoothed the cool potion over his injured flesh with her fingertips. *One more visit.*

He took deep breaths, his fingers squeezing into fists as he tried to focus his thoughts elsewhere, but it was no use. Mariah's touch ignited fires that willpower simply couldn't control. He drew in deep gulps of air and slowly let it out. His desire was building, becoming fierce and urgent, demanding to be slaked.

"Unless you want a repeat of yesterday, you'd better finish that in a hurry," he warned her through clenched teeth.

Mariah glanced up at him, her mouth forming the word *oh*. Quickly, she cut fresh gauze and applied it to his skin. When she rose and began to put away her medicine, Jake saw a slight tremble in her hands.

He turned his back and fastened his pants, forcing down the urge to pull her into his arms and take her mouth in a crushing kiss.

What the hell—why shouldn't he?

At the sound of the door opening, he swung around. Mariah had gone.

Chapter 13

Mariah hung her hat on a peg and went back to the kitchen to make herself a cup of chamomile tea to steady her nerves. Lazarus followed her, tail wagging, undoubtedly hoping she'd have time to play.

"You'll have to settle for a good brushing tonight, Laz," she told him, taking a thickly bristled brush from the pantry.

While the water heated, Mariah knelt down to groom the dog, her thoughts on Jake. Telling him she would return one more time had been foolhardy. She was losing her ability to be objective, to treat him as she would any other patient. And Jake had made abundantly clear what his feelings were.

Would she have the strength to resist him?

* * *

"Good morning, Annie," Mariah called, as she tied on her apron the next morning.

" 'Morning, honey," Annie replied, walking toward her. "Livvy Adams is waiting to see you, but first I want you to check on Willy. He's feeling out of sorts. I'm afraid he may have picked up something from the Pullins kids."

Mariah walked through the curtain and sat down on the chair beside the bed. Willy was propped up on two pillows, his gaze following her listlessly.

"Don't feel up to snuff today?" Mariah asked, placing her hand on his forehead.

He gave a slight shake of his head. Annie walked in with a thermometer, and Mariah took the child's temperature. "It's up slightly," she told Annie. "You'd better ask Mrs. Pullins if any of her children are ill."

"Feel like eating anything?" she asked Willy, stroking his hair. When he merely shook his head, Mariah instructed Annie to give him some peppermint tea and keep a close watch on his temperature.

She had just shown Livvy Adams out of the surgery and was standing at the open door when a wagon came up the street at full speed.

"Doc!" one of the men yelled. "We've got an injured man."

Mariah hurried over to the wagon and glanced in the back, where one of the quarry men lay unconscious, his face ashen, his clothes damp from sweat. "What happened?" she asked.

"He was shoveling stone and just keeled over," the driver volunteered.

"Can you tell me your name?" she asked the patient, lifting his eyelids, hoping to get some reaction. When he didn't respond, another man said, "His name is Floyd Burns."

Mariah felt the pulse in Floyd's neck and found it fluttering erratically. "Bring him inside."

They carried him into the surgery and gently placed him on the table. Mariah had Annie stand by as she listened to Floyd's heart with her stethoscope. The beats were weak and erratic as the organ strained to pump blood. Mariah had seen the condition many times in the hospital in Chicago. Unfortunately, there was no good treatment for a failing heart.

She looked up to find the two men watching her anxiously. "I'm going to give Floyd something to make him more comfortable," she told them. "Annie, would you get the foxglove tonic, please?"

"What's wrong with him, Doc?" one of the men asked.

While Annie took a key from her pocket and opened the medicine case, Mariah motioned the men to one side.

"It's his heart," she told them quietly. "I'm afraid there's not much I can do. Sometimes foxglove helps."

Mariah took a measuring spoon and the dark glass bottle from Annie. But before she could pour a dose of the tonic, Floyd suddenly gasped, and his eyes bulged as he fought for breath. Mariah quickly handed the spoon and bottle to Annie and lifted Floyd's shoulders off the table, trying to make it easier for him to breathe. Despite her efforts, he gasped again, his arms flailing, and then his body went limp.

Mariah put the stethoscope to Floyd's chest but could find no beat. She checked his pulse, and that, too, was still. She told herself she could have done nothing more to help Floyd, yet Mariah still felt the burden of her failure.

Jake's deep voice broke the silence. "What happened?"

Mariah swung around in surprise as Jake strode to the table. "His heart gave out," she told him. "I was told Floyd fell over while shoveling stone."

Jake showed no emotion as he gazed down at the dead man.

While Annie covered the body with a blanket, Mariah pulled a sheet of paper and pen from a drawer and began to make notes for the death certificate. "How old was Floyd?"

"About fifty-two, Doc," one of the men supplied.

Fifty-two years old, and the poor man was laboring for fourteen hours a day in the summer sun. Mariah simmered at the injustice of it.

"Tom, get Floyd's wife and bring her here," Jake said in a dispassionate voice. "Ed, on your way back to the quarry, stop at the undertaker's."

His blatant callousness fired Mariah's indignation. She waited until Annie and the two men had left the room, then she turned to face Jake. "You had no business working a man that age from dawn to dusk shoveling heavy stone. Is that road worth more than his life?"

Jake's closed expression told her everything. Without replying, he swiveled and strode out of the room.

Mariah forced herself to take calming breaths as she opened the cabinet and put away the medicine. How could she have ever been in love with such a cold-hearted man? How could she have even felt any desire for him?

"Doc, it ain't Jake's fault."

Mariah turned to find one of the stone men standing sheepishly at the surgery door.

"Floyd wanted to do that work," he told her. "Nobody forced him."

"You're saying he chose to do that backbreaking work for fourteen hours a day?"

"What I'm saying is that he could'a chose not to."

"Wouldn't he have been fired?"

"Naw! Jake would'a just given him some lighter work at the mill, but Floyd wanted the extra money. He'd planned to retire next year."

Guilt stabbed her for the angry words she had hurled at Jake. Why hadn't he told her that?

"Hey, Jake, want a ride back?"

Jake glanced around to see Ed slowing down the wagon. Grateful for the chance to get off his injured leg, he climbed up and sat on the bench.

"Thanks."

"Jake, the doc didn't know what she was saying about Floyd. I set her straight, though. It just wasn't fair for you to take the blame."

"Doesn't matter. But thanks."

Jake knew he was kidding himself. It did matter, not only what Mariah had said, but also what she had implied—that he had caused another death, another in a seemingly continuous line of deaths.

Jake walked into his office and slumped down in his chair. Another life lost because the damned road had to be finished by October. Bracing his elbows on the desk, Jake rested his head in his hands.

Suddenly he caught sight of an envelope lying on the desktop. He tore it open and read the letter inside, then folded it and stuck it in his pocket. Finally, he'd managed to do one thing that would please Mariah: he'd found Willy's relatives.

Over a late supper that evening, Jake listened to Emeline chatter nonstop about her wedding plans while Owen sat quietly, picking over his food. Jake tried to engage him in conversation, but he seemed in a fog.

Excusing himself as soon as he could, Jake left and headed for Mariah's house. He had no intention of trying to see her; he'd just put the envelope under the door for someone to find in the morning.

But as he approached the house, Lazarus began to bark. He saw the dog watching him through a window. "Quiet, Laz," he whispered. "It's just me."

Suddenly, Mariah's front door opened slightly, and he saw an eye peer through the crack. "Jake?" Mariah opened the door. "What are you doing here?"

He held up the envelope. "I got an answer from Willy's relatives. I was going to leave it for you to read."

There was a hesitation, then she said, "Come in," and opened the door wider.

Given her earlier frame of mind, Mariah's invitation came as a shock. As Jake stepped inside, he saw her quickly tuck her hair behind her ears and run her palms down her skirt, as though suddenly conscious of her appearance. She had taken her hair down, and it lay like a beautiful curtain of blond silk on the shoulders of her light green blouse. She looked soft and vulnerable, like the lovely sixteen-year-old he'd been madly in love with, and nothing at all like the prim, professional doctor.

Lazarus's tail wagged furiously as he waited for Jake to acknowledge him. As Jake bent to scratch the dog behind the ears, he glanced around the parlor. The familiarity of the room squeezed the air from his lungs. He had once been a regular visitor there, at first with Ben, then later to see Mariah. How long ago that had been, yet it seemed like only yesterday.

Spotting an open notebook on the desk, he asked, "Am I disturbing your work?"

"I've just finished. What does the letter say?"

Jake handed her the envelope. Donning her spectacles, Mariah seated herself on the sofa, while Jake wandered over to the small sideboard set against one wall to look at the framed photos on it. He saw one of Mariah, Eliza, and Ben, and turned away.

"So Willy has an aunt and uncle living in Fort Wayne," Mariah said, removing her glasses.

"From the sound of it, they'll be here sometime next week to pick him up."

Mariah took her time folding the paper and inserting it in the envelope. "I think I'd like to meet them first."

"They're his kin, Mariah. We can't stop them from taking him."

"I can't just hand Willy over as if he were a parcel of merchandise, either. I want to interview them to make sure they're suitable."

A sudden tapping noise brought Mariah to her feet with a gasp. She glanced at the window, a look of alarm on her face.

"What is it?" Jake asked, starting toward her. Lazarus gave a friendly yap and bounded past him, heading for the kitchen. Mariah's body sagged in relief as she started after him.

"Annie's at the kitchen door," she called over her shoulder.

Jake followed, wondering what had caused her fear.

"Honey, Willy's temperature is up," he heard Annie say. "I've given him tea and broth and put a cold cloth on his forehead, but I can't get the fever down. You'd better come take a look."

Annie peered around Mariah. "Jake!" she exclaimed in surprise. Her puzzled glance shifted to Mariah.

"I'll explain later." Mariah put Lazarus in the backyard, then turned back to Jake. "Thank you for bringing the letter."

"I'd like to see Willy to make sure he's all right, if you don't mind."

"I don't mind," she told him, surprised by his sudden interest.

Willy lay on the narrow bed, tossing restlessly and moaning, his body shaking from fever. Mariah took the thermometer from Annie and tried to get it in the child's mouth, but his teeth were chattering too violently. She put her hand on Willy's back, which radiated heat.

"Annie, we need a washbasin filled with tepid water."

From the corner of her eye, Mariah saw Annie sink down on the chair. "I don't feel so good myself, honey."

Mariah took a closer look, noting the unnatural flush to her cheeks. "You have a fever, too, don't you? Why didn't you tell me?"

"You've got enough worries without me adding to them."

"I'll get the water for Willy," Jake offered. "You see to Annie."

Despite her friend's protests, Mariah saw Annie settled in her spare bedroom with a cool cloth and cold peppermint tea. Hurrying back to the dispensary, she found Jake bathing Willy's face and neck with a wet cloth, talking soothingly to the child.

"Is Annie all right?" Jake asked.

"I think she's caught whatever Willy has." Mariah sat down next to him on the side of the bed and said quietly, "I can't tell how serious it is yet, but you shouldn't be here. It's probably contagious."

"Don't worry about me." He met her gaze evenly. "Let's get this fever down."

Mariah tried to coax Willy to drink water, but he thrashed about to much, muttering incoherently. For half an hour she and Jake applied cool cloths to his body, but they couldn't bring his temperature back to normal.

"I'll have to immerse him," Mariah said, rolling back her sleeves.

Jake rose, starting for the door. "Tell me where to find the buckets."

"Beneath the sink in the supply room. The tub is in my kitchen pantry. I'll meet you there."

While Jake pumped water from the well outside, Mariah heated more on her range. When the temperature in the tub was right, Jake carried Willy in and lowered him into the water. Instantly the boy began to struggle. Between Mariah's soothing words and Jake's strong arms, they were able to calm him. After nearly an hour, his fever had gone down enough to put him back to bed. Willy fell asleep almost at once.

Mariah brewed another pot of peppermint tea while Jake stayed at the child's bedside. As she stood in her kitchen waiting for the tea to steep, her foot tapped anxiously against the floor. She suddenly realized that her anxiety was not completely attributable to Willy's condition. She was in a hurry to get back to Jake.

Mariah paced the kitchen, unable to stand still. She had to stop what was happening to her.

Why couldn't she get it through her head that the boy she'd once loved was gone and there could never be a future for her with the man he'd become? As much as she wanted to keep the past from intruding on her life, what had happened that summer afternoon long ago would always be with her, preventing her from ever fully forgiving him. And without forgiveness, there could never be love.

With new determination, Mariah carried the teapot in on a tray and placed it on a small table in the corner. As she poured the tea, she noticed that Jake had brought in a chair from the waiting room and placed it next to his.

"You needn't stay any longer, Jake. I'm sure you're tired."

"No more so than you. In any case, if Willy's fever spikes again, you'll need help."

"I'll manage," she told him.

"I'm going to stay." Jake waited until she met his gaze, then he said quietly, "Whether you believe it or not, Mariah, my concern is genuine."

Oddly, she wanted to believe him. They drank the rest of their tea in silence.

After that, the tension between them seemed to

lessen. Soon Mariah found herself telling Jake about the many trials, tribulations, and calamities of her sister, Eliza, in Chicago. "That town will never be the same," Mariah said, shaking her head. "I do miss her, though."

For a moment Jake said nothing. Then, in a voice husky with emotion, he asked, "Why did you come back to Coffee Creek, Mariah?"

His question caught her off guard. Mariah's stomach gave a sudden lurch as she remembered the words he had thrown at her after the newspaper article came out. *Why did you come back? To torture me? To make my life miserable?*

"You know why," she said evenly, keeping her gaze on Willy. "To take my father's place."

"Is that the only reason?"

Mariah found herself suddenly defensive. "I came because my father wanted me to," she replied. "I wouldn't have come otherwise."

"I thought so." There was a long pause, then Jake said quietly, "I wasn't surprised to hear that you'd become a doctor."

She turned her head to gaze at him. "You weren't?"

"You're smart. Compassionate." He studied her for a long moment. "It suits you."

His praise was so unexpected that Mariah was momentarily at a loss for words. She'd never thought of her career choice in those terms. She'd just felt obligated to become a doctor because Ben hadn't been able to. But Jake was right. She enjoyed her work. It did suit her.

"Thank you," she said finally.

After another cup of tea and another hour of maintaining a vigil, Mariah felt her eyelids drift shut. She came awake with a jerk, nearly dropping her cup. She quickly set it down and rose to check Willy's temperature.

"How is it?" Jake asked, rubbing his eyes.

"His temperature is slightly elevated but nowhere near where it was before."

Jake got to his feet.

"Are you leaving?" she asked, feeling a sudden, sharp sense of disappointment.

He gazed down at her with warm blue eyes. "Do you want me to?"

"You stood up. I thought—"

"I don't have to go."

"Don't."

Mariah stared into his eyes, unable to look away. *Why did I say that? Why didn't I just let him leave?* The answer frightened her.

"I need some fresh air," he told her. "I'll be back in a moment."

Mariah checked Willy, then sat down again, twisting her hands together. She caught herself glancing at the back door, waiting for Jake to return. She fidgeted in her chair for what felt like an eternity and finally got up, telling herself she was only going to check on the dog.

Mariah stepped outside, where a warm breeze lifted her hair. The night was alive with the sounds of insects and the lush, grassy smells of summer. The moon cast a pale glow over the ground, illuminating the fence, where Jake reached over to pet Lazarus. The dog had his paws on the top rail, his tail wagging excitedly.

Mariah couldn't stop herself from walking over to the fence. "You've made a friend," she told Jake, reaching over to stroke Laz's head.

"He's a good dog."

She didn't know what to say next and wasn't even sure why she had come out. Mariah studied Jake's strong profile. It was on just such a night that she had fallen in love with him.

"Why did you ask me to stay?" he said suddenly.

Once again he caught her by surprise. "I suppose I wanted the company."

"No supposing."

Mariah hesitated, then said quietly, "I *wanted* the company."

"Are you that desperate?" he asked ironically.

"I don't put up with anyone or anything unless I choose to."

He stared off into the darkness. "I wish I could say the same."

"I learned it from you," Mariah answered softly.

Jake looked around at her, the bleakness of his expression startling. "Mariah, I—"

She saw him swallow, then he glanced away and shook his head, as though it was impossible to get the words out.

Unable to help herself, Mariah reached out to him, putting her hand on his arm. "What is it? Tell me."

For a moment, Jake said nothing. Then he

brought his hands to her face, cupping it between his warm palms as he gazed down at her.

Mariah's heart began to gallop. She searched his eyes for a clue to his thoughts, but, as usual, he kept them well hidden.

"Some things are better left unspoken," he whispered, and slowly dipped his head toward her.

Chapter 14

Mariah closed her eyes as Jake captured her lips in a long, smoldering kiss. Her thoughts whirled madly as his kiss became deeper, hungrier. *Stop him*, her conscience ordered. But his lips were so firm and demanding, his hands so warm and gentle, that she ignored the warning and kissed him back.

His hands slid down her shoulders and over her back to cup her derriere, bringing her tightly against his hard body. Desire surged through Mariah's veins, driving out every other thought. She draped her arms over his shoulders and entwined her fingers in his thick hair, reveling in its coarse texture, in the minty taste of his mouth and musky scent of his skin.

Jake lifted her long hair away from her neck as his lips forged a hot trail across her cheek to the sensitive spot below her ear, where his tongue drew lazy circles. His mouth slid down one side of her throat and up the other, and suddenly he was kissing her again, coaxing her lips apart, his tongue searing hers as it probed and stroked. Liquid heat knotted deep inside her, bringing on a delicious throbbing that left Mariah weak and wanting.

Jake broke away to stare down at her, as though stunned by the passion vibrating between them. Then he kissed her again, more intensely, and Mariah melted against his hardness. She gripped his shoulders as his tongue flickered lightly over her lips then plunged into her mouth, tantalizing her with excitement and the hint of pleasures yet to come.

Slowly, the sound of Lazarus's whining broke through the thick fog of desire, reminding Mariah of where she was and who she was with.

She broke the kiss suddenly, breathlessly, and stepped back, rubbing her fingers across her swollen lips as she realized the magnitude of her actions. What if Annie had seen them? She'd behaved scandalously—and with Jake Sullivan!

Too shocked to speak, she turned and fled.

Jake's heart sank as Mariah hurried inside the dispensary. The shock and repulsion on her face had told him all he needed to know. Why hadn't he left well enough alone? What had happened to his common sense? He'd worked so hard to tame that reckless, impetuous side of his nature, but one moment of passion had brought it all out again.

Jake headed home just as the first faint light of morning tinted the sky. Although bone-tired, he was almost glad of the dawn. He wouldn't have found any solace in sleep.

After washing and changing into fresh clothing, Jake left for the mill, arriving just as a newsboy delivered the *Coffee Creek Gazette*. Jake flipped the boy a coin, tucked the paper under his arm, and climbed the stairs.

Sitting down in his chair, he opened the paper, put his feet on the desk, and leaned back to read it. The headline proclaimed:

SENATOR COFFMAN APPALLED BY PARTNER'S CARE-LESSNESS.

Jake swung his legs down and sat up, his fury building as he saw himself described as a hard taskmaster determined to finish the road at all costs, forcing the men to work punishing hours, mistakenly and foolishly believing the senator's seat depended on it.

"Son of a bitch!" Jake rolled the paper into a tube and threw it as hard as he could against the wall. How dared his partner betray him! He stalked across the room and back several times, trying to think what to do. Finally, he yanked open the door, summoned a clerk, and began dictating a letter.

As the young man took down his words, Jake paced the room, his hands clenching and unclenching, his stomach in knots. Then he strode to the desk, signed his name at the bottom, and handed the pen back to the clerk. "Take it to the post office at once."

"Luther!"

At the sound of his mother's sharp voice, Luther set the cup of tea on the tray and hustled into her bedroom. She'd complained of pain in her belly that morning, so he'd left the quarry at noon to come home and check on her.

"Here's your tea, Mama."

"Where's my soda water?" she cried, as he placed the tray on her lap. "You know I have to have soda water for my digestion."

"I'm sorry, Mama. I didn't think of it. I'll go down to the store and get it right now."

"You should have gone this morning. It's Monday, you know. You're supposed to get it on Monday."

"All right, Mama. I'm going now. Calm yourself."

"Don't tell me to calm myself. You always do this to me, Luther." She rubbed a thickly veined hand over her left breast. "You get me riled, and you know that's not good for my heart. What have I done to deserve a child like you?"

Luther dropped his gaze. He hated disappointing her. She'd always done so much for him. "I'm sorry, Mama. I promise I won't let you down again."

"Ha! As if I could ever believe you."

As he headed into town, Luther spotted Mariah and her dog walking in the opposite direction. She carried her black bag; she was probably on her way to make a house call.

Leaving her own house empty.

Excitement surged through his veins. It was just the opportunity he'd been waiting for. Quickly, Luther bought the bottled soda water at the general store, then headed down the street toward the dispensary. His mama would just have to wait a few more minutes for her tonic.

Ahead, he saw Oscar Drubb sweeping the empty sidewalk in front of the barber shop. As he drew even with Oscar, Luther made a barking noise that sent Oscar scuttling into the shop.

With a snicker, Luther continued on to Mariah's house. He glanced around to make sure he wasn't being watched, then stole around the side, keeping low and hugging the wall. Jumping the fence, he crossed the backyard, opened Mariah's door, and slipped inside.

For a moment, Luther stood in the middle of her kitchen, inhaling the scents, wishing he had time to familiarize himself with all the room's details. But the sound of a distant ticking clock reminded him that he had to hurry. He headed for her bedroom, where he began opening drawers, looking through her belongings.

This would be the best surprise yet.

Mariah felt the first symptoms of fever as she headed back to the dispensary at lunchtime. She tried to tell herself she merely needed rest, that the hot flush on her cheeks was a result of her heated kiss with Jake, but she knew better.

"Hello, Mariah," someone called from behind.

Mariah turned to see Mrs. Drubb, Oscar's mother, standing in front of the milliner's shop. She returned the greeting and waited for the elderly lady to catch up.

"I've been wanting to talk to you about Oscar," Mrs. Drubb began. "I'd appreciate it if you could come by our house to see him."

"Is he ill?"

"No, dear. It's about the explosion. Oscar mumbles about it all the time. He's even had nightmares. I don't know why it has affected him so much."

"I'll try to stop by in the next day or so."

By the time she reached the dispensary, Mariah felt dizzy and weak. Gertrude Johnson was filling in for Annie at the desk. Thankfully, no patients were waiting to see her.

"How's Willy?" Mariah asked, as she headed back to wash her hands.

"He's sleeping now. I was able to get him to eat some beef broth. I made it myself."

"Good. And thank you so much for taking Annie's place. How is she, by the way?"

"Weak, but at least her fever is gone. She wanted to work, but I wouldn't let her."

Mariah went to the back and splashed cool water on her heated face. Her muscles ached, and she was starting to feel a chill. "After I check Willy,

I'm going home to lie down for a while, Mrs. Johnson. Will you keep Laz here with you?"

"You know I will. Are you feeling poorly, dear?"

"Just a little warm," Mariah told her. "I'll be all right after a quick nap. I didn't get any sleep last night."

As soon as she'd satisfied herself that Willy was doing well, Mariah opened the connecting door and stepped into her kitchen, thinking only of crawling into bed. But as she closed the door behind her, the hairs on her neck suddenly prickled.

Mariah turned with a jerk, her gaze sweeping the room, her heart thudding in sudden trepidation. Yet as before, no one was there.

Cautiously, Mariah opened a cabinet, took out her mother's wooden rolling pin, then tiptoed to the parlor doorway and glanced around. Her desk was closed, but she checked it anyway. She found her notebook undisturbed and her papers in order. Nothing in the room seemed out of place.

Still feeling ill at ease, Mariah checked the front bedroom and then her own room at the back. She told herself the fear was simply the product of her tired mind, yet she couldn't shake the eerie feeling that someone had been there.

Standing at her dressing table mirror, Mariah examined her flushed face and stuck out her tongue, which she was dismayed to see was coated. She couldn't fall ill; she didn't have time.

Her head throbbed as she opened the buttons down the front of her blouse. She took it off, then unfastened her skirt and let it drop to the floor, her petticoat and stockings following a moment later. Laying them over a chair, Mariah walked to her bed wearing only her chemise and corset. One hour's rest, she told herself, and she'd be fine. She grabbed the coverlet, folded it down—and jerked her hand back with a gasp of alarm.

A sheet of her personal stationery lay on the pillow.

Mariah stared at it in shock. She hadn't seen the distinctive blue-bordered paper in years. She'd even forgotten where she'd stashed it.

She tried to reassure herself that Annie had probably left it or even Gertrude. But she knew that was illogical. There was only one rational conclusion: someone had been in the house. Worse yet, he'd gone through her personal things.

Mariah stretched out a trembling hand and drew the paper toward her. A feeling of dread crawled up her spine as she unfolded it.

Jake is a murderer.
Leave now, Mariah, or you'll be next!

Mariah dropped the letter, her heart pounding in fear as the paper floated to the floor. Who was trying to frighten her?

She tried to think what to do, but her head began to swim, and she felt like she was about to faint. Crawling onto the bed, Mariah pulled the coverlet around her and lay shaking, teeth chattering and body aching, her fevered mind trying to sort out the implications of that terrifying message. Was she becoming delirious? Perhaps if she closed her eyes for a moment, she'd be able to focus on the situation.

Sometime later, she heard Annie calling her and realized she'd dozed off.

"In h-here," she answered.

In a moment, she felt Annie's hand on her forehead. "Oh, goodness, honey, you're burning up. You must have caught the fever from Willy, too."

"Annie, th-there's a letter on the floor."

"Where, honey? I don't see anything. I'm going to get you a cloth for your forehead. You stay put."

There had to be a letter. Annie must have missed it. Mariah pushed herself to her elbows, then sat up and slowly swung her aching legs to the floor. She stood with great effort and looked around, bewildered. Lowering herself to her hands and knees, she peered under the bed. She couldn't possibly have dreamed it.

"Mariah, what in heaven's name are you doing?" Annie exclaimed. "Come on, honey, let me help you."

"You sh-shouldn't be up, Annie. You're still r-recovering yourself."

"Don't you worry about me. I'm much better."

Mariah allowed herself to be guided back to bed, where the coverlet was pulled up around her and a wet cloth was laid across her forehead.

"I hope Jake didn't catch the fever, too," Annie mused. "Perhaps I should send someone around to alert him."

Jake is a murderer. Leave now, Mariah, or you'll be next!

Mariah scrunched her eyes shut. Was someone trying to frighten her—or warn her?

Chapter 15

Standing on the floor of the Franklin quarry, Jake watched with relief as a small crew successfully cut neat grooves with the new channeling machine.

"Good work!" he called above the noise, then turned when a boy ran up to him and handed him a letter. Jake tore it open and began to read, but got no farther than the second line. Mariah had been struck down by a fever. He didn't bother to read the rest.

When he charged in through the front door of the dispensary, Gertrude looked up with a gasp. "Good gracious, you nearly frightened me to death!"

"Where's Mariah?"

"She's at home in her bed, but—"

Jake strode to the back and opened the connecting door.

"You can't go in there!" Gertrude finished.

He got as far as Mariah's doorway, where Annie blocked his path. "She's not up to visitors," Annie said in a hushed voice.

He peered around her, but Annie pushed him farther back, pulling the door closed behind her.

"Is Mariah all right?" he asked impatiently.

"Yes, her fever is coming down. I told you that in my note. We were just concerned you might have caught something, too."

Mariah was concerned. "I'm fine," he told her.

"Good. Then go back to work," Annie said, guiding him to the door. "She should be up to visitors tomorrow."

"I'll be here. Tell her I'll be here."

"I will," Annie assured him. She shut the door after him, shaking her head. Poor Jake. He'd never gotten over Mariah.

Luther quietly opened the door to his house and stepped inside, carefully maneuvering around the squeak in the floorboards. No matter how he tried, his mother always seemed to know when he came in. It had become a game with him to see if he could fool her. Today he just wanted to be able to think without her nagging him.

He'd had good and bad luck that afternoon. Besides leaving Mariah his clever note, he'd managed to get a look at that book she was always writing in. That's where he'd found her record of the explosion.

"Not an accident," she'd written. Seeing those words in black ink had angered him so much that he'd nearly ripped out the page. But that would have been a stupid thing to do. He didn't want her to make the connection between her scares and the explosion.

Dang it! Mariah didn't know it wasn't an accident. She couldn't. Except for the senator, no one knew anything. Luther clenched his fists as the inferno inside him grew. Now he had to find out why she had written it. What did she know that he didn't?

"Luther? Is that you?"

"Yes, Mama. I've got your soda water."

"It's about time. Where'd you have to go for it? Ohio?"

Luther took a glass of the water into the bedroom. "Here, Mama. This will make you feel better."

"I doubt it. You took too long. I could have died before you returned." She scowled at him as she sipped the water, then set it down with a bang, sloshing water onto the table. "It isn't fresh. You take it back right now and see that you bring me a fresh one."

"I have to get back to the quarry, Mama. You know how they depend on me there. I'll have to bring it after work."

"Hmpf! Never mind. I'll just make do with what

I've got. It's what I've had to do with you, all these years."

Luther bent down to press a light kiss on her forehead, but she only jerked away. "I'll see you later, Mama. You rest and get better now, all right?"

"As if you cared," she muttered. "It's no wonder your father went to an early grave."

Luther felt the sharp sting of her words all the way back to the quarry, but he knew she didn't really mean it. She was just feeling poorly. She always talked mean when she was feeling poorly.

"Hey, Luther," the foreman called. "Where did you go? I've been looking for you."

Luther hesitated. He'd told the same story so many times it made him ill. *I had to go home. Mama's not feeling well.* And every time he said it, he knew people were laughing at him. But he couldn't help it that his mother had ailments. "I had to go to the outhouse."

"For an hour?" the foreman asked, causing the few men standing nearby to chuckle. "If it takes you that long, son, you'd better have the doc check you out."

"I guess you're right, Dan. Thanks for the advice." Luther walked away from him and headed for the derrick. *Bastard*. Dan's jeers fueled the rage inside him. The foreman didn't know it, but he'd just sealed his own fate.

Luther could thank Dan for one thing, though. He'd come up with a great way to get close to Mariah: he'd become her patient.

* * *

Mariah was back on her feet the next afternoon, though she hadn't gotten over the shock of the letter. She'd told Annie about it, and they'd both searched the house, but it hadn't turned up. She knew Annie thought she'd simply dreamed it, but Mariah was sure it was real. Where had it gone?

The most logical explanation scared her to death.

For the first time in her life, Mariah felt unsafe in her own home. As soon as she was up and dressed, she walked down to the cabinetmaker's shop and purchased a wooden bar for each of her windows.

With her windows and doors secured and her mind more at ease, Mariah turned her attention to other matters. Annie had told her about Jake's surprising visit and his promise to return. Mariah wasn't sure she wanted to see him.

She had thought long and hard about their passionate embrace, trying and failing to find some justification for her own behavior. All she really knew was that she couldn't love Jake. She *wouldn't* love him. It tortured her to think she could feel such desire for the man who had ended Ben's life. Yet how could she deny the passion Jake aroused?

She had to find a way to stop those feelings. The next time she saw him, she had to view him as the person he was: a hard, ruthless man who cared more about profit than human life.

Mariah was working at her desk that evening when Lazarus raced to the door and began to bark.

With a thudding heart, she rose just as someone knocked on the door. She moved slowly toward it, glad she had thought to throw the bolt.

"Who's there?" she called.

"Jake."

Relief washed over her, followed by a sudden excited fluttering of her stomach—and then dismay. She braced herself to resist his potent appeal and opened the door.

Yet as Mariah gazed up at him, so splendidly masculine in a pair of black pants and a blue cotton shirt, she knew she could no more control her reaction than she could change the seasons.

He handed her a bouquet of wild daisies. "I thought these might cheer you up."

Mariah brought them to her nose, inhaling to catch their fragrance—and to hide the blush that colored her cheeks. "That's very kind of you."

"You're feeling better?"

"Much better, thank you." She pretended to examine one of the blooms. It was difficult to think badly of Jake when he was being so sweet.

Remember who he is, Mariah.

"I'm glad you're better." Jake gazed at her for a moment, as though he was waiting for her to say something. Mariah blushed harder. She couldn't invite him in; being alone with him was too risky.

But she couldn't just let him walk away, either.

Quickly, Mariah tried to think of something else to talk about, wanting to keep him there—and knowing she shouldn't. "You didn't catch the fever," she blurted.

"No. I was lucky. How's Willy doing?"

"He seems completely recuperated." Seeing a potential conversation, Mariah came outside and sat on the stoop. "I've been giving his situation a great deal of thought."

She was relieved when Jake sat beside her. "What have you decided?"

"Willy is a bright little boy," she said. "He just hasn't had the education to bring it out. I want to make sure these relatives of his will promise to see that he has schooling. I don't want him treated like a farmhand."

"And if they won't?"

"They can't have him."

"How will you stop them?"

"I don't know yet. I'll have to see a lawyer, I suppose."

"You may have a fight on your hands," Jake warned. "Are you prepared for that?"

"Willy has lost the people he loved most in the world. I know precisely what he's suffering, and I'll go to any length to keep him from being hurt further."

She was so fiercely protective that Jake's insides ached. "I hope it works out the way you want it."

Mariah searched his eyes as though trying to peer into his soul. "So do I," she said softly.

Jake's gaze dropped to her mouth. He desperately wanted to taste her, to hold her in his arms, to stir her desire as she stirred his. He leaned toward her, intending to kiss her. Her eyes widened, but she didn't pull back.

Slowly, he touched his lips to hers, feeling the electricity spark between them. Then she did draw back, as though that spark had been too intense, too frightening. Instantly, she rose and opened her door, calling out a hasty "Good night, Jake."

Luther brought two work horses out to the Jefferson quarry the next morning, taking his time with their harnesses while keeping his eye on the twenty-odd men on the floor. Stealthily, he slipped his knife from his pocket, switched it open, and cut a deep gash in his left forearm, slicing through the shirt, relishing the sudden sting of air hitting raw flesh.

For a moment Luther watched, transfixed, as red blood pooled in the gash and soaked through his shirt. With a satisfied grin, he wiped the blade on the torn sleeve and put it away.

Glancing over his shoulder, Luther grabbed the derrick rope overhead and drew it through the open wound, making sure to embed hemp fibers in the cut.

"Dang it!" he said loud enough for others to hear. He saw one of the men look over at him. "I'm hurt," he called, slumping to the ground. "Where's Dan?"

"Hey, Dan!" the man yelled out. "Luther's been hurt."

As Luther leaned his back against the derrick and pressed his handkerchief against the gash to stem the blood, he saw the foreman heading toward him.

"What happened, Luther?"

"Aw, the derrick rope sliced me a little, is all." Luther removed the cloth and showed the fore-man.

"How the hell did it cut so deep? You'd better see the doc right away." He turned and motioned to one of the men. "Bill, take Luther over to the dispensary."

Luther let them help him into a wagon, then he put his head down so they couldn't see the smile on his face.

Mariah spent part of the noon hour teaching Willy how to write his letters. As he stuck his tongue between his teeth and bent over the small slate, earnestly copying Mariah's writing, she couldn't help but compare him to the skinny waif he'd been when they first brought him in. Willy had gained weight, his brown hair was clean and neatly combed to one side, and he sported a new yellow shirt and a pair of plaid knickers.

"How's that?" he asked, glancing up eagerly.

"It's perfect, just perfect." Mariah ruffled his hair. "You keep practicing. Tomorrow we'll finish the alphabet."

"Can I play with Laz now?"

"Sure you can. He's out in the backyard. Just don't get winded; you're still recovering from a fever."

"I won't."

Mariah watched him go, pleased that Willy was regaining his youthful enthusiasm. She had engaged Gertrude to come every morning to teach him arithmetic. Willy now slept in Annie's spare bedroom, where the two women thought he'd feel more settled. Willy had also made a friend of Lazarus, who had at first shied away.

Mariah found herself dreading the upcoming visit from Willy's relatives. The thought of strangers taking him away worried her sick.

"You've got a patient, honey," Annie said, as Mariah washed her hands. "A stone man injured at the quarry."

Mariah pulled her apron on over her head. "Willy is out back with Laz."

"I'll keep an eye on him," Annie told her.

She walked through the waiting room to the surgery, but stopped suddenly just outside the room when the hairs on the back of her neck began to prickle. From the doorway she could see a man in profile sitting on the examining table. He had on the customary workers' outfit of white shirt, brown suspenders, and dusty brown work pants; certainly nothing to cause alarm. As she walked toward him, she saw that he was cradling his left arm and that his sleeve was blood-soaked.

Hearing her come in, he turned his head—and smiled.

Chapter 16

"What do we have here?" Mariah asked crisply.

"I sliced my arm with a rope." He announced the injury almost as though he was proud of it. He peeled off a bloody handkerchief and held out his wounded arm.

Mariah put on her spectacles. The gash ran about five inches down his left forearm, halfway between wrist and elbow. Coarse fibers clung to the clots of blood in the wound, giving evidence of the damage done by the rope. And yet the skin looked too evenly severed to have been caused by a rope.

"Pretty bad, huh?" he asked. His voice was calm, as though he was not at all disturbed by his injury, yet his feet waggled as if he had too much pent-up energy.

"How did it happen?"

"There's a line that hangs from the derrick mast on a pulley. I grabbed it and tugged it down, but it snapped up and caught my arm."

Mariah studied him as he talked. He looked familiar, but she couldn't remember his name. He was near her age, with wiry brown hair, a thin face, and light brown eyes that watched her with strange intensity.

"What's your name?" she asked, turning to open her medicine cabinet.

"Luther Sinton."

"Mr. Sinton, I'm going to have to clean the wound before I stitch it up." Mariah poured a vinegar solution onto a piece of cloth. "This will hurt. I can give you a shot of whiskey or a few drops of laudanum if you'd like."

"I'd like it if you'd call me Luther."

Mariah turned to put the bottle of solution away. The odd request made her uncomfortable, though she didn't understand why. She decided to simply ignore his request.

"You remember me, don't you?" he asked with a confident grin. "I was a year behind you in school."

"Did you want something for the pain?"

"Naw," he said. "I don't want you to go out of your way for me."

"It's part of my job," she assured him.

"I can take the pain."

"If you change your mind, let me know." Mariah began to clean the wound, using her pincers to

carefully pick the tiny fibers from the raw flesh.
She knew it had to hurt, yet when she looked up,
his eyes were half shut and his mouth was curved
in the barest hint of a smile, almost as if he were in
a dreamlike state.

She threaded a surgical needle. "Are you sure
you don't want anything?"

"I'm fine."

Luther quietly watched her work for a few
moments, then he said, "I saw Joe Krall yesterday.
He's doing pretty good, considering what he went
through. That was too bad about the explosion,
wasn't it?"

Mariah paused to glance up at him, ever inter-
ested in hearing a new opinion on the blast. "Yes, it
was a terrible tragedy. Were you at the quarry that
morning?"

"Sure I was." He held up his right palm to show
her the tiny scars. "My hand got cut up pretty
bad."

"What do you think caused the explosion?"

Luther grinned. "You've been listening to all
that gossip, haven't you?"

"Then you believe it was just an accident?"

"What else could it have been?" he asked, with a
shrug.

"That's what I'm trying to find out." Mariah
began to wrap his arm with gauze. "I hope you're
not left-handed."

"No, Mariah, I'm not."

His familiar use of her name annoyed her. "I'd
prefer you to call me Dr. Lowe." She put away the

gauze and walked to the open doorway. "I'll have to check your arm tomorrow. Will you be able to stop by during your lunch break?"

With a sullen look, Luther got down from the table. "I'll be here."

Mariah waited until the door closed behind him, then she turned to Annie sitting at the desk. "What an odd experience. That's the first time I've ever seen anyone smile while being stitched up."

"Dang it!" Luther said as he headed back to the quarry, causing a pair of ladies to turn around on the sidewalk with an indignant gasp. He hadn't found out what he needed to know. Somehow he had to get Mariah to talk about the explosion.

Luther lifted his hat to the ladies and gave them his humblest smile. "Beg pardon. I didn't mean any offense. I got my arm hurt real bad down at the quarry this morning, and it hurts something fierce. I just came from the doc's."

They murmured sympathies and clicked their tongues like they felt sorry for him. Luther patted the knife in his pocket. *Watch out, old biddies, or you won't have any tongues to click.*

With a smile, he sauntered on, calling friendly greetings to people on the street. He hadn't lied; his left forearm hurt like the devil—but he liked the pain. It made him feel alive.

Jake kept his eye on his sister as they ate supper that evening. Emeline had high color in her cheeks, and her movements seemed jerky. Twice she sloshed water onto her lap and three times she dropped her fork, startling Owen out of his doldrums when it clattered to her plate.

"Holy terrors!" Owen exclaimed irritably. "What's the matter with you?"

"What's the matter with *you*?" Emeline retorted. "Can't a body drop a fork?" She rose with a huff and threw down her soggy napkin. "Oh, stop pouting, Owen. I'm leaving you to eat in peace. Are you happy now?"

Jake gave his brother a cold look to silence any reply he might make. "Is something wrong?" he asked, following his sister into the hallway.

"Wrong?" Emeline replied snidely, starting up the staircase. "What could possibly be wrong? In a matter of days I'm getting married to a wonderful man. I'm the happiest girl alive." She broke into tears, lifted the hem of her skirt, and dashed up to her room.

Jake started up after her, cringing at the loud slam of her door. He knocked softly, but her sobs muffled it. Opening the door, he peered in. She was lying on her stomach on the bed, her arms folded beneath her head.

"Go away, Jake! You can't help me."

"If you don't want to marry Percy, just say so."

She turned to look at him, her eyes swollen and red. "Then who am I going to marry?"

"You don't have to marry anyone."

"You want me to be an old maid?" She threw herself down again, crying harder.

Jake decided to leave before he made things

worse. He stuffed his hands in his pockets and headed back to the dining room, where Owen was pouring himself a whiskey from the decanter at the sideboard.

"I don't think she wants to marry Percy," Jake commented.

"No one else is going to marry her," Owen muttered. "She'd better not let him get away."

Jake sighed wearily. "I wish I knew what to do."

"Have a drink. It won't seem so bad, then."

Jake frowned as Owen tilted back the glass and drained it. "You'll kill yourself on that rotgut."

"I doubt I'd be that lucky." Owen held up his glass in silent salute and walked out of the room.

With a frustrated shake of his head, Jake sat down and stared blindly at his plate. He didn't know how to help Owen—he wasn't even sure Owen wanted to be helped—but he was at even more of a loss with Emeline. She needed a woman to talk to, someone knowledgeable and caring.

Perhaps Mariah would help her.

In his senate office in Washington, D.C., Hugh Coffman leaned back in his chair, picked up Jake's letter with a frown, and read it again.

Ah, well, he'd wire Jake tomorrow and simply tell him the truth: that he'd said what he had to say to the reporter to keep from losing votes. Jake understood how important that was.

But in another few weeks, it wouldn't matter if he understood or not. The deal had already been made with Bernhardt. Hugh was quite proud of his business acumen. He'd led Bernhardt to believe Jake had the capital to buy him out, forcing Bernhardt to raise his offer several times. An unethical move to some, but he simply considered it a shrewd business decision.

Nothing was official yet, of course, but he had Bernhardt's word on it. C & S Indiana Limestone was about to be history.

Mariah's first stop the next morning was to see Oscar Drubb. She left Lazarus on the porch and accompanied Oscar's father to the kitchen, where his mother was serving a breakfast of potatoes fried in butter, and bacon.

"Look, Oscar," his mother said, "the doctor has come to see us."

Oscar stopped shoveling potatoes into his mouth and stared at Mariah.

"Please sit down," his father said, pulling a rickety chair out from the small pine table.

Mariah sat across from Oscar. "How are you feeling? Good?" At his nod, Mariah asked, "Are you sleeping soundly at night?"

Again a nod.

"No nightmares, Oscar?"

He dipped his head and began eating again, ignoring her question.

"Oscar, you must tell the doctor the truth," his mother prodded. "She wants to help you."

Mariah tried again. "What are your nightmares about, Oscar?"

He looked up at Mariah, then his gaze shifted past her, his eyes growing wide. "Mad dog. Mad dog."

"The nightmares are about a dog?"

"Mad dog. Arf, arf." He picked up a slice of bacon and bit into it.

Mariah didn't know what to make of his words. "Do you have nightmares about the explosion, Oscar?"

He dropped the meat and scooted back his chair as though he was getting ready to flee. His father quickly put his hands on Oscar's shoulders. "You're safe here, son. Calm down, now."

"Oscar, do you know why the explosion happened?" Mariah asked.

He shook his head adamantly, then suddenly changed it to a nod. Mariah glanced at his mother for confirmation.

"Did you see something, Oscar?" his mother asked. "No? Did you hear something?"

"Mad dog. Arf, arf," he repeated.

After several more attempts, with the same response, Mariah gave up. Whatever Oscar knew, it would remain locked in his confused brain forever.

She returned at noon from her house calls to find all five chairs in the waiting area occupied. Lazarus followed her inside, tail wagging, as he pranced over to receive his pat on the head from Annie.

"Good afternoon," Mariah said, glancing around at her patients. "I'll be with you in a moment." As she started toward the back room she heard Laz growl and turned to find him standing with legs braced, hackles raised, and teeth bared, facing someone in the room.

"Come here, Laz," Mariah called firmly, as Annie got up and tried to shepherd him toward the supply room.

Lazarus wouldn't budge. Instead, he moved forward, his growl turning more ferocious, causing the people in the room to gasp and scoot their chairs back. Even Annie backed away. Shocked by the dog's frightening behavior, Mariah ran to the supply room, grabbed a rope, and hurried back.

By that time, all three female patients had climbed onto their chairs, while one elderly man had backed into the corner. But they weren't Lazarus's target. At the opposite side of the small room, Luther Sinton sat calmly in his seat, grinning at the dog.

Chapter 17

Luther's reaction was so bizarre that Mariah simply stared at him. It seemed almost as if he was daring Laz to attack.

Looping the rope around the dog's neck, Mariah pulled Laz to the back and shoved him through the connecting door into the kitchen. Annie stood just behind her.

"I've never seen Lazarus behave that way," Annie said in a whisper. "What could have caused it?"

"Did Luther provoke him?"

"Not at all. I was petting Laz—you know how he has to have attention when he comes in—when all of a sudden he turned around and began to growl."

"It's very odd," Mariah remarked. "Laz singled Luther out."

"Why don't I put Luther into the surgery first?" Annie suggested. "He's probably shaken up."

Mariah wasn't so sure. She washed her hands and returned to the waiting room to apologize to everyone for the disturbance and to assure them that Lazarus was safely confined.

"I'm very sorry about my dog," she told Luther, as she walked into the surgery. She put on her spectacles and unwrapped the gauze covering his arm. "I don't know what made him behave like that. He's normally quite friendly. I apologize if he frightened you."

"I wasn't frightened."

Mariah glanced at Luther curiously, but he merely smiled as though he thought the whole incident was amusing.

"At least your arm seems to be on the mend," she commented.

"I don't think so. It's giving me lots of pain."

Mariah examined the stitches again. "I don't see any signs of infection. I'll give you some salve to put on it twice a day. Just make sure you keep it covered."

"I'll come back and let you take care of it."

She opened the medicine cabinet and took out a jar of the pungent salve. "There's really no need for me to see you again."

"Yes, there is. I don't want to get blood poisoning."

"All right, Mr. Sinton; come back tomorrow and I'll look at it again."

"It's Luther, remember?"

Mariah said nothing as she returned the jar to the cabinet. She couldn't explain why Luther made her so uneasy.

"My mama said to thank you for fixing up my arm," Luther told her as he hopped off the table. "She really liked your daddy, you know. He used to come see her once a week. She's got lots of ailments. She was just saying today how your daddy always took care of the stone men—not just their ailments, but their problems, too. You know what I mean. I wonder what your daddy would have said about the explosion, especially what with the gossip going around about it not being an accident and all."

Mariah folded her arms and studied him. "My father didn't take much stock in gossip. He always went after the truth."

"That's why everyone liked him. That's what you're doing, too, isn't it? Going after the truth?"

"I'm trying my best."

"I think people like to gossip so they feel important. I know a lot about dynamite, you know. My daddy was one of the first charge men to work for C & S. You'd have to be awfully smart to set the dynamite off and make it look like an accident. None of those men down at the quarry could do that."

"I'll keep that in mind." She walked to the doorway. "I'll see you tomorrow."

Dang it, his arm was healing too quickly. Luther hid his annoyance behind a friendly smile as he sauntered through the waiting room and stepped outside, the bell over the door tinkling as it shut behind him. He had to do something to infect the wound so he had a reason to come back.

Mariah was starting to trust him; Luther could tell she'd been impressed by his knowledge. But he had to build up that trust quickly. The election was getting close.

The only problem was that Mariah's stupid mongrel kept getting in the way. He needed to get rid of the dog once and for all.

His mind preoccupied, Luther nearly collided with Jake.

"What are you doing here, Luther?" Jake asked.

Luther held out the bandaged left arm but kept moving past him. "Derrick rope sliced me up. Doc wants to see me every day 'till it's healed." He turned his back on Jake and continued down the street. *Go ahead and glare at me, bastard. You'll get what's coming to you real soon.*

Mariah came out of the surgery to call her next patient and saw Jake standing next to Annie's desk, casually leaning against the wall, watching her with hooded eyes. His white shirt was smudged with dust, yet the garment stood out like fresh snow against his tanned skin and blue eyes.

Although she tried to remain calm, Mariah's heart was doing cartwheels as she moved toward him. She was dismayed to feel a blush color her face.

"Did you need to see me?" she asked him, keeping her tone purposely brisk.

"If you have a moment."

Mariah reluctantly drew her gaze away. "Annie, will you take the next patient into the surgery while I wash up? Jake, you may come to the back with me, if you'd like."

She tried to still the excited beat of her heart, but as she scrubbed her hands, she knew he was standing behind her so close that she could feel that strong magnetic current between them and smell his sun-warmed skin. Mariah grew weak all over, imagining him pulling her into his arms and inundating her with burning kisses. Reaching for the towel, she squared her shoulders and turned to face him. "Have another burn you need tended?"

His eyes darkened, letting her know exactly where his thoughts lay. "Got a match?"

For a long moment, their gazes locked, his with an intensity that brought on a startling and overpowering desire in Mariah to feel his hands and mouth on her bare flesh. Jake ran his knuckles lightly down the side of her face, causing every nerve ending under her skin to tingle in anticipation. Her eyes closed as he lowered his head and lifted her chin to meet his lips.

Then Lazarus began to whine and scratch on the connecting door, breaking the spell. Mariah's eyes flew open in horror as she realized where she was. Thank goodness Annie hadn't come upon them.

"Why is Laz in the house?" Jake asked, stepping

back as though he, too, realized the peril of being discovered.

Mariah opened the door, and Laz came bounding through, running immediately to Jake, his tail wagging happily.

"He nearly attacked one of your employees this morning."

Jake crouched to rub the dog's head. "Has Laz ever done that before?"

"Not that I know of. I can't imagine what set him off."

Jake walked to the curtained doorway and peered inside. "Where's Willy?"

"At Gertrude Johnson's house. She's been giving him instruction in arithmetic."

At that moment, Annie came up the hallway. Mariah pushed a strand of hair away from her face, hoping she didn't look as guilty as she felt.

"Mrs. Beech is here, honey. Will you have time to see her this afternoon?"

"I'll see her." Conscious of Annie's curious gaze, she turned back to Jake. "I'm sorry you missed Willy. I'll tell him you were here. You can visit him tomorrow, if you'd like."

Jake's forehead furrowed slightly, as though there was something else on his mind. But all he said was, "That's fine."

"Was there anything else you needed?" she asked hesitantly.

"You've got patients to see. It'll keep."

* * *

Mariah ate supper with Annie and Willy, a delicious sausage and potato soup that had simmered all afternoon on Annie's range. When they finished, Willy took Lazarus over to Mariah's backyard to play, while Mariah helped Annie with the dishes.

"Auntie Annie, Mariah, come look at the tricks I taught Laz," Willy called through the open window.

The two women walked across the yard behind the dispensary to Mariah's backyard fence, where they watched Willy put Laz through his paces.

"I know it's for the best, but I'm sure going to hate to see that boy go," Annie said quietly.

"He's not going anywhere if his aunt and uncle aren't suitable," Mariah insisted.

She was still musing on that subject as she sat at her desk that evening updating her notebook. Chasing those thoughts away, she reread the entries she'd made for Luther Sinton. "Deep cut to left forearm," she had written on his first visit. Mariah frowned in thought. Luther had indicated that he was right-handed. Wouldn't he have been holding the rope with his right hand?

Then again, she didn't have the experience to say whether that would be likely or not. Mariah made a mental note to ask Jake about it.

"Laz, come back. Come back!"

Hearing Willy's panicked cries, Mariah put down her pen and ran to the back door. Willy was standing at the open gate, calling into the woods, "Laz, come back here! Please be a good dog. You might get lost."

"What happened?" she asked, hurrying out to the gate.

"I threw the stick for Laz, and he ran to fetch it. Then he saw the gate was open, and he went right out it, barking like he was chasing something. And now he won't come back."

"Did you open the gate, Willy?"

He shook his head, tears filling his eyes. "I swear I didn't. It was already open." Putting his small hands over his eyes, Willy cried, "He's gone, just like Pa. I did something bad and now he's gone."

Mariah pulled him against her, stroking his head. "You didn't do anything bad, Willy. Laz probably caught a rabbit's scent and went after it. He'll be back soon. He never stays away very long." She glanced around at the gate, wondering how and when it had been opened. She knew it had been closed earlier in the day.

Willy scrubbed his eyes, hiccuping. "You promise he'll come back?"

"I promise. You don't need to worry about Laz."

By midnight, though, the dog still hadn't come home. Mariah paced the floor from front door to back, unable to take her own advice. She was worried.

Jake was talking to his foreman on the quarry floor the next afternoon when he was handed a telegram. He brushed the dust off his hands, tore open the envelope, and scanned the message inside.

"Bad news?" Dan asked.

"Nothing important." Jake crumpled the paper and jammed it in his pocket. "I'll be back." He strode across the quarry floor and started up the ramp, simmering with fury. Who in blue blazes did Coffman think he was fooling? Jake knew he was being used as a scapegoat.

He reached the top of the hill and paused to looked down at the bustling activity. Against his own better judgment, he was putting his men through hell for Coffman. He should have called a halt to the road project weeks ago. Instead, he'd pushed his workers to their limit.

By God, he wasn't going to be used as a whipping boy. They were partners; they would share the blame equally. He'd wire Coffman immediately and tell him—

"Jake?"

He swung around to find Mariah hurrying up the grassy slope toward him. She had on a yellow straw hat and a white and yellow print dress, looking much like a daisy—an unhappy daisy. Crossing his arms, Jake geared himself for another lecture. He'd witnessed that look before.

"Have you seen Laz?" she asked.

Jake held up his hands in mock surrender. "If he's here, I had nothing to do with it."

"He got out of the gate last night and hasn't come back." Mariah twisted her fingers together anxiously as she turned to scan the area below. "I've looked all over town and by the creek. I was hoping to find him here with you."

She hadn't come to lecture; she'd come for help. "Let's check the mill," he said.

They circled the quarry, Jake matching his stride to Mariah's. "How did Laz get out?"

"Willy was playing with him in the backyard. Somehow the gate was left open, and Laz ran through."

They walked around the mill, then checked all through the inside. Jake questioned several stone cutters, but none had seen the dog. "Keep your eye out for him," he told the men.

Mariah stood outside the building, nibbling her lower lip. "I suppose I'll go home and wait. Maybe he'll show up at supper."

"Do you have any patients to see?"

"Not for a while."

"Let's take the path through the woods. Maybe we'll find him playing in the creek."

Mariah felt immense relief as she set off beside Jake. It eased her mind to have his help. Knowing how hard he was working to get the road completed, she was amazed that he would take time out to hunt for her dog.

They followed the trail from the quarry to Coffee Creek, then tramped up and down the water's edge, calling Laz's name. An hour passed, and still there was no sign of the dog. Mariah's spirits sank. She had a feeling in the pit of her stomach that something terrible had happened.

Finally, she paused to open the watch pinned to her bodice. "I have to get back," she said dejectedly. "I have patients coming in this afternoon."

Jake cupped her chin and gazed down at her through eyes charged with determination. "We'll find Laz," he promised.

Mariah blinked away tears. "If there was any way possible, he'd be home by now. I know something has happened to him."

Jake jammed his hands into his pockets as he watched her turn and head down the narrow path. Feeling the crumpled telegram, he cursed silently. He didn't have time to hunt for Laz. He needed to get a reply out to Coffman, and he'd told one of his foremen that he'd be out to inspect the progress of the road.

Yet he couldn't stand seeing Mariah in such distress. Jake turned and scanned the woods. The dog couldn't have just vanished. He had to be out there somewhere.

Hiking back to the Jefferson quarry, Jake pulled two of his men off the floor. "Go through town and ask around about Dr. Lowe's golden retriever. Someone may have seen him. I'm going to head back to Coffee Creek and check the woods. If one of you finds the dog or knows his whereabouts, go straight to the doctor's house and let her know. Then come get me."

Jake took the path back to the creek, pausing every few minutes to call. Once he'd reached the water, he headed off the path and wove through the trees. He came out by a hill where two small openings led to limestone caverns inside. As a boy he'd explored both caverns, but they'd proved too small to hold his attention.

He crouched in front of each opening and called, then waited for a long while, listening for a bark or whine. A cave would have been a likely spot for an injured animal to hide.

As the sun moved lower in the west, Jake's stomach rumbled with hunger and his neck itched from mosquito bites, but he refused to give up. It wasn't only the image of Mariah's tearful face that kept him going; he'd also grown fond of the dog. Yet after covering most of the forested area on the north side of town, Jake couldn't help but fear the worst.

There was only one place he hadn't searched: the cave where Ben had drowned.

Chapter 18

～∽◯∽～

With a heavy heart, Mariah trudged toward the backyard and stopped to open the gate. Willy had been playing with a hoop and stick, but as soon as he heard the creak of the hinges, he dropped the toys and ran, until he realized that Lazarus wasn't there. Instantly, he stopped, his body stiffening as though he'd been struck.

"Laz's gone, ain't he?"

Mariah pulled Willy close as he began to weep, "He's gone. I'll never see him again. Just like my ma and pa."

"Jake is still looking," Mariah assured him. "We haven't given up yet." She glanced up at Annie, who had come out to hear the news.

"I've been telling everyone I see," Annie reported. "And Jake sent two of his men around town to look for Lazarus."

"Did you hear that, Willy?" Mariah asked. "Everyone is looking for Laz."

The boy lifted his head to gaze at her, his grief-stricken face nearly breaking her heart. "Jake'll find him," he whispered. "He has to find him."

Mariah left Willy with Annie and returned to the dispensary, where she found Luther waiting to see her. Hearing the bell tinkle, he jumped to his feet and hastily yanked his cap off his head. His presence immediately put her on edge; once again she wondered why.

"How is your arm today?" she asked, as she took him into the surgery.

"It hurts like the dickens. I can hardly move it."

For someone in such pain, Luther certainly seemed in a jovial mood. Mariah put on her spectacles and unwrapped the gauze bandage, instantly noting a putrid smell, like that of horse dung. She was shocked to see that the stitches were crusted with what appeared to be dried pus. "Have you unwrapped this?"

"No, ma'am. I can't even look at it."

Trying not to wrinkle her nose in distaste, Mariah doused the wound with a strong vinegar solution and washed it thoroughly. How had it become so grossly infected if he had kept it wrapped? She pulled out a drawer at the bottom of the glass cabinet and took out a magnifying lens.

"What've you got there?"

"It's a magnifier." Mariah held the lens over the wound.

"What d'ya need it for?"

"I want to make sure I've cleaned out all the infection." She studied the injury closely and soon discovered what she'd suspected: there was dung embedded in the stitches. Yet the bandage was clean on the outside.

Luther had lied to her. He'd deliberately infected his wound.

Mariah had heard of patients purposely injuring themselves; but whatever his reason had been, she had to discourage him from further jeopardizing his arm. She applied a poultice to the area and put fresh gauze on it, determining the best way to handle the situation.

"If it gets infected again, I'm going to have to send you to Bloomington for treatment," she told him gravely. "I wouldn't want you to lose your arm."

"I don't need to go there," he said with a smile. "You're doing a good job."

"Oh, but I'll have to insist," Mariah said, replacing the lens in the drawer. "If you come back tomorrow with more infection, it's off to Bloomington you go."

"It'll be all right by tomorrow." He jumped down from the table as though he had too much energy to sit still. "Say, that's too bad about your dog."

Mariah glanced around at him curiously. "What's too bad?"

"I heard he was lost. That happened to my dog once."

"Did you find him?"

"No, he died."

"How do you know he died if you didn't find him?"

"I just knew. Don't you know inside when something bad is gonna happen?"

Something about his question made her extremely uneasy. She closed the cabinet and looked around at him, but he only gave her an innocent smile. She walked to the door and opened it. "Thank you for your concern about my dog, Mr. Sinton. I'll see you tomorrow."

His smile faded, and his strange eyes seemed to grow flat. Almost in a whisper, he said, "I asked you to call me Luther."

The barely restrained anger in his voice took her aback. Before Mariah could even think how to react to it, his mood suddenly switched.

"You want me to help you search for your dog, Mariah? I'm real good at finding things."

Mariah looked him straight in the eye. "If you want me to continue treating you, Mr. Sinton, then you'd better respect my wishes and call me Dr. Lowe."

He gave her a slow smile. "Sure. I'll do that. And I'll be back tomorrow so you can check my arm."

Goose bumps dotted Mariah's arms as she stood at the window and watched Luther saunter down the sidewalk. If Luther never came back again, it wouldn't bother her in the least.

Luther strutted down the street, feeling quite

pleased with himself. Offering to help Mariah find the mutt had been a stroke of genius. Too bad she hadn't agreed to it. He'd have asked her to come with him. He would have liked to have been there when she found the body.

With a sudden scowl, Luther glanced down at the bandaged arm. That hadn't turned out as he'd planned; he'd never imagined that Mariah would send him somewhere else. And he still couldn't understand why she didn't want to call him Luther.

He just had to build up a little more trust. Shoot, given enough time, Luther was certain that he could even get Mariah to like him.

Too bad there just wasn't enough time.

Jake rubbed his clammy hands down his pant legs and stared at the gaping mouth of the cave. He knew he couldn't go back without at least making an attempt. But now that he was actually faced with it, the thought of going further made his insides roil.

He began to shake and quickly sat down, beads of nervous perspiration dotting his forehead. He sat ten yards from the entrance, unable to move closer.

"Lazarus," he called, his voice tight with tension. "Laz, come here, boy." He'd repeated it so often, his throat ached. Jake knew he'd have to head back before night set in. But how could he tell Mariah someone else she loved was gone?

An image flashed before Jake's eyes—the mo-

ment he'd told Mariah of her brother's fate. He'd
been completely numb, unable to feel sorrow or
pain, unable to shed tears, utterly without emotion, as though he had died right along with Ben.
At the funeral, he'd felt as though it had all happened to someone else and he'd been just an
onlooker.

The guilt had come later. But Jake had learned to
live with the guilt and turn it to anger. Anger pre-
vented him from feeling anything painful.

But Mariah's return had changed all that.

Dusk was settling over the forest. He had to go
back; he had only a quarter of an hour or so until
all light was gone. Jake wiped the sweat off his
forehead and stood.

"Lazarus," he called again, listening for an
answering bark.

Instead, he heard a whimper.

For Willy's sake, Mariah pretended a hopeful-
ness she didn't feel as she sat down for supper that
evening. She and Annie kept up a constant chatter,
but she ate little, spending most of the time pushing her food around her plate. Jake hadn't returned. She feared he had given up and gone
home.

Sitting at the rolltop desk afterward, Mariah
stared at her notes about Luther, trying to keep her
mind off Laz. Many things about Luther's accident
didn't make sense, starting with the fact that he'd
injured the left arm instead of the right. Then there
was the evenness of the cut and the dung in the

stitches. Mariah wrote, "Self-inflicted?" and underlined it twice.

She had a sudden feeling of being watched, and she quickly shut and barred the window. Laz should have been there, standing guard for her, and the thought brought tears to her eyes. She loved the dog. She couldn't bear to think she'd never see him again.

So many strange things had happened in the past several weeks that Mariah was beginning to feel on edge all the time. Were they nothing more than a series of coincidences, or was someone deliberately trying to frighten her? Any why?

"Laz. Here, boy!" Jake called again. Had he imagined it? Drawing a steadying breath, he forced himself to move closer to the entrance—eight yards, five yards—until he could see a few feet inside. He couldn't bring himself to go further.

"Lazarus!"

Another whimper, fainter this time, seemed to come from the left side of the entrance, where several thick bushes grew. Jake pushed branches aside, and his heart sank.

Lazarus lay on his side, too weak even to raise his head. Dark, sticky blood matted his golden fur from neck to belly. For the first time in more than ten years, tears filled Jake's eyes. He swiped them away with his sleeve and bent to lift the dog in his arms.

"Stay with me, Laz. You're going to make it, boy. You've got to make it."

He walked as gently and as swiftly as possible, holding the animal to his chest, mindless of the blood that oozed onto his shirt. He wanted to pray but feared he'd forgotten how.

Darkness descended before he reached the edge of the forest. Jake pushed on, his face scratched by branches he couldn't see or push aside, aware only of the injured pet in his arms.

He came out behind Mariah's backyard and began shouting. "Open the gate. I've got Laz."

Mariah had just tied the sash of her night robe when she heard Jake's shout. A sob rose in her throat as she ran to the kitchen, flung open the back door, and saw a dim figure at the gate.

"You found him!" she cried in relief, running to meet them. But as she drew near, she saw the blood, and her heart stood still.

"He's hurt badly, Mariah."

Mariah gulped back tears. "Let's get him to the surgery." She grabbed a lamp inside the house and ran ahead to open the door.

Jake eased Lazarus onto the table while Mariah lit more lamps. She put on her spectacles and began moving her fingers through the dog's matted fur. Jake kept one eye on her progress as he continued to talk to Laz in a soothing voice.

"Where did you find him?" Mariah asked.

"Near the cave."

There was no need to explain which cave. "He's been stabbed," she said, separating the fur. "Right here, in the chest. I'll have to close it up." She glanced up at Jake briefly. "It's going to be messy. If you're not up to it, I can get Annie."

"I'll stay."

Jake watched as Mariah prepared for surgery. In her night robe and with her long hair unbound, she looked more like a student than a doctor. He could almost pretend that ten years hadn't passed, that they were still sweethearts, that Ben hadn't died. But that only made the reality harder to bear.

It was after ten o'clock when Mariah finished stitching up the opening in Laz's chest. She bound him with a gauze bandage, then pressed her stethoscope against the dog's side. "His heartbeat is steady."

Jake ran his hand over the dog's golden head. "I can't imagine why anyone would want to harm him."

As Mariah placed Laz onto a thick blanket on the floor, she had a sudden vision of Luther sitting in the waiting room chair with that strange smile on his face. Would Luther have hurt Laz? Why would he have any reason to hurt him?

"I'll check the latch on your back gate," Jake promised. "I don't want Lazarus to get out again." He studied her for a moment. "Do you have any idea who might have done this?"

Mariah hesitated, sawing on her lower lip. "Remember that strange incident I told you about where Laz nearly attacked one of my patients? That patient was Luther Sinton, one of your employees."

Jake gave her a dubious look. "I don't know

why Laz would have wanted to harm Luther. I'm going to alert the sheriff about this tomorrow."

Jake rubbed his eyes as he spoke, and for the first time Mariah noticed how tired he looked. He was still wearing his bloody shirt and pants, and beneath the day's growth of beard, she could see many cuts and scratches. Her heart swelled with emotion—merely gratitude, she assured herself.

She pulled up a chair and patted it. "Sit down, please."

He gave her a wary glance. "What are you going to do?"

Mariah removed several jars from the cabinet. "I'm going to take care of those scratches on your face."

He ran a hand over his chin and jaw. "It'll be all right."

"It'll be better if I put something on it. Sit."

Grudgingly he sat—and scowled—as Mariah leaned down in front of him to gently clean his face. Then she smoothed a salve onto the cuts, working from jaw down to the base of his throat.

She stopped to open the top button of his shirt and fold back the collar, then applied more salve to the scratches on his neck. Being that close, Mariah couldn't help but admire the strong, handsome planes of his face, the deep, intense blue of his eyes, and the thick, wavy texture of his hair.

But it was the musky scent of his skin and the feel of his warm, firm flesh beneath her palms that flooded her with memories of their last kiss.

Her hand stilled as liquid heat poured through

her veins. All she had to do was lower her head and press her lips against his to experience that kiss again.

Did she dare?

Chapter 19

Mariah closed her eyes and inhaled slowly, searching for the will to resist those traitorous thoughts. When she opened her eyes, Jake was watching her. His expression was unreadable, but his mesmerizing gaze glowed with an inner fire that made her knees weak and her cheeks flush with color. Did he know what she was thinking?

Jake was so hard with need he had to hold onto the seat of the chair to keep from pulling Mariah down on his lap and taking her mouth in a lusty kiss. Her touch, her sweet scent, her body so close to his, had him out of his mind with desire. To see that desire reflected in the darkening of her eyes and the blush of her cheeks pushed him dangerously close to the edge.

She frowned in concentration as she returned to

her task, pretending to ignore the potent attraction between them, yet Jake knew better.

But when she touched the scar on his cheek, a jolt went through him. Immediately, he put his hand over hers, halting her movements. "That's enough."

Mariah eased her hand from beneath his. "I have to finish, Jake," she said softly.

Her tone and the determined set of her jaw told him she wouldn't stop until she had completed the job to her satisfaction. Slowly, reluctantly, Jake put his hand on his lap and let his body relax, but he kept his gaze on her face, waiting for the moment when her expression changed.

Mariah's touch was gentle and reassuring as she applied the last dab of her salve to his cheek. His desire flared again, hot and urgent, as she wiped her hands on a cloth and stood back to scrutinize her work, the delicate fabric of her night robe outlining her curves.

"That should take care of your cuts," she said, removing her spectacles. "Now we'll see to your stomach. I'll wager you haven't had supper."

She was so beguiling, so utterly feminine, that Jake couldn't resist her. "I'm hungry, Mariah," he said, his voice husky with passion, "but not for food."

Her eyes widened, but she didn't protest when Jake took her hand and drew her toward him. He pulled Mariah onto his lap and ran his hand down the side of her face, feeling the fine, silken texture of her skin, gazing into her captivating eyes. Then he met her lips in a bold, lusty kiss, wrapping his arms around her to hold her close. Her bottom nestled against his engorged penis, driving him wild with desire.

As he stroked the inside of her mouth with his tongue, Jake opened her robe and unbuttoned the front of her nightgown, slipping his hand inside the gossamer material to caress a supple breast. His lust rocketed as he circled her nipple with his thumb and felt it tighten.

Unable to resist her, he broke their kiss to take the taut bud in his mouth and suckle it, causing his penis to throb heavily, demanding relief. Mariah clutched his shoulders, gasping, letting him know she was as ready as he.

Desperately wanting her, Jake was on the verge of taking her right there, seated on his lap, but his conscience stopped him. Mariah wasn't an object on which to slake his lust; she was the woman he loved. She was just beginning to trust him; he refused to jeopardize that for his own gratification.

He lifted his head and cupped her face in his hands, his gaze absorbing those beautiful features he knew so well. He waited until the passion had faded from her eyes and clarity returned, then he said, "I want you to understand something, Mariah. You're not obligated to repay me in any way for finding Laz. I didn't search for him for my own gain."

She met his gaze with no hesitancy. "You saved his life, Jake. How can I ever thank you for that?"

Jake studied her for a long moment, almost

afraid to trust his vision. He blinked again, but there it was. Her green eyes shone with gratitude and, for the first time in years, not a trace of bitterness.

"You already have," he told her.

It was barely dawn when Mariah ran across the backyard to Annie's house. "Laz is back," she announced happily.

Annie threw her arms around Mariah and gave her a hug. "Thank the Lord."

"Jake found him in the woods. He'd been stabbed in the chest, but he's holding his own this morning."

"Stabbed! Oh, my poor Laz! I don't like this one bit." Annie handed Mariah a cup of coffee. "First someone gets into your desk, then you find a letter that later disappears, and now Laz turns up wounded. I'm telling you, honey, you need to tell the sheriff everything that's been going on."

"What can he do, Annie? I don't have any evidence to show him."

"At least he can keep an eye out for you."

"I wish I had that letter."

"That's another thing that bothers me," Annie remarked. "I keep asking myself who in town would write such a cruel, frightening note."

"Leaving an unsigned letter is the act of a cowardly person, Annie, and I refuse to let a coward intimidate me." Mariah finished her coffee. "Let's go tell Willy that Laz is back."

Willy had just awakened and was sitting up in

bed sleepily rubbing his eyes. When both women walked into his room, his eyes grew round. "I ain't in trouble, am I?"

"Don't be a goose!" Mariah chided him playfully, sitting down on the edge of the bed. "We just wanted to tell you the good news. Laz is home. Jake found him in the woods."

"He is? I knew Jake would find him!" Willy cried, bounding off the bed. "Can I go see Laz?" Glancing at Annie, who had been working on his manners, he added hastily, "Please?"

"You can see him this afternoon," Mariah told him. "He's resting now. He was hurt, Willy, so we have to be careful with him."

"He got hurt? What happened to him?"

"He was cut across his chest."

The color drained from Willy's face, and he swallowed hard. "Was there blood?"

"Yes, but he's all bandaged now."

He clasped his hands tightly together, and when he spoke, his words came out in a whisper. "D-do you know w-who did it?"

"No."

Wordlessly Willy stared at her, stricken by some unknown fear. He walked slowly back to the bed and sat on the edge, his face turned toward the window.

"Willy, what is it?" Mariah asked, stroking his hair. "What's troubling you?"

"Nothin'."

"Do you know something about Laz's injury?"

The child shook his head, but he wouldn't meet her gaze.

"If you know anything at all, please tell me." Mariah waited a moment, then finally rose and went to stand beside Annie.

"He's keeping a secret," Annie whispered.

Mariah sighed. "I know. I wonder why."

Despite his weariness, Jake's step was light as he strode to the quarry that morning. Even the feel of the telegram in his pocket couldn't diminish the warmth he felt inside. Laz was safe, and Mariah was relieved. At last, he'd accomplished something good.

He wrote a letter to his partner, stating firmly that he would never again allow himself to be made a scapegoat. If such an article appeared in the newspaper a second time, Jake would make sure a counter-article was printed that wouldn't be flattering to the senator.

"Hey, Jake," one of his foremen called, as he walked through the cutting mill, "any word on the doc's dog?"

"He's back."

"Did you hear that, boys?" the foreman called. "The dog's all right."

There were cheers and whistles all around. By the time Jake got out to the Jefferson quarry, the news had spread.

"Did he step in a trap?" one of the men asked.

"Someone stabbed him," Jake replied.

At that, the men near him stopped working to gather around, peppering him with questions.

"Is the dog going to make it?"

"Who'd do something like that?"

"How'd he get out of his yard?"

Jake held up his hands. "I don't have any answers. I'm going to turn it over to the sheriff."

"I'll bet the doc was upset that someone stabbed her pet, wasn't she?" Luther asked.

One of the men gave his arm a hard nudge. "Cripes, Luther, wouldn't you be?"

"Sure I would. Same thing happened to my dog, you know. Only he died."

"When did that happen?" Jake asked.

"Oh, golly, it was a long time ago, maybe eleven years back. Yep, it had to be, 'cause I was fourteen."

"Did you ever find out who did it?" Jake asked.

Luther lowered his head. "No one ever found out."

Luther ambled into the dispensary at noon and found two women waiting to see Mariah. He stopped at the desk to ask Annie how Willy was getting along, then sat down to wait his turn.

"How's your mother, Luther?" one of the women asked.

"Her stomach's been bothering her a bit," he replied with a friendly smile, "but I take good care of her."

"You're a good son, Luther," the woman said, patting him on the cheek.

When it was his turn, Luther sauntered into the

surgery and sat on the table. "My arm's doing better."

Mariah unwrapped the gauze and examined it. "Yes, it is. I think it's safe to say you don't need to come back anymore."

"It's no bother to come back. The foreman doesn't mind if I take a bit longer than my half-hour."

"There's truly no reason for you to come back."

"I heard your dog is all right. Strange thing, isn't it? I mean, not knowing who tried to kill him? I'd be pretty shook up if I were you, thinking there was someone in town who could do a thing like that. You probably felt safer up in Chicago, didn't you?"

"I'm just very glad Laz is back," Mariah answered.

After stopping to make a report to the sheriff, Jake arrived home shortly after sundown. He stripped off his soiled clothes, bathed, and dressed, and went down to the dining room for a late supper. The house was silent save for the kitchen help.

As Jake served himself from a platter of ham at the sideboard, he glanced at his reflection in the mirror hanging above it, grimacing at the bleary-eyed man who peered back at him.

"What happened to you?" Owen asked, giving him a puzzled look as he walked into the room. "You're starting to look like me."

"I was up all night last night."

"Now you even sound like me." Owen filled his plate and sat down. He didn't seem the least bit curious as to the reason for Jake's appearance. "Emie's ill," he said between mouthfuls of food.

"What's wrong with her?"

Owen shrugged. "She doesn't have an appetite. She didn't even want to see Percy this evening."

"I'd better go up and talk to her."

Jake knocked softly on his sister's door and heard a faint, "Come in." He opened the door and peered in. Emeline was lying in her four-poster bed, nearly hidden under the mountains of down quilts and pillows.

"It's me, Em," he called.

"Jake?" she said in a faint voice.

"Owen said you weren't feeling well."

Emeline removed a cloth covering her eyes and squinted up at him. "I've had a dreadful headache since yesterday afternoon. It won't go away."

"I'm sorry to hear that."

She sighed, the gauzy pink sleeves of her bed jacket billowing as she flopped her arms down on the bed. "I can't eat, I can't sleep. How am I ever going to be able to go through with the wedding? Oh, I wish it would just go away!"

"Do you want me to talk to the doctor?"

"Yes," she said with a sigh. "Perhaps she'll give me some laudanum."

Mariah was working at her desk that evening when a knock startled her.

"Who's there?" she called through the door.

"Jake."

Her instant relief gave way to caution. Several times now, she'd come dangerously close to giving in to her own passion. Did she dare trust herself around him?

Mariah exhaled sharply. She could either send him away or gird herself to resist his charm. The first seemed the act of a coward, the second of a fool. Which was she?

With a resigned sigh, she threw back the bolt and opened the door. "Come in."

He shut the door behind him and examined the bolt. "You're locking your door now?"

Mariah was reluctant to tell him about the strange occurrences, though she wasn't quite sure why. "Habit," she answered, with a shrug. "We always locked our doors in Chicago."

"How's Laz?" he asked, glancing around the room for the dog. Jake, too, seemed somewhat guarded, but perhaps he sensed her mood.

"He's doing fine. He's been sleeping most of the time, but he did have some water earlier." Mariah led the way back to the kitchen, where Lazarus was stretched out in a long basket near the big black range.

Jake crouched down beside him. "Hey, Laz. How are you, boy?"

The dog attempted to lift his head a few inches. His tail thumped once. Jake soothed him with a gentle stroke of his broad hand. "Easy, boy. You're doing fine."

Mariah felt something soften inside her as he

talked quietly to Laz. Then he rose and came toward her, causing her pulse to flutter erratically.

"I didn't mean to come by so late, but Emeline hasn't been feeling well. Today she's complaining of bad headaches. She thought perhaps you could give her something for it."

She turned away so he wouldn't see the excited flush on her cheeks and reached for a canister on a high shelf. "I can send some willow bark tea for her to drink tonight. I don't want to give her anything stronger until I know for certain what she has. Tell her I'll stop by after church in the morning."

Jake was relieved. "I'll tell her."

"Willy was so happy that you found Lazarus," Mariah told him as she measured the tea into a jar. "He said he knew you could do it." She handed him the tea. "Steep a heaping spoonful of this in hot water for a good ten minutes, then strain it and have her drink it all down at once."

His hands covered hers, and for long a moment, he gazed down into her eyes. "She'll appreciate this, Mariah."

With a blush, she eased her hand out from beneath his. "I hope it gives her some relief."

Jake hesitated, trying to figure out the best way to ask Mariah to talk to his sister. Perhaps a hint would do the trick.

"Emeline's getting married in eight days," he said as he walked with her to the front door.

"Yes, I'd heard. That's wonderful for her. I'm sure all the excitement and preparations are causing some of her tension."

"It seems more like misgivings than excitement."

"I suspect that's normal," Mariah replied. "Marriage is quite an undertaking."

Jake tried again. "It'd be easier for her if she had her mother around to talk to—or some other female."

"I'm not sure how much good I can do, but perhaps Emeline will confide in me when I see her tomorrow."

That was exactly what Jake had hoped she'd say. He started to thank her when he suddenly caught sight of a wooden bar on the floor beneath the window. With a puzzled frown, he strode across the parlor and picked it up. "What's this for?"

"The window."

Jake glanced around and spotted a second piece of wood. "Why are you barring your windows?"

Mariah took the wood out of his hands and tucked it beneath the sofa. "It's that old habit again." She looked away, as though she were hiding something.

"We've never had to bar our windows or bolt our doors in Coffee Creek, Mariah."

She rocked back and forth on her heels, her hands clasped behind her back. "That's not to say we never will."

Ever so gently, Jake lifted her chin and forced her to look at him. "When Annie knocked on the kitchen door the other night, I saw the fear in your eyes. What are you afraid of?"

Mariah gazed into those probing blue eyes and

wanted to drown in them. His strength, his over-whelming masculinity, gave her such a sense of security that her fears suddenly seemed ridiculous. Too ridiculous to share.

Jake folded his arms across his chest. "I'm not leaving here until you tell me."

Mariah sighed. She knew how stubborn he could be. "This may sound unbelievable to you, but I know someone has been watching me. I sensed it in the woods before I fell, and I've sensed it several times while I was sitting here at my desk. The bars and locks help me sleep better."

"Have you ever seen anyone?"

Mariah shook her head. "I just feel a—presence."

Jake glanced toward the window. He hated the thought of someone following her or staring into her windows at night. His first instinct was to camp out at her house until he caught the culprit, but he knew Mariah wouldn't stand for that. He searched for some other way to protect her. "Do you have a gun in the house?"

"No, and I don't intend to, either."

"Don't be stubborn."

"You're calling *me* stubborn?" she spluttered. "Do you actually believe that as a doctor I could actually shoot someone? My father never picked up a gun in his life and wouldn't have even if he'd needed one."

"You're not your father, Mariah. You need a gun for protection."

"It's for my protection *not* to have one, Jake."

"Mariah—"

"Besides, I can't shoot," she admitted with a frown.

"Why didn't you say so? I'll teach you."

Mariah gazed up at that handsome, serious face and was sorely tempted to say yes. But then she pictured him standing behind her with his arms around her, his mouth close to her ear, his hands covering her hands as they aimed at a distant target. She imagined him taking the gun out of her hands, then laying her down in the grass and ravishing her with his hungry mouth and stroking fingers until she gave herself up to him.

Mariah suppressed a shiver of pleasure. She knew she'd be making a dreadful mistake if she let that happen.

"My house is safe now," she assured him. "I'll be fine." She opened the door for him. "Tell Emeline I'll see her in the morning."

Luther waited in the shadows across the street from Mariah's house until he saw Jake leave, then he crept across the road and ducked down beneath the window. He was in a black mood—he hated it when his plans didn't work. The damn dog shouldn't have lived.

Luther was just about to poke his head up when he heard the sound of the sash being lowered. Moments later, he heard the same sound from the side window. Cautiously, he straightened to peer into the parlor, but she'd closed the curtain. And a thick piece of wood was wedged between the sash and the top of the window frame.

Luther crouched down and moved around the house, checking the other windows. They were all barred. Fury raged like an angry tempest within him.

Did Mariah think she could keep him out?

Chapter 20

After church on Sunday morning, Mariah stopped to get her medical bag, then headed to the Sullivans' house. The housekeeper let her in and showed her to Emeline's bedroom.

The room was decorated in pinks and yellows, with gauzy curtains, lace-edged linens, and an ornate four-poster bed with a canopy, reminding Mariah of an elaborate dollhouse. In the middle of the bed on a cloud of downy comforters, the doll herself lay with a damp cloth over her eyes and a petulant frown on her face. Her corkscrew curls were spread in disarray on her pillow, and one pink-silk-clad arm hung lifelessly off the bed.

"How is your head today?" Mariah asked, perching on the edge of the bed.

Emeline lifted one side of the cloth and peered at her through a bleary eye. "Not much better at all."

"Did the tea help?"

"A bit," she said peevishly.

It still amazed Mariah that this pampered child had been her sister's best friend. She calmly opened her bag, put on her spectacles, and took out a tongue depressor. "Open your mouth and stick out your tongue."

With a huff, Emeline removed the cloth and opened her mouth. "Ah-h-h."

Mariah took her temperature, felt the glands in her neck, checked her eyes, and listened to her heart. "Everything seems fine." She sat back and studied the girl. "Jake tells me you're getting married in a week."

With a groan, Emeline clapped the cloth over her eyes. "Thinking about it makes my head hurt worse."

"Are you having misgivings about the marriage?"

"Percy is a wonderful man," Emeline snapped. "Why should I have misgivings?"

"Because suddenly you'll be a wife, living in a strange home with new responsibilities."

Emeline jerked the cloth down. "Well, wouldn't you have misgivings if you were me?"

"Absolutely."

Her mouth fell open. "You would? Truly?"

"Of course I would."

Emeline scrambled to sit up. "What would you do about them?"

Mariah pondered her question for a moment. "I suppose I'd talk to someone to help me sort out which were worth worrying about and which weren't."

Emeline studied her warily, then flopped back on the bed. "You have a sister to talk to. I only have brothers, and you know how heartless they can be." There was a pause, and then Emeline's eyes rounded. "Oh, Mariah, I'm sorry. I forgot about Ben. Oh, now my head hurts worse." She reached for the cloth and pulled it back over her eyes.

"You do have a doctor to talk to," Mariah said quietly.

Emeline peered at her again. "You?"

Mariah glanced around. "I don't see another doctor, do you?"

That brought a grin to Emeline's face. She sat up again, looking contrite. "I'm sorry I was sharp with you. I'd really like to talk to you about— well—things, when my head doesn't hurt so."

"Perhaps I can come by this evening after supper."

"Oh, yes! You can say I've invited you for coffee."

"I'll be here." Mariah tucked her glasses in the bag and closed it. At the door, she paused to glance back. "Do you want any medicine for your head?"

Emeline felt her temples. "It feels better already," she said in some amazement.

Mariah smiled. "I'll see you this evening."

"Afternoon, Dr. Lowe."

The sound of Luther's voice chafed Mariah's

nerves like burlap on a sunburn. She stopped outside the dispensary and glanced around at him.

"I thought you'd probably want to check my arm again."

Mariah silently counted to ten. Luther just didn't seem to understand. "That's really not necessary unless it's bothering you."

"It's not bothering me. Aren't you going to go inside?" he asked, gesturing toward the door.

"Is there something you need?"

"I wanted to talk to you about my mama. She's been having terrible bellyaches lately. I give her soda water, but that doesn't seem to be working."

"Would you like me to pay her a call tomorrow?"

Luther beamed. "Sure I would. But do you think you could come today? She likes for me to be there, and I'll be at the quarry all day tomorrow."

Mariah tried not to attend to any but the very ill on Sundays, but she had a feeling Luther wouldn't go away until she gave in. "I'll stop by later this afternoon."

"Thanks, Dr. Lowe," he called, backing away. "I know Mama will like you. She really liked your daddy, you know."

Gritting her teeth in annoyance, Mariah stepped inside and closed the door. "Luther Sinton tries my patience, Annie," she said, shaking her head. "I hope his mother isn't as irksome as he is. I have to go see her this afternoon."

"Wait 'til you meet her," Annie said, rolling her eyes. "You'll wonder how Luther turned out as well as he did. I'm sure your father kept notes on her medical condition. Why don't you check them?"

"If I have time." Mariah walked to the back and parted the curtain. "Where's Willy?"

"At Gertrude's for his arithmetic lesson," Annie called. "She's really taken with that boy. She always wanted to have children of her own, you know. Too bad her husband died so young."

When Mariah entered her kitchen, Lazarus's head came up and his tail thumped the floor. "Well, look at you!" Mariah said, stooping to pet him. "You're feeling better today, aren't you?" She checked his injury, then hand-fed him, relieved to see that his appetite was returning. "You gave me quite a scare, Laz. I sure wish you could tell me what happened."

Before Mariah could knock on the weathered wooden door of the Sinton's tiny house, the door swung open.

"Dr. Lowe, come in," Luther said, as though thrilled by her visit. He stepped back, beaming, as she entered.

"Who's that, Luther?" a raspy voice barked.

"It's the doc, Mama." Luther leaned close to Mariah and said, "She's been so excited all afternoon. I had to keep calming her so she wouldn't get herself worked into a state. She has a weak heart, you know."

Mariah knew much more than that. She'd finally checked her father's records for information on Dolly Sinton. Luther's mother was a hypochondriac who used her imagined illnesses as a way to control her husband and later her son. Mariah had also discovered that her father had used harmless sugar pills to treat her—with spectacular results.

Luther led the way through the dismal parlor to the bedroom, where his mother reclined on several lumpy pillows on a high, stiff bed. A white eyelet nightcap covered her head, and a faded pink nightdress hung on her bony shoulders. The only natural light came from one narrow window, which was covered by a heavy, dark green drape. The air smelled stale and musty.

"Here's Doc Lowe, Mama," Luther announced, unnecessarily for the woman stared straight at her.

"Hello, Mrs. Sinton." Mariah set her bag on the bed, put on her spectacles, and took out her stethoscope. "Luther tells me you're having gastric problems."

"Luther, you get out of here," the woman ordered, waving a clawlike hand at him. She waited until he had slunk out of the room, then she turned her baleful glare on Mariah. "That boy will be the death of me yet. Such irresponsibility. Huh!"

Mariah walked to the window, threw back the drape, and opened the window.

"What are you doing? I hate bright light," Dolly snapped.

"There's nothing like natural light and fresh air to make a person feel better. Now, what kind of stomach pains are you having?"

"Bad ones. Right here." She poked a gnarled index finger into her belly.

Mariah gently pressed on her stomach. "Does that hurt?"

"Yes."

"Sharp pains or dull ones?"

"Sharp. Always sharp. Like a knife stabbing me."

Mariah listened to the woman's heart, then checked her eyes and the glands in her neck. "Do you get these pains before or after you eat?"

"Sometimes before, sometimes after."

Mariah had her take deep breaths. Both her heart and lungs seemed strong and healthy. "Any pains in your chest?"

"Always. Especially when that boy is around. He's enough to send me to an early grave."

"I think you have a nervous stomach, Mrs. Sinton." Mariah put away her stethoscope and took out a paper packet. "I'm going to give you some pills that should take care of it. Take one with every meal."

The woman opened the packet and eyed the pills. "These aren't the same ones your daddy used to give me."

"These are even stronger."

Dolly wrapped them up and put the packet on the table beside her. Surprising Mariah, she clasped her hands. "God bless you, girl. You're a good doctor, just like your daddy. He'd be proud of you." She dropped Mariah's hand, and instantly her eyes narrowed. "Not that like boy of mine. Huh! What have I got to be proud of? A lazy good-for-nothing!"

Mariah closed her bag and stood up. "Take your pills faithfully, Mrs. Sinton. If you need me again, send for me."

There was no sign of Luther, so Mariah let herself out into the bright sunshine. Taking a deep breath of fresh air, she headed for home, glad to be away from the Sintons.

When Mariah arrived at the Sullivan house that evening, Jake was waiting on the front porch. The sun had set and the night was warm, with a dry breeze that carried the fragrant scent of petunias. Jake leaned against one of the stone columns, his arms folded, his face expressionless. But his eyes . . .

Mariah swallowed. His eyes raked over her, stripping the clothes away, bringing a sudden excited flutter to her stomach. *Remember who he is, Mariah.*

"Evening," he said in his low, husky voice, nearly making her forget why she'd come.

"Hello, Jake."

She started past him, but he reached out and put his hand on her arm. His touch made her heart skip a beat, made her skin hot where his fingers lay, and made that deep, intimate core of her throb lustily. She kept her gaze down out of fear he'd see the passion he aroused.

"It's kind of you to do this for Emeline," he said quietly.

Mariah gave him a brief nod. She couldn't admit she was doing it mainly for him. "Where is she?"

"In her room."

He stroked two fingers down her cheek, tipping her chin up until Mariah met his gaze. Her breath caught at the hot desire blazing there.

"Jake?" Emeline called from her second floor window. "Is Mariah here yet?"

"She's here," he replied, his gaze never leaving Mariah's face. In a low voice, he said, "I'll see you home tonight."

His words sent tingles of excitement racing up Mariah's spine, even though she knew she would be courting danger. *Are you a coward or a fool, Mariah?* Wordlessly she turned and followed him into the house.

Jake took her up to Emeline's room at the end of the hallway on the second floor. Mariah tapped lightly, then opened the door. Emeline was still in bed.

Mariah closed the door behind her and took a chair from the writing desk to pull up near the bed. "Are you still having headaches?"

"Not now. But Percy came over and, well, I didn't wish to see him just yet . . ." She glanced at the silver pot on the table beside her bed. "Do you want some coffee?"

"Yes, thank you. I would."

"Do you mind pouring?" She stretched out her hand. "It's a little far for me to reach."

It was on the tip of Mariah's tongue to tell her what a spoiled brat she was. Instead, Mariah counted to ten as she poured two cups and handed one to Emeline, who then eyed the sugar bowl longingly. Mariah held it out so she could plop four sugar cubes into the fragrant brew.

Mariah added cream to her own cup and took a sip, studying the girl over the rim. "Tell me about Percy," she said.

Setting down her cup, Emeline related how they'd met and told Mariah all about his background and future goals, including what his yearly profits were. Weeding through all the boasting, Mariah gathered that Percy was a likable fellow with infinite patience, yet she noted that Emeline kept plucking at the comforter as she spoke.

"Do you want to get married?"

"Well, I don't want to be a spinster, so I suppose I do."

"Do you love Percy?"

"I don't know. I like him an awful lot, and he does treat me well." Emeline smiled a dreamy smile. "He says I'm all his fantasies come true." But that thought seemed to make her even more distraught. She twisted her fingers and looked away with a worried frown.

Mariah pondered the matter as she drank her coffee. "Are you ready to be a wife?"

"Do you mean can I run a household? I won't have to. Percy has a housekeeper who runs everything."

"That's not exactly what I meant. There are wifely duties other than keeping a house."

Emeline grew pale. Quickly, she sipped her coffee. "My head is hurting something fierce. Perhaps we should talk when I'm feeling better."

"I think I know why your head is hurting, Emeline."

"You do?"

"What do you know about procreation?"

"Oh, Mariah, don't even speak of such things."

"For heaven's sake, Emeline, you'll be a wife in seven days." At the girl's groan, Mariah said, "Do you know how babies start?"

"I don't want to know," she whined, sinking down into the bedcovers.

Mariah was losing patience. Emeline behaved more like a twelve-year-old than a fully grown woman. "Then I suggest you call off the wedding."

"Call it off?"

"It seems quite clear to me you're not ready."

Emeline sat up. "I can't call it off. I'd be the laughingstock of town. Who would marry me then?"

"If you're going to act like a child, no one." Mariah stood up and walked to the door. "You have seven days. If you want to talk, send for me."

"Mariah, wait!" In a little girl's voice, she said, "Will you come tomorrow? I promise to be ready to talk then."

Mariah studied her a moment, wondering if another visit would be worth the bother. But she was doing this for Jake. "I'll be here."

There was an immediate look of relief on Emeline's face. "Thank you, Mariah."

Mariah found Jake sitting in a chair on the porch, reading the newspaper. For a moment she observed him quietly, admiring his strong, lean body and handsome profile, then she cleared her throat. Instantly, he was on his feet. He tossed aside the paper and strode toward her, all virile six feet of him.

"How's my sister?"

"Mostly scared."

He nodded toward the street. "Shall we?"

Despite her trepidation, Mariah couldn't help but delight in the beautiful August evening. She strolled at a leisurely pace beside Jake, tilting her head to gaze heavenward, where stars twinkled like tiny crystals in the inky sky. Around them, fireflies flashed tiny beams of yellow light, and crickets chirped in rhythm.

A sudden breeze enveloped Mariah in Jake's clean, musky scent, causing her pulse to quicken. She closed her eyes and inhaled slowly, filling herself with that scent, imagining that it was a summer night ten years ago, when she and Jake were so much in love.

Jake began to talk, breaking her reverie. "I worry about Emeline. She's been coddled all her life. She's very naive."

"Perhaps it's time to stop coddling her."

"I don't know how." He stuck his hands in his pockets and frowned. "All I want is for her to be happy. If she doesn't care for Percy, then she shouldn't marry him."

His deep concern for his sister was yet another

surprise, showing a protective side of Jake. Mariah had once believed she knew everything about him. She was slowly realizing how much more she had to learn. That she truly wanted to learn astonished her.

"I think Emeline likes Percy well enough," Mariah assured Jake. "She's just frightened because she doesn't know what to expect in terms of . . ." Mariah paused. "Emeline's just nervous about her—wifely duties." Mariah felt Jake glance at her and quickly added, "But I suppose all women experience that before their wedding night."

"Were you able to put her fears to rest?"

"She didn't feel much like talking tonight," Mariah answered diplomatically. "She's asked me to come back tomorrow evening, when she's feeling better."

Mariah didn't tell Jake that she had some doubts about whether she'd be able to reassure Emeline. She knew the basics of sex, but her knowledge was limited to medical textbooks and her studies of animal husbandry. Everything else was pure speculation.

But then perhaps that was why Jake had asked.

As they came to a stop in front of her door, Jake turned to gaze down at her, his face hidden in shadows cast by the street lamps behind him. "I'm glad Emeline has you to talk to." His voice had deepened, taking on that husky tone that sent electrified thrills throughout Mariah's body.

She suddenly found herself wondering what it

would be like to let Jake teach her about sex. She felt a hot blush color her cheeks and quickly glanced away. Was he wondering the same thing?

From the corner of her eye, Mariah caught a movement behind her and turned with a gasp.

"What is it?" Jake asked, swinging around.

" 'Evening, folks," the sheriff said, as he strolled past.

" 'Evening," Jake replied.

Mariah let out her breath. She had to stop jumping at shadows. She had finally told the sheriff about the strange incidents, and he was no doubt making a point of walking past her house every evening. She glanced up to find Jake scowling at her.

"I don't like you being frightened, Mariah. You shouldn't have to live with barred windows and doors, jumping at the least little sound. What kind of life is that?"

"I'm not particularly fond of it, either."

"You'd feel better if you knew how to use a gun."

"And just how am I going to learn? You're too busy to teach me."

"I'll make time."

His expression was so determined, his words spoken with such sincerity, that Mariah regretted her sarcasm. "I didn't mean to be short with you. I really do appreciate your offer, but I just can't bring myself to own a gun. Thank you for seeing me home."

There was a long pause, and then he said, "It was my pleasure."

Once again the huskiness of his voice sent those delicious currents coursing through her. She dared not raise her head for fear of seeing her own desire reflected in his gaze.

"Good night, Jake," she said softly. But instead of going inside, Mariah hesitated, wanting to hold onto the moment, yet fearing what might happen if she did.

Her fears were realized when Jake cupped her face and raised it, bending his head toward her. Despite her resolve, Mariah wound her arms around his neck, leaning into him, pressing her breasts against his hard-muscled chest, eagerly lifting her mouth to meet his. Her thoughts ran wild as her passion soared. She felt an urgent need to know what it would be like to lie naked in his arms, to take him inside her until she had slaked her desire for him.

All she had to do was invite him into her house.

Chapter 21

Mariah fought hard to rein in her reckless emotions. She was playing with fire, tempting herself and Jake with something that could go no further than lust. And that was something she would not do. She wouldn't give her most precious gift to a man she couldn't marry.

She broke the kiss and turned away, hurriedly fumbling for the key in her pocket.

"Mariah?"

How could she explain her behavior when it made no sense to her, either? She turned the lock and opened the door. "Good night, Jake," she said again without looking back.

"Mariah."

She stepped inside and waited, afraid to turn around.

His voice was husky with passion. "I'll see you tomorrow." It was said as a promise.

At noon the next day, Mariah was making her house calls when she spotted Luther half a block up on Center Street, chatting with the barber outside his shop. Mariah stopped and pretended to study a store window, not wishing to encounter him. Luther started off down the sidewalk, smiling and nodding to others as they passed by.

Ahead of him, Oscar Drubb was washing the window of the tannery. As Mariah watched, Luther paused just behind Oscar. At once, Oscar dropped his bucket and cloth and scurried into the shop. It was such an odd sight that Mariah could only stare in bewilderment. What had Luther done to frighten him?

As soon as she saw Luther turn into the general store, Mariah went to the tannery. "Is Oscar here?" she asked the cobbler.

"He's getting a broom." The man shook his head. "He spilled a bucket of suds all over the sidewalk."

Mariah waited outside until Oscar returned. When he saw her, he ducked his head and began to sweep.

"Hello, Oscar. How are you feeling today?"

He gave a quick shrug and continued sweeping.

"Oscar, what made you drop the bucket?"

"Don't know," he said nervously, shaking his head as he whisked the sudsy water off the sidewalk.

"I saw Luther Sinton stop behind you. Did he say something to upset you?"

Oscar's gaze darted nervously about, then he muttered quietly, "Arf, arf. Mad dog."

He'd said the same thing when she'd questioned him about the explosion. "What does that mean, Oscar? I don't understand."

Suddenly, his eyes grew wide and he fled into the store. Mariah swung around to see Luther strutting up the sidewalk toward her, carrying a bottle of soda water.

"Dr. Lowe," he called cheerily, "I was just thinking about you."

Mariah glanced inside the shop, but there was no sign of Oscar.

Jake received a telegram from Willy's aunt and uncle that afternoon. As soon as he could get away from the quarry he took it to the dispensary, where he found Mariah just finishing up with her last patient.

"I thought you should see this."

Mariah put on her spectacles and opened the telegram.

WILL ARRIVE TO COLLECT WILLY WEDNESDAY.

Two more days. With a heavy sigh, she handed it back and removed her spectacles. "I'll have to prepare Willy."

Jake studied her for a long moment. "You don't want him to go, do you?"

Mariah felt her throat tighten. She shook her head, afraid her voice would give away her emotion.

At that moment, Willy burst through the door, followed by Gertrude. "Hi, Jake! Mariah, can I visit Laz now?"

Mariah ruffled his hair. "Of course. Just be calm around him. He shouldn't get excited."

Willy held his finger up to his lips. "I'll be quiet," he whispered. Mariah laughed as he tiptoed down the hallway to the connecting door.

"He's such a bright boy, Mariah," Gertrude reported. "He's a delight to teach. Do you know he already has his multiplication tables memorized? I told him we'd start long division next week."

She was so enthused that Mariah hated breaking the news to her. "His aunt and uncle are coming for him on Wednesday, Mrs. Johnson."

Gertrude put a hand to her throat. "He's leaving us?"

"Jake was kind enough to find Willy's family. They're coming to take him back to their farm near Fort Wayne."

"That far?" She went to stand at the window, a bleak expression on her face. "I didn't know," she said in a quavering voice. "I suppose it's the best thing for him—to be with family." She tried to smile, but it didn't work. "I must get back," Gertrude said woodenly. "I'd like to see Willy off on Wednesday, if you don't mind."

"Not at all." Mariah followed her to the doorway, watching as Gertrude hurried along, dabbing her eyes with a handkerchief.

Mariah closed the door and turned toward Jake. "I dread Wednesday. It's going to be difficult to let Willy go. If I wasn't completely convinced this was in his best interests, I wouldn't give him up."

Jake studied her for a moment, then suddenly took her hand. "Come with me. I have something to show you."

"Where are we going?"

"You'll see."

"But patients may come in, Jake."

"They'll wait. This won't take long."

He led her through the backyard, opened the gate, and waited for Mariah to pass through before shutting it behind her. Without saying a word, he strode down the path until they came to a small clearing in the woods just before the creek. "What do you see down there?" he asked, turning her shoulders until she was facing in the right direction.

"A tree."

"Anything else?"

Mariah squinted. "Something hanging from a branch. Tin cans?"

"Targets."

"Targets?" She turned, but he was already heading toward the creek.

She marched after him, holding up her long skirt to keep from tripping in the grass. "I told you how I felt."

"Are you afraid to learn?" he called over his shoulder.

"I don't like guns, Jake."

"Neither do I. But sometimes we have to do things we don't like."

"Where are we going now?"

"Nowhere in particular. I just thought you needed to get away for a little while."

She caught up with him when he stopped by the creek. As Jake crouched to pick up a smooth pebble from the water, Mariah studied him wonderingly. It seemed she had much to learn about Jake Sullivan.

A breeze stirred the trees, shaking leaves from the branches, the first hint of the coming autumn. Mariah tipped back her head, closed her eyes, and inhaled slowly, filling her soul with the clean, fresh air, listening to the water gurgle as it flowed over stones. She let out her breath on a sigh. How she loved this place.

"Remember when we used to fish here?" Jake asked, turning to gaze at her. "I always had to bait your hooks."

Mariah laughed. "And I always caught bigger fish than you did."

He rose and walked toward her. "Just once."

"I set a record," she boasted. "You told me so yourself. All-Time Coffee Creek Fishing Champion."

"You believed me?"

"Do you mean to say you made that up?"

Jake tipped back his head and laughed, a real, genuine, from-the-heart laugh.

"You beast!" Mariah cried.

"Brat."

The smile slowly dissolved from Jake's face as he stared deep into her eyes. Suddenly Mariah was in his arms, kissing him with the passion and intensity of a lover. She didn't want to think about what she was doing. She knew it was foolish, yet she couldn't help herself. His taste was familiar, yet immeasurably exciting. His mouth was firm and hungry. His hands burned where they touched her, making her body pliable and willing. They were teenagers again, madly in love.

When they broke the kiss, Mariah wrapped her arms around Jake's waist and laid her head on his shoulder, confused by her feelings. Her conscience chided her for being disloyal to her brother's memory. Yet during moments like these, she could shut out those bitter thoughts and pretend nothing had ever come between her and Jake.

But her mind was too logical. She couldn't pretend her brother hadn't drowned or that Jake wasn't responsible. She could only wish.

The sound of snapping twigs jolted Mariah back to the present. She turned with a gasp as the hair on the back of her neck began to prickle. "Someone's out there," she whispered.

Jake swung around. "I don't see anyone."

"I can feel him." She rubbed her arms as a shudder racked her body. "Let's go back."

By the dubious expression on his face, Mariah could tell Jake didn't believe her. But she knew what she sensed. She glanced up at the branches above her. No breeze stirred the leaves; no crickets chirped. The air fairly quivered with menace.

Someone was still watching them.

After Mariah had seen her last patient of the afternoon, she and Annie sat down with Willy in his bedroom. As Mariah explained about his relatives, an alarmed look flashed across his face. "Did I do something bad?"

"No, Willy, not at all," Mariah assured him. "Your family wants you to live with them."

"Don't you want me to live here anymore?"

Annie's voice quavered as she answered. "We'd love for you to stay with us, Willy, but you should be with family."

His little fingers twisted together as his panic rose. "You could be my family."

Mariah saw Annie turn away and pull out a hankie. Blinking back her own tears, she said, "Your aunt and uncle live on a farm, Willy. You'll get to meet cousins and have pets. It'll be a wonderful experience for you."

"I don't want cousins. I don't need pets. I have Laz."

Mariah gave him a fierce hug. "Wait until you meet them before you decide anything."

He pulled away, giving her a defiant glare, though his lower lip trembled. "I won't like them."

"Come along and eat supper now, Willy," Annie coaxed. "I've made your favorite cornbread and ham."

Mariah watched as Annie took his hand and led him into the kitchen. How were they ever going to send him away?

Late that afternoon, Mariah paid a call on Emeline, who was seated on a pale green Queen Anne-style sofa in the parlor, an array of delicacies on the table before her.

"Coffee?" she asked, picking up the silver pot.

"Please." Mariah sat down on one of the wing-back chairs opposite her and accepted a cup.

Emeline waved a hand over the pastries. "Help yourself."

Mariah nibbled on a scone as Emeline chattered about everything except her upcoming nuptials. Finally, Mariah turned the subject to the matter at hand. "Have you been thinking any more about your wedding?"

Emeline nodded, her mouth stuffed with a tea biscuit. She chewed quickly and swallowed. "I have to marry Percy. That's all there is to it. Just tell me in the simplest terms what I must do."

"You mustn't think of it as a chore to be gotten over with."

Emeline used the tip of her napkin to wipe the crumbs from her mouth. "Then how shall I think of it?"

Mariah sighed. How best to explain passion? "Did you enjoy eating that biscuit?"

"Yes, but what has that to do with anything?"

"Describe the sensations of eating it."

Emeline scrunched her eyebrows together. "Well, it was sweet and delicious—and I want another." She immediately reached for the plate.

"Exactly," Mariah said with a satisfied smile. "That's what passion is like."

"A tea biscuit?" she asked in bewilderment.

"Like something delicious that makes you want more."

"Really?" Emeline sat forward. "How do you know, Mariah?"

Mariah set her cup down with a clatter. She didn't know, she could only imagine. The trouble was that she imagined it with Jake. "I—studied it in medical school."

"You studied passion? That's amazing. But just exactly how do you go about"—she leaned close to whisper—"*it?*"

Mariah explained as gently as possible the physical positioning of the bodies as well as the scientific explanation of conception. When she had finished, Emeline sat back with a frown.

"That doesn't sound delicious at all. It sounds painful."

"You'll have to trust me—there are too many babies conceived for it to be painful. On the other hand, a lot of the pleasure will be up to you. You must not just lie back and expect Percy to know what to do. You must take the initiative. Be bold, Emeline. Guide him, tell him what feels good, where you want to be touched, and then you must ask him to tell you those same things. Percy seems to be very eager to please you, so I doubt you'll have any problems."

"You're quite sure it will be pleasurable?"

"If you make it so. It's like that biscuit: you can dip it in frosting and make it more enjoyable or in vinegar and sour it."

Emeline smiled cannily. "Well, in that case, I suppose I'll try the frosting."

"That's the right attitude."

Emeline took a sip of her coffee, then patted her lips dry. "They certainly teach a lot about passion in medical school."

Mariah smiled obliquely. "Do you have any more questions?"

"Not right now. You've given me a lot to think about. But if I do, may I call on you?"

"Of course." Mariah stood up. "Thank you for your hospitality."

Emeline rose and sailed around the table to her, surprising Mariah by bussing her on both cheeks. "Thank you, Mariah. I appreciate your help. I know you've never liked me."

Mariah was so stunned by Emeline's blunt admission that she couldn't think what to say. She needn't have worried, however, because Emeline continued on. "You know I've invited your sister to the wedding. I'd like you to come, too."

"That's really not necessary."

"I know. I would truly appreciate it if you would."

Flustered, Mariah said, "Thank you. I'd be delighted to attend."

"I'll have a handwritten invitation sent around tomorrow. I'm so looking forward to seeing my dearest Eliza and Eileen again."

"Eileen is coming home?" Mariah asked as they walked to the front door.

"I haven't heard otherwise. I'm sure she would have written if she can't make it." Emeline paused to glance around, then said in a conspiratorial voice, "Perhaps my marriage will encourage my brother to renew his courtship of you."

A jolt ran through Mariah's body. "I'm afraid that's not possible."

"Of course it's possible. He isn't courting anyone else, although I know a certain young lady in town who would like nothing better than to be courted by the handsome Jake Sullivan." Emeline's eyes widened. "Oh, but maybe you're the one who's seeing someone. Who is it? I promise I won't tell a soul."

"It's not that, Emeline. I just can't marry—"

She swung around as the front door opened and Jake walked in. He didn't even seem to notice his sister. His gaze was on her.

"Evening, Mariah," he said with a nod.

Mariah's heart began to pound. He was so stunningly male, so excitingly rugged—and so dangerously close. "Hello, Jake," she said, in a voice she knew was too breathless. Blushing hotly, she turned to Emeline, who was gazing at her with a curious expression. "Emeline, thank you again. If you have any more questions, please feel free to call on me."

She stepped outside and heard Jake follow her onto the porch.

"I'll see you home."

Mariah paused, imagining a kiss at her door, Jake's strong arms pulling her close, his hard body pressed against hers, tempting her to discover the sensual pleasures she had described to Emeline. She drew in a shaky breath. "It would be better if you didn't."

Before he could argue, Mariah hurried down the sidewalk. She had to put distance between them quickly before that powerful attraction pulled her back.

It was only when she finally turned onto Center Street that Mariah felt herself relax. Talking about passion with Emeline reminded her too much of the desire Jake aroused in her. Seeing him only heightened those emotions. But letting Jake court her? To what end?

Even had the past not held so much pain, they were still miles apart in their thinking. Mariah would never tolerate marriage to a man who thought nothing of treating his employees like slaves for his own profit. It went against everything she was raised to believe. A union between them would be impossible.

The sound of Lazarus's whimpering woke Mariah from a restless sleep. She lit a lantern, slipped on her wrapper, and hurried to the kitchen, where Laz was attempting to get up.

"Stay still, Laz." She sat beside him on the floor and tried to calm him, but he kept whining and trying to get up. She knew something had disturbed him.

Carrying the lantern, Mariah made sure the bolt on the back door was thrown, then she walked through the house, checking all the windows. When she came to the front door, the hairs on her neck suddenly rose. Instantly, her heart began to race. Was someone on the other side?

Mariah pressed her ear to the door, but all was silent. Did she dare open it to check?

Suddenly, Lazarus began to growl. Mariah grabbed her desk chair and propped it beneath the doorknob, then ran to the kitchen and found the dog struggling to his feet, fangs bared, staring at the back door.

Mariah pressed a hand to her chest to still her racing heart. She couldn't get out through the dispensary. She would have to exit onto Center Street, and there was no way to know who waited outside.

A shadow moved stealthily past the kitchen window, revealing the outline of a man. Nearly dizzy with fear, Mariah dropped down to the floor, opened a cabinet, and grabbed the heavy rolling pin. She was trapped in her own house.

Chapter 22

Cradling her makeshift weapon in trembling hands, Mariah sat for hours with her back against the kitchen door. Lazarus had finally stopped growling, but Mariah remained at her post, dozing on and off, afraid to leave the door unguarded.

If she made it through the night, she was going to have Jake teach her how to shoot.

Lazarus's cold nose against her cheek woke her. Mariah jerked upright with a gasp, then uncurled her legs, groaning at the stiffness of her muscles. Light filtered through the curtains at the window, and Mariah had never been so happy to see the dawn.

She rose slowly and put the rolling pin on the table, then turned to find Lazarus sitting at her feet, tail wagging, gazing up at her hopefully. He seemed to have forgotten all about his wound as well as their fright in the night. She knelt down to put her arms around him. "I'm so glad you're better."

As soon as she'd fed him, Mariah went through the house to satisfy herself that everything was all right. She opened the front door and cautiously poked her head out to look around. In the street a delivery wagon passed by, while further down the block, the newsboy was delivering papers. Everything seemed perfectly normal.

With a sense of relief, Mariah returned to the kitchen and opened the back door, then recoiled with a cry of alarm. On her stoop lay the headless remains of a large brown rat. Lazarus came running to see what the disturbance was about, but Mariah grabbed him and pulled him back.

With a shudder of repulsion, she shut the door, then hurried to her bedroom to get dressed. This time she had something to show the sheriff.

An hour later, Mariah and Annie stood in the backyard watching as Sheriff Logan disposed of the remains in the woods.

"Looks like a prank to me," he said, pulling off his heavy gloves as he trudged back across the yard. "Wouldn't surprise me if it wasn't the work of that young hooligan Bill Newton and his gang. I'm going to round him up and bring him over here to see what he has to say for himself."

"With everything else that's happened, leaving a

dead rat on my doorstep seems more like a threat than a prank."

The sheriff gave her a dubious glance. "Any reason why someone would be threatening you?"

"Tell him, honey," Annie said, giving her an encouraging nod.

"To be honest, Sheriff, I've been asking a lot of questions around town about the explosion. Perhaps someone doesn't want me to find the answers."

The sheriff pushed his hat back on his head and frowned at her from beneath wrinkled brows. "I asked a lot of questions, too, Doc, and I examined the quarry myself. No one has made any threats to me. If I wasn't satisfied that it was nothing more than a terrible mistake, I'd have to agree that might be a reason to threaten you—but I am satisfied, and so is everyone else I've talked to, including Jake Sullivan.

"Now, I'm going to bring Bill Newton down here, and we'll get this settled once and for all. Okay?"

Mariah had no choice but to agree. But as soon as he'd gone, she huffed in frustration. "It wasn't a prank, Annie. Someone was giving me a warning."

"Honey, I'd feel a whole lot better if you moved in with me."

Mariah gave her a hug. "I appreciate your offer, but I refuse to let these threats chase me from my home. Do I have any patients to see?"

"Not this early."

Mariah started for the back gate. "If anyone comes in, I'll be back in half an hour."

"Where are you going?" Annie called.

"To hire a teacher. It's time I learned to shoot."

Jake was surprised to see Mariah pacing in front of the mill when he rode in that morning. Her blue skirt whipped about her legs, the full sleeves of her white blouse billowed in the strong wind, and she had to hold on to her straw skimmer to keep it from blowing away. Gray clouds covered the sky, giving the day a grim cast that matched the look on her face.

He dismounted and led the horse toward her. "Morning."

"Good morning."

"I'll take the horse for you, Jake," Luther called, striding out of the mill. "Hello, Dr. Lowe," he said cheerfully.

Mariah gave him a brief nod of acknowledgment. Jake watched her as Luther led the horse to the stables. She had dark circles beneath her eyes, her lower lip was caught between her teeth, and her hands trembled as she clasped them together. Mariah wasn't angry; she was distressed.

"I want to learn to shoot."

"What changed your mind?"

Mariah glanced around, as though to be sure they were alone. "Someone left a present at my back door last night."

Jake's gut tightened in apprehension at the emphasis she put on the word *present*. "What was it?"

The color drained from her face as she spoke. "A decapitated rat."

Jake clenched his jaw in anger. If he ever found out who did it, he'd choke the bastard. "Did you tell the sheriff?"

"He thinks it's a prank. He's going to bring Bill Newton over to talk to me."

"What do you think?"

"I think it's a warning."

Jake listened as Mariah explained her theory. Privately, he had to side with the sheriff. It sounded like the kind of disgusting juvenile prank a bunch of hooligans would come up with. But whatever it was, he couldn't stand to see Mariah so fearful.

Mariah peered up at him from beneath the brim of her hat. "Is your offer still open?"

"We'll start this evening."

Mariah made her morning house calls and headed back to the dispensary around noon. She wasn't surprised to see the sheriff's buggy parked in front. Inside, she found Logan waiting with a stocky, blunt-nosed youth wearing knee breeches and a sullen expression. The room was empty except for them.

The sheriff rose and ordered the youth to do likewise. "Morning, Doc. I brought Bill Newton to see you." He nudged the boy.

" 'Lo, Doc," the lad muttered, keeping his gaze down.

Mariah stood in front of him and waited until he finally looked up at her. "Bill, did you leave something on my doorstep last night?"

He shook his head adamantly. "I already told the sheriff I didn't. I don't have nothin' against you, Doc. You can ask my ma. She'll say I was at home."

"She always says you were at home," the sheriff drawled.

"Well, this time it's true. I swear it is." He gave Mariah an imploring look. "Your pa saved my pa's job, Doc. I wouldn't prank you. I'll even help you find out who did."

Mariah studied him for a moment, then turned to the sheriff. "I believe him."

Logan gave her a dubious frown. "Are you sure?"

"I'm positive."

"Thank you, Doc!" Billy exclaimed.

"And I'm going to take you up on your offer, Bill," Mariah said. "I want you to do everything you can to find out who did it."

"I will. I swear it. I'll get started right now."

Logan tipped his hat back and sighed. "I guess I'd better get started, too."

Supper at Annie's house was a glum affair. Mariah and Annie tried their best to cheer Willy, with dismal results. He wouldn't listen to talk about living on a farm, meeting new people, or traveling on a train. He moped through his meal and then lay on the floor beside Lazarus, one hand on the dog's back.

Mariah watched him guiltily. Though she was delivering the child into the hands of strangers, she had only Willy's best interests at heart. But was it the right thing to do?

Jake arrived at Mariah's house promptly at seven o'clock. He'd brought a shotgun with him, a weapon he thought would be her best safeguard against an intruder.

"A shotgun?" She stared warily at the weapon. "I'd pictured something a bit smaller, one of those little guns—derringers, I think they're called."

"The barrel is too short, and it only holds two bullets. You'd have to be standing next to the person for a derringer to do any harm. I don't think you want to get that close if you're in danger." He patted the shotgun. "This is your best means of protection."

At her grimace Jake said, "You don't have to go through with the lessons."

"I'm sorry; I'm out of sorts this evening. I just feel so guilty about sending Willy away."

"He'll get used to his new home."

"I'm sure he will. Right now he thinks we don't want him."

Jake led her to the clearing, stopping about fifty feet from the hanging cans. "Are you sure you want to do this tonight?"

He saw her draw in a breath and square her shoulders. "Yes, I want to learn."

Jake was relieved. He knew Mariah would feel much better knowing that she didn't have to live in constant fear of someone breaking into her house. He showed her how to load the shotgun, then had her repeat his actions. After demonstrating how to aim and fire the weapon, he held it out to her. "Your turn."

Mariah stared at it for a moment as if it would bite her. Then she pressed her lips together and took it from him. With quick efficiency, she inserted the shells and closed the chamber. But when it came time to fire it, she balked.

"I can't do it."

"Don't be afraid. Let me help you." Jake placed her hands correctly and had her aim for the cans. Mariah scrunched her eyes as she pulled the trigger, then jerked back from the recoil.

"Tarnation!" Scowling, she rubbed her shoulder. "I didn't even come close."

"It helps if you keep your eyes open." Jake began to unbutton his shirt.

Mariah stepped back warily. "What are you doing?"

"You'll see." He removed his shirt, rolled it up and placed it between the butt of the shotgun and her shoulder. "Try it again, but hold it up higher." He stood behind her and put his arms around her to help her hold the gun steady, trying to ignore the soft curve of her backside pressed against his groin. "Now, aim down the sights. Fix your eye on the center can. Have you got it in view?"

At Mariah's nod, he said, "Squeeze the trigger." An instant later, they heard several metallic tings as the shell exploded and peppered the cans with shot.

Mariah's mouth dropped open as the cans swung from the impact. "I hit the target!"

Her enthusiasm made him smile. "You sure did. Let's try it again and see if you can do it twice."

Jake waited until she'd reloaded, then he put his arms around her once again. He breathed in the clean honey scent of her hair and felt the heat of her body against his. Her skirt brushed provocatively against his thighs, and the soft roundness of her backside tantalized him, causing his thoughts to wander far from the task at hand.

"I did it again!" Mariah said, with a triumphant laugh.

"One more time," Jake told her. Though it was unnecessary, he couldn't resist putting his arms around her.

As Mariah got the can in her sights, he imagined drawing his hands up her arms to her shoulders, running them down her back, beneath her rib cage, and under her breasts as he nibbled the delicate skin beneath her earlobes. He pictured himself opening her blouse, freeing those delectable ivory mounds, and cupping them in his hands as his lips moved down her throat toward those rosy nipples.

Jake took deep breaths, trying to regain his composure, but other parts of him wouldn't obey.

Desire coursed through his veins until he was drunk with it. All he could think of was laying Mariah down in the grass, stripping off his own clothing, and making wild, impassioned love to her.

Mariah fired, the recoil pushing her back against him hard. Jake was so aroused he was in agony.

"Did you see that?" she cried, swinging to face him. But the joy on her face dissolved as she stared at him. "Did I do something wrong?"

"You did very well," he said in a strained voice. He took the shotgun and turned away, trying to hide the evidence of his wayward thoughts. "That's enough for the first lesson."

Silently, Mariah handed him his shirt. Jake slung it over one shoulder, and they walked back in the waning daylight. Neither spoke. Jake guessed that Mariah's thoughts were still on Willy's departure. His thoughts, however, were totally selfish: he was aroused and he wanted her. He knew he'd get little sleep that night.

When they reached her house, Jake handed her the shotgun and a box of shells. "Put these in a handy spot near the front door."

"When shall we meet for another lesson?" Mariah asked, gazing up at him.

"Tomorrow evening, if you feel up to it."

"I think it'll be good for me to keep my mind occupied. Tomorrow will be a difficult day."

"Will you send someone to the quarry to let me know when Willy's aunt and uncle arrive? I'd like to be there to say good-bye."

"I'll do that."

Jake stood looking down at her for a moment, longing to kiss her. "Good night, Mariah."

"Jake," she called, as he strode away. "Thank you."

He turned and pressed the ends of two fingers to his lips, throwing her a kiss.

His gesture was so surprising yet so achingly familiar that Mariah could do nothing but stare at him, her heart in her throat. Had Jake even realized what he'd done?

She closed and bolted her door, then leaned against it, remembering a time when Jake couldn't leave without throwing her a kiss. Melancholy swept through her at the thought of those sweet, simple days, when her only concern was when she would see him again. She glanced over at her brother's picture, wishing she could turn back the clock and change history.

Frowning, Mariah pushed away from the door. She had to stop wishing for the impossible. The past couldn't be erased. All she could do was concentrate on the present and the problems it held— which, at that moment, seemed a formidable task.

Wednesday arrived too soon. Mariah had a knot of dread in her stomach all morning. She saw several patients at the dispensary but canceled all house calls to wait for Willy's relatives. She brought her notebook to the surgery so she could work and keep watch at the window at the same time. Willy played quietly with a spinning top in the back room; his bag sat ready on the other side of the connecting door. Annie and Gertrude hovered nearby, unable to stay away from him for longer than ten minutes at a time.

At noon, both women came up front and stood at the window, forlorn expressions on their faces. "Perhaps they won't come today," Annie said, with a hopeful sigh.

Gertrude brightened at the thought. "Perhaps they had train trouble."

"Perhaps I won't even like them." Mariah walked past the window and went to the back to check on Willy. He jumped to his feet when she came through the curtain, his eyes round with fear.

"Are they here?" he whispered.

"No. I just wanted to talk to you about something."

He sat down on the narrow bed, pressing his hands between his knees, staring at her with big, solemn eyes.

"Willy, I asked you this before. I want you to think very hard and answer me honestly. Do you know who might have hurt Laz?"

He shook his head, sucking in his cheeks and pinching his lips together.

"Are you positive?" At his nod, she asked, "Do you remember anything about the explosion?"

Again he shook his head. The bell over the door tinkled in the front, and a moment later Mariah heard a man begin to talk. She frowned in disgust. Luther!

Willy, too, heard his voice. At once, his eyes

opened wide, and he drew back with a gasp, staring at the doorway in alarm.

"What's wrong?" Mariah asked.

He opened his mouth, but no sound came out. As his breathing grew shallow and his color turned ashen, Mariah pressed his head between his knees so he wouldn't pass out. "Willy, tell me what's wrong."

"I c-can't."

"Yes, you can."

Outside the room, they could hear Luther chatting with the two women. Willy threw himself into Mariah's arms, his body shaking with fear. "Don't let on that I'm here. Please, Mariah. I didn't mean to be bad. I was only playin' with my soldiers."

Chapter 23

M ariah glanced at the top on the floor as she rocked him in her arms. "When were you playing with your soldiers, Willy?"

The bell tinkled again, and this time they heard two strange voices, a man's and a woman's. A moment later, Annie came to the back and peered through the curtain. "His aunt and uncle are here."

"I'll be out shortly, Annie." She took the child by the shoulders. "You have to tell me why you're afraid, Willy."

He stared at her, his eyes wide with terror, then he whispered, "I h-have to g-go."

"Is that why you're frightened? Because you have to go away? It wasn't Luther's voice that frightened you?"

He hesitated, then shook his head. Mariah gazed at him skeptically. "You wait here," she told him.

Mariah followed Annie to the front, where a middle-aged couple stood by the desk. Luther sat in a chair nearby.

"Excuse me for a moment," she said to the couple and walked over to Luther. "Did you need something?"

"I just wondered if you could come check on my mama today."

"I have a very busy day," she told him firmly. "I'll stop by tomorrow."

"Around noon?"

"Yes, around noon."

"That'd be fine. I'll tell her to expect you then." He walked to the door and nodded to the strangers. "Nice meeting you folks. Good luck with Willy."

While Annie performed the introductions, Mariah sized up Willy's relatives. His uncle, Thomas Burton, had the leathery skin and sinewy frame of a hardworking farmer. His aunt, Sophie, was as wide as Thomas was spare, with ruddy cheeks, a small nose with a round tip, and eyes that looked much older than her years. Both people were polite and soft-spoken and seemed almost intimidated by their surroundings.

"Let's go to my kitchen," Mariah suggested. "I've just brewed some coffee."

"When can we meet the boy?" Thomas asked.

"He'll be here soon."

She ushered them past the supply room, where she caught a glimpse of a small eye peering at them from behind the curtain. Over coffee, Mariah subtly questioned them about their children and their beliefs about religion and education. To her relief and disappointment, she could find nothing wrong. After nearly an hour, she felt satisfied that Willy would be well taken care of.

"Wait here, please, and I'll get Willy."

Mariah left her kitchen and went to the curtained room, where Annie and Gertrude waited with him. "They're good people," Mariah assured them. "They want to meet him now. But I'd like to speak to Willy alone for a moment first."

She waited until the women had left the room, then she sat beside Willy on the bed. "You said earlier that you hadn't meant to be bad, that you'd just been playing with your soldiers. When was this?"

He squeezed his hands between his knees. "The morning my pa died."

"What did you think you'd done?"

The color drained from Willy's face. "Nuthin'. I was just playin', honest."

"Where?"

"At the Jefferson quarry."

"Do you remember that day?"

"Just that I went down early to play with my soldiers."

"Then why were you frightened earlier?"

He stared at her but wouldn't answer. Mariah sighed in frustration. "Willy, it's very important for you to tell me if you remember anything more. It could help me find out why the accident happened."

"I don't remember anything else," he said stubbornly.

"All right, but promise me you'll let me know if you do."

Willy hesitated a long moment, then gave a reluctant nod. Mariah put her arms around him and hugged him. "Let's go meet your aunt and uncle."

Holding his little body stiff and straight, Willy walked into the kitchen with Mariah. His uncle immediately scooted back his chair and stood.

"Hello, Will," he said, sticking out his big, callused hand.

"It's Willy," the child corrected him.

Mariah recognized that defiant thrust of Willy's lower lip and gave him a slight nudge. Willy reluctantly put his small hand in his uncle's large one. "Hello, Uncle Thomas."

He turned to face his aunt, who motioned him over. Willy obediently complied, stiffening further when she put her arms around him. "Hello, Aunt Sophie," he said in a flat voice.

She held him away from her and looked him over. "We're going to fatten you up," she promised, pinching his cheek. "We eat good at our house, as you can see." She gestured toward her ample girth. "You'll like it on our farm."

"When do you have to go back?" Mariah asked them.

Thomas opened his pocket watch and checked the time. "There's a train that leaves at two o'clock."

That left only one hour. Mariah forced a smile. "Well, then, Willy, let's take your aunt and uncle over to Annie's. She's made a nice going-away meal for you."

Mariah escorted them to Annie's house, then hurried to the cutting mill. "Is Jake here?" she called to one of the men.

"He's at the Jefferson."

Mariah nearly ran all the way. She saw Jake on the floor below and hurried down the ramp. "Jake."

He glanced around and instantly dropped what he was doing to stride toward her.

"They're here," she said breathlessly. "They'll be taking Willy back on the two o'clock train."

"Just a minute," he said, then went to speak briefly to the men loading stone. In a few moments he was back. "Let's go."

Letting Willy board the train with strangers was one of the hardest things Mariah had ever done. The odor of burning coal permeated the air, thunder rumbled in the distance, and the sky had darkened with the threat of rain, making the day even more dismal.

Mariah waited on the platform with Jake, Annie, and Gertrude, while Willy and his new family found their seats. Around them others, too, had gathered to see loved ones off.

Biting anxiously on her lower lip, Mariah watched the windows. In a few moments, she saw a small face pressed against one of the glass panes.

Willy opened the window and stuck his head out, motioning for her to come near.

Mariah hurried toward him.

"I have to tell you a secret," he said.

She stood on tiptoe as he leaned closer and cupped his hands around his mouth. "I did do something bad. I wasn't supposed to be at the quarry before anyone else got there."

"What happened?"

"Swear you won't tell."

At Mariah's nod, he said, "I hid behind a pile of stone to play with my soldiers." His voice dropped to a whisper. "Only he caught me."

"Who caught you?"

"All aboard," the conductor shouted. A piercing whistle blocked Willy's next words. The train hissed steam and began to chug as it pulled out.

"Willy, what was his name?" Mariah called above the noise, walking alongside the moving train.

"I couldn't see him. I could only hear his voice."

She had to walk faster to keep up. "Was it the voice you heard this morning? Was it Luther's voice?"

As the train picked up speed and coal dust filled the air, Willy's uncle pulled him back inside and shut the window. Willy stared at Mariah, his palms flattened against the glass—and nodded.

Mariah stopped. Luther had been at the quarry early. Why had that frightened Willy so? Was it significant to the explosion?

As raindrops dotted the wooden platform, she

turned and began to walk back. Jake stood with Annie and Gertrude, who were both holding handkerchiefs to their eyes and umbrellas over their heads.

Jake unfurled an umbrella and held it over Mariah. "Is he all right?"

"He wanted to tell me he remembered something about the morning of the explosion." Mariah stood with her hands on her hips, watching in frustration as the train chugged out of the station.

"What did he remember?" Annie asked.

"He said he went down to the quarry early that morning to play with his soldiers and someone caught him at it. He didn't know who it was, he'd only heard a voice. But today, when he heard Luther, he recognized him." Mariah tilted her head to gaze up at Jake. "He was so frightened he couldn't speak."

"I can't imagine Luther saying anything mean to him," Gertrude offered.

"Where was Willy playing?" Jake asked. "Luther usually goes down to the stables early to take care of the horses before they have to be out on the quarry floor. Maybe Willy got in his way and he scolded him."

"That wouldn't have caused the kind of fear Willy showed today. Besides, Willy said he went to the quarry, not to the stables."

"Honey, are you sure Willy just wasn't afraid of leaving with his aunt and uncle?" Annie asked.

"No, Annie. I'm sure. He was afraid of Luther."

As Annie and Gertrude whispered between

themselves, Jake said, "If it will make you feel better, I'll talk to Luther."

Mariah pursed her lips. "No, not yet. I need more information first." Besides, she wanted to question Luther herself in a way that wouldn't arouse his suspicions.

She gazed down the tracks and watched the train as it grew smaller. It looked like she was going to have to take a trip up to Fort Wayne to talk to Willy.

The railroad station stood one block away from the cutting mill. The tracks ran directly in front of the mill, so that the heavy stone slabs and carved moldings used in construction could be easily loaded and shipped. From the second floor, the station's platform was visible.

Luther squinted his eyes to watch Willy board the train, then he turned and headed down to the main floor. The brat was finally out of the way. That left only Mariah.

Hugh Coffman balled up the letter in his hands and sent it hurtling across his office. Who did Jake think he was, issuing threats to a senator?

"I will not tolerate being your scapegoat," Jake had written. "If such an article ever appears in the newspaper again, I will see to it that a counter-article is printed that won't be flattering to you."

Hugh got up and paced his office, fuming. What he really wanted to do was to inform his partner that he was selling out and there wasn't a damn thing Sullivan could do about it. But he couldn't risk it. The road had to be completed first.

Soon, however, Jake would get his comeuppance.

"Hey, Jake, you've got visitors," Dan called from the mill doorway late that afternoon.

Jake had been inspecting the carvings on twenty limestone columns that were being shipped to Washington, D.C. Hearing his foreman call, he turned to see two gentlemen wearing city suits standing inside the mill, looking around curiously.

Jake strode toward them. "Jake Sullivan," he said, extending his hand. "What can I do for you?"

One of the men stepped forward and shook it. "Josef Schultz," he said, with a trace of a German accent. Schultz introduced his companion, then said, "We would very much like to see the mill in action. Do you mind if we look around?"

"I don't allow strangers in the mill during working hours. It can be dangerous at times. Why don't you come back after we're through for the day? I'll have one of my foremen give you a tour."

Schultz grinned, as did his companion. "We're quite familiar with mills, Mr. Sullivan."

Something about the way he answered put Jake on alert. "Why are you here?"

"Your business is up for sale, is it not? Herr Bernhardt wants to see what he's buying."

Bernhardt! Jake clenched his teeth in fury and

took a step forward, causing the men to shrink back in alarm. "Tell Mr. Bernhardt," he ground out, "that Jake Sullivan says it's *not* for sale."

They left, shaking their heads and muttering.

Dan came up behind him and asked quietly, "What's going on, Jake?"

"Coffman is trying to sell."

"Damn!" the foreman said under his breath. "You'll stop him, won't you?"

"I'll do what I can." Jake let out a tense breath. "This news can't go any farther than you. Got that?"

"All right, Jake."

Jake returned to his office and pored over the accounting ledger. After two frustrating hours, Jake slammed it shut and sat back, rubbing his temples. He still didn't have enough capital.

Perhaps he should just sell the company and walk away from it. He'd be guaranteed a sizable sum for his shares, and he could go anywhere he liked and start afresh. But that meant his men would end up working for Bernhardt, and Jake would lose the company his father had worked so hard to establish.

Could he do that to his men and to his father's memory?

When Jake walked into the house that evening, Emeline was in a state of high anxiety. She sailed out of the parlor, shaking her curls in consternation.

"Owen is going to ruin my wedding. He's drunk

as a skunk *again*. He even embarrassed Percy at dinner this evening. I've begged and begged Owen to please not drink at my wedding, but I just know he'll do it, anyway. You've got to do something, Jake."

She held her head in her hands and groaned. "Oh, I feel a headache coming on. This wedding is going to be a disaster, I just know it."

"Where is Owen?"

Emeline picked up her skirts and ran up the staircase, calling back, "I don't know and I don't care."

Jake headed straight for the gazebo and found his brother lying on one of the benches encircling the structure, snoring loudly, emanating whiskey fumes. Jake shook his shoulder. "Get up, Owen."

"Leave me 'lone."

Jake hauled him to his feet. "I said get up, damn it. What's wrong with you? You've been drunk for five straight days. Do you know how frightened Emie is that you're going to ruin her wedding?"

"Emie's gettin' married?" Owen smiled crookedly. "Aw, isn't that just swell? Who's the lucky fellow?"

Jake shoved him down on the bench and stood glowering over him. "You're a disgrace. You should be thankful our parents aren't here to see what you've done to yourself."

His brother just curled up on his side, drew his knees to his chest, and closed his eyes.

"What's the use?" Jake said in disgust, sitting down beside him.

"Yeah, what's the use?" Owen mumbled. "I might as well be dead. Hell, I'm already dead inside."

Jake gazed at him for several long moments, then rose, picked up his brother, and slung him over his shoulder. He trekked up to the house, carried Owen to his room, and deposited him on the bed. After removing his shoes and clothing, Jake pulled the quilt over him and walked out.

What was he supposed to do? He couldn't keep emptying liquor bottles; Owen would just buy more. He'd tried to keep him busy working, but Owen simply stopped showing up at the mill. He'd tried reasoning with him. He'd tried scolding him. Nothing worked.

It wasn't until Jake had taken a seat on the porch that he remembered Mariah's shooting lesson. Cursing under his breath at his forgetfulness, he headed for her house.

Mariah sat at her desk staring at the pile of letters she had yet to answer. All she could think about was Willy's confession. Her instinctive feeling was that Willy held the key to what had happened the morning of the explosion, even though he probably didn't realize it. She just had to ask him the right questions to find the answers. But that meant taking time off to travel to Fort Wayne.

A sudden knock at the door caused Mariah to jump. She rose quietly and tiptoed over.

"Who's there?"

"Jake."

Her heart skipped a beat. Jake hadn't forgotten her, after all. She opened the door and found him standing on the stoop, looking very contrite—and weary.

"I'm sorry I didn't make it in time for your lesson."

"I had work to do, anyway. Did you get delayed at the mill?"

He raked one hand through his hair. "You could say that."

Mariah could tell that something weighed heavily on his mind. She was tempted to invite him in, but thought better of it. She stepped outside and pulled the door shut behind her. "Do you want to sit and talk for a while?"

He sighed, as though he'd hoped she would ask. "If you don't mind."

Jake waited until Mariah had arranged her skirts, then he sat beside her, careful to avoid crushing the material. She had on a rose-colored blouse that buttoned down the front and a gray striped skirt. She'd taken the pins from her hair and had tied her long blond locks with a shiny pink ribbon, which made her look much like the young girl he'd loved so fiercely.

"How are you getting along?" he asked her.

"I'm trying to keep busy. Is everything all right at the mill?"

Jake wasn't sure if he should burden her with his troubles, but he suddenly felt as though he would burst if he couldn't talk to someone. "Hugh Coffman is trying to sell the company."

"Can he do that?"

"He owns more of the business than I do."

Mariah frowned thoughtfully. "If he sells, what will happen to all the men who work for you?"

"That depends upon what the new owner decides. He might keep them, or he might fire them all."

"Jake, that's terrible. What are you going to do?"

"I haven't figured it out yet."

"You have to stop the sale," she said, gazing at him in concern. "You can't put all those men out of work. It would devastate them, not to mention what it would do to Coffee Creek."

"I know. And I'm worried about Emie's wedding, as well—if there *is* a wedding."

"Emeline hasn't changed her mind, has she?"

"I hope not." Jake couldn't bring himself to talk about Owen's problem, because of the association with her brother's death.

Mariah put her hand on his shoulder. "I don't know if I can do any good or not, but I'll pay another call on your sister before Saturday—in case she needs to talk."

Just knowing that Mariah was offering her help eased part of his burden. Jake put his hand over Mariah's and rubbed his palm over her smooth skin. It felt so good to be able to talk to her again. He hadn't realized how much he'd missed that.

Had it not been for Ben's death, he wouldn't have had to miss it. Mariah would be his wife now. They'd be going to bed together every evening, where they could talk over their problems and make love and sleep contentedly wrapped in each other's embrace.

Jake imagined her undressing, slipping between snowy white sheets, her honey-blond hair cascading down her back, a sultry smile on her face as she waited for him to join her. Jake lifted her hand to his mouth and pressed his lips against the dewy skin, feeling his desire begin to build.

To his surprise, Mariah gently eased her hand away and stood up. "I have early calls to make in the morning."

Jake got to his feet. "I didn't mean to keep you up."

She gazed up at him with those lovely eyes, and all he could think of was making love to her. "I'm glad you came," she said softly. "I would have been worried."

Jake searched her earnest expression. Could the past be behind them, after all?

He curved his fingers around her shoulders, his gaze roaming the contours of her face—her arched eyebrows, her delicately sculpted cheekbones, her pointed little nose, her luscious lips. "I had to come, Mariah. I had to see you tonight." Then he dipped his head toward her.

"Jake," she whispered, but he silenced her with a deep kiss. Her mouth was so tender and sweet that he couldn't stop. He threaded his fingers in her long hair and looped it around his hands, glorying in its silken texture as he nibbled her lips and then her earlobes. Her soft, honeyed fragrance filled his nostrils, inflaming his passion even further.

"What if someone sees us?" Mariah whispered in a panic.

He reached behind her, felt for the doorknob, and opened it, backing her into the house as he ravaged her mouth with hungry kisses. He kicked the door shut with one foot and pressed her against it, his mouth moving down her throat. He unfastened the top buttons of her blouse, then slipped a hand inside to stroke the velvety smooth surface of her breast. When he eased his thumb beneath her corset to caress her nipple, he heard her gasp of surprise and then a ragged sigh of pleasure that sent his desire rocketing out of control.

Tonight Mariah would be his.

Chapter 24

The intimacy of his touch scandalized her, yet Mariah's own overwhelming desire made her powerless to stop him. She arched her back, thrusting her breast into his palm, moaning as his fingers caressed her nipple until it tightened into a hard bud. Her skin tingled where he touched it; her body throbbed with mounting excitement; and her mind emptied of logical thoughts. There were no sounds except for her own sighs of pleasure, no scents except for Jake's, no sensations except for his passionate kisses and erotic strokes.

Jake's mouth glided from her neck down to her open blouse, where her breasts overflowed her corset. In the next instant, he had peeled her blouse back and lifted one breast in his hand, bending down to capture it in his mouth.

Gasping, Mariah clutched Jake's shoulders as he

fondled the nipple with his tongue, then suckled, causing wave after wave of pleasure to ripple through her from the tip of her breast to her womb. He lifted his head and captured her mouth once again, taking her hand and placing it over his swollen manhood.

"Do you feel that, Mariah? Do you feel how much I want you?"

Before she could frame a coherent reply, Jake swept her up in his arms and started for her bedroom.

"I'm going to make love to you." He kissed her eyelids, her cheeks, her ears. "Let's mend the rift between us. Then we can forget the past."

"Forget the past . . ." she repeated dreamily. Then his words broke through the fog, and her thoughts instantly cleared. "Jake, stop! We can't do this. It would be a terrible mistake."

The panic in Mariah's voice cut through Jake's passion-besotted brain like a razor. He halted at her bedroom doorway and gazed at her dumbly, her words ringing in his ears: *It would be a terrible mistake.*

Her voice shook with emotion. "Please put me down."

Jake's desire evaporated in an instant, and he set her down. "I'm sorry, Mariah. I thought we could put the past behind us." He gazed down at her, hoping she'd tell him he was right. When she didn't, he strode to the front door and walked out. What kind of fool was he to think the past could ever be laid to rest?

Mariah stared unseeingly at the door, ashamed that she still ached with need. She could understand that Jake's desire was strong—her own surely matched his—but how could he believe their differences could be made to evaporate simply by their joining bodies? Or that she could forget the past on account of one carnal moment?

She was still shocked by his declaration: *I'm going to make love to you.* Had she not come to her senses, their rashness would have cost Mariah her virginity.

Shaken deeply, she walked to the front door and bolted it, then returned to her bedroom, where she faced herself in the mirror. What had she said that had given him the impression she'd been willing to make love with him?

The answer stared her in the face. It wasn't what she'd said; it was in her eyes, as clear as if she'd spoken it: she wanted him, too.

The next morning, Jake pulled half his crew off the road project and sent them to the Washington quarry under the pretense of needing more limestone blocks for a construction project. Then he dictated a telegram to inform his partner that there had been a delay in the completion of the road. He offered no excuse and made no mention of the visit by Bernhardt's men. He was sure Coffman would find out from Bernhardt himself soon enough.

Jake was counting on the election to buy him some time. Coffman desperately needed that road finished. He'd have to hold off making any move until after it was completed or risk the voters' wrath.

Jake wouldn't allow himself to think about Mariah or about what his foolhardy behavior might have cost him. Next to worrying about the company, his focus had to be on his own family, and for the moment, that meant getting his sister married.

By three o'clock that afternoon, Jake was too exhausted to think clearly. He started for home, then changed his mind. Emeline was to have her last bridal gown fitting that day and was sure to be in the midst of some crisis or other. Owen hadn't come to work at all, and at that moment, Jake didn't feel he could handle his brother without losing his temper.

He cut into the woods and headed for the creek. He found a large, flat, sunny rock, took off his shirt and undershirt, shoes and socks, and stretched out in the warm sunshine.

Mariah spent a restless night filled with erotic dreams of Jake and nightmares about her brother's death. She awoke bleary-eyed and out of sorts. As she lay in bed reviewing her dreams, Mariah realized her ill temper wasn't directed at Jake but at herself. She had disregarded all her own warnings and let herself get carried away by that potent attraction. She couldn't blame Jake for that; the problem was how to fight it.

The church bell tolled the noon hour as Mariah headed for Luther's house, timing her arrival for when she knew he'd be there. She'd decided to disarm him with friendliness to find out what she needed to know.

Luther must have been watching her approach from the window, for as she raised her hand to knock, the door opened.

"Hello, Dr. Lowe," he said, flashing his cocky smile.

Mariah smiled back as she stepped into the gloomy interior that smelled of sweat and stale air. "How's the wound on your arm?"

"It's great. You did a fine job of fixing it up."

"Luther?" his mother called. "Is the doctor here?"

"Yes, Mama. I'll bring her back now."

"Your mother is very lucky to have a son like you," Mariah flattered, following him to the bedroom.

"Yeah, I take good care of her."

Mariah had to wait for her eyes to adjust to the dim light. "Hello, Mrs. Sinton."

"Thank heavens you're here," the old woman snapped. "My back has been aching something terrible. Luther, go away."

As Luther slunk out of the room, Mariah opened the curtains and lifted the window sash, breathing in clean air.

"Mrs. Sinton, I do wish you'd get some fresh air every day. You'd feel much improved in spirits."

"My spirits are fine. It's my back that needs tending."

Mariah had her turn over on her stomach, then she pressed several points along her spine, causing the woman to groan and complain.

"Can you stand, Mrs. Sinton?"

"Of course I can stand."

"Then please do." Mariah waited until Dolly had climbed out of bed, then she had her turn around so she could examine her back. "I see what the problem is. You're spending too much time in bed."

"Well, of course I'm in bed. I'm sick."

"I'm going to prescribe a fifteen-minute walk every afternoon."

Dolly's sagging jaw dropped. "Walk? Can't you just give me some pills for it?"

"I'm afraid this is something pills won't cure—although a mustard plaster may give you some immediate relief."

Dolly climbed back into bed and pulled up the cover. "Have that worthless son of mine get me a mustard plaster, then. I need all the relief I can get."

"I have one back at the dispensary. I'll send it home with him."

She found Luther sulking outside the front door. He immediately put on a cheerful face when he saw her.

"How's my mama?"

"Your mother needs a mustard plaster. Do you

want to walk back with me to the dispensary to pick one up?"

"Sure."

As they walked along, Mariah let Luther chatter about what a good doctor her father had been and brag about how he took such great care of his mother.

"Won't the foreman be angry with you for taking so much time off work?"

"Naw! They like me down there. They understand about mama's illnesses."

Mariah kept her tone casual and friendly. "How long have you been with C & S?"

Luther stuck his hands in his pockets and thrust out his chin. "Since I was fourteen. The senator asked me personally to come work for him, running errands and the like."

"I'm surprised he didn't hire you to be a water boy, like Willy."

"He needed me for more serious work. When I turned sixteen, he moved me to the stables, but I still run errands for him—the important ones."

"I would have thought he'd train you to be a charge man like your father."

Luther shrugged. "He had his reasons. But I could have done it. I know a lot about dynamite."

"From your father?"

"Yeah, and from helping the other charge men sometimes."

"Really?" Mariah lifted her eyebrows, pretending to be impressed.

He puffed up like a peacock. "Yeah. I could do their job."

"It's awfully dangerous work. You're much safer where you are. I'm relieved that Willy won't be in danger anymore." She heaved an exaggerated sigh. "Poor boy. He took his father's death hard."

"Yeah, I felt the same way when my daddy died."

"Well, then you and Willy have something in common. Too bad you didn't get to know him." She paused, then said, "But I guess you did know Willy, didn't you?"

"I didn't have much to do with him," Luther said quickly. "I practically never saw him."

Mariah stopped at the dispensary door. "That's odd."

Luther smiled, but the smile didn't reach his eyes. "Why is it odd?"

"Someone told me you'd talked to Willy the morning of the explosion."

"I don't know who could've said that. I wasn't around the quarry that morning. I had work to do at the stable."

Throwing him a doubtful glance, Mariah opened the door. "I'll get the mustard plaster."

Luther paced back and forth, his hand nervously gripping the switchblade in his pocket. Who could have seen him with the brat? No one else had been in sight. He'd made sure of it. It had to be the kid who told her.

Luther simmered in a barely contained rage. Mariah knew more than she was letting on—but how much did she know? He heard the door open and quickly turned, his smile in place, but it was only Annie.

"Here you go, Luther. This is for your mother."

Stunned, he stared down at the package in his hand. "The doc's not coming out?"

"She had a patient waiting to see her."

"But she has to tell me how to use this."

Annie stepped out onto the sidewalk. "It's very simple. Apply the plaster directly over the area on your mother's back that's hurting her and wrap gauze around her to keep it from slipping."

"But what if it doesn't help?"

"Then let me know."

That wasn't good enough. He had to talk to Mariah. Luther gripped the paper wrapping until it crinkled in his fingers. He felt as though he was going to explode inside.

"Can you ask her to come to the house tomorrow? Same time?"

"Well, I—"

"She'll say yes. She always does."

Annie gave him a sympathetic smile. "All right, Luther. I know you're worried about your mama. Tell her the doctor will come again tomorrow."

He gave a nervous laugh. "Sure, that's all right, then. Thanks." Luther turned and strutted down the street, but inside he could barely control his fury. He wanted to open his knife and jam it in someone's throat. Just the thought of it made his heart race and his groin tighten with excitement.

Suddenly, he caught sight of Oscar on the opposite side of the street washing the barber shop window. Luther stopped to let a buggy clatter by, then he strode across toward him.

A young boy and his mother came out of the barber shop, nodded a greeting, and continued past while Oscar wiped the glass with a thick cloth, oblivious to Luther's approach. Luther fingered his knife, imagining the thrill of driving it into Oscar's neck. He couldn't do it here, but he could give him a little scare.

Oscar must have seen his reflection, for he suddenly wheeled around and began a high-pitched keening. Luther clapped his hands over his ears to block the sound, but it buzzed through his head until he couldn't think.

"Mad dog, mad dog!" Oscar yelled at the top of his lungs, bringing the barber running.

Luther took off, heedless of the barber staring at him. He had to get away from the noise.

"Did Luther give you any problems, Annie?" Mariah asked. Her patient had left, and the waiting room was empty.

"He seemed very upset that you didn't come out to explain the plaster."

"I doubt that was why he was upset. I questioned him about Willy and caught him in a lie. I'm sure he was hoping to talk himself out of it."

"What did Luther say?"

"I mentioned that I knew he'd talked to Willy the morning of the explosion. He denied it, of course. He said he'd been nowhere near the site.

He was also bragging about how much he knew about dynamite."

"What do you think it means?"

"I have a nagging suspicion that Luther was somehow involved in the explosion."

"Oh, honey, I sure hope not. I can't imagine Luther doing such a terrible thing."

"Then let's hope I'm wrong."

"Mariah, if Luther was involved, you shouldn't be questioning him. What if he catches on?"

"I can take care of myself, Annie."

"You stay right there," Annie told her.

She left the dispensary and returned a few moments later. Taking Mariah's hand, she tucked a double-barreled derringer and a small bag of cartridges into it.

Mariah stared at the small pistol in surprise. "Where did you get this?"

"I've had it for years. I keep it in my bureau drawer. I want you to have it now."

"Jake's already taught me how to use a shotgun."

"You can't carry a shotgun in your medical bag. Go on, take it now. I'll feel a whole lot better if you do."

Mariah accepted it with thanks, but she had no intention of keeping it with her medical tools. It just seemed wrong.

Mariah had no patients to see that afternoon, so she took some time off to spend outdoors with Lazarus. He was able to move around more easily now, so she opened the gate and took him for a leisurely walk.

Lazarus was soon bounding after a squirrel, his injury forgotten, leading Mariah deeper into the woods. She didn't mind. The forest was alive with the cries of blue jays, robins, blackbirds, and even whippoorwills. She breathed in the fresh, pine-scented air and enjoyed the delights of stretching her legs and swinging her arms, of just being alive.

But feeling so alive was also a poignant reminder of her brother's death. She tried to picture what Ben would have looked like now and what he'd have been doing. No doubt, he'd have been working at the dispensary in her place.

Unbidden images of Ben after he'd been pulled from the underground pool flashed in her mind. Feeling the deep ache of sorrow, Mariah forced herself to remember instead his winning smile and infectious laugh.

Her brother had always had such zest for life. Ben had dreamed of being an adventurer, of traveling deep into the heart of some faraway jungle and making an important discovery that would have been his claim to fame. He'd even sent for literature on Africa. She remembered him showing it to her one evening.

"Look, Mariah," he'd whispered, opening a pamphlet, "this is where I'm going."

"Father will never let you," she had chided.

"He won't know until it's too late to stop me."

Mariah hadn't believed him; they never disobeyed their father. But the truth was, Ben had never really wanted to be a doctor.

Mariah stopped as she realized what she'd just thought. *Ben had never really wanted to be a doctor.* But he'd been too afraid to tell their father.

She sat down on a nearby rock, stunned by the revelation. Why hadn't she seen it ten years ago? Why had she felt such a responsibility to go to medical school in Ben's stead when she'd surely had some inkling he'd never intended to go himself?

Somewhere near the creek up ahead, Lazarus began to bark excitedly. Her stomach automatically tightened in dread.

"Laz, come here," Mariah called, hurrying after him. She stopped at the water's edge and looked downstream. The dog was standing beside a large slab of limestone, tail wagging, gazing adoringly up at Jake.

Mariah's pulse raced; she just couldn't stem that rush of excitement.

Jake was stretched out on a large rock, his chest bare and brown from the sun, and his dark hair ruffled by a warm breeze. As she started toward him, he leaned on one elbow and watched her with that familiar, guarded expression.

Mariah came to a stop several feet away, trying to still her racing heart. Keeping his gaze fixed on her, Jake swung his legs over the edge of the rock and sat up. She noticed he wore no shoes or socks, either.

Damp heat throbbed deep between her thighs as her gaze traveled up his long, lean legs. She paused at that bronzed, well-muscled chest, then continued slowly up to his mouth, remembering the inviting taste and feel of it.

Mariah took a steadying breath. "What are you doing out here?" she asked cautiously. "I thought you had to work until dusk."

"I needed a break." Jake leaned over to pet Lazarus, affording her a glimpse of his sleek, strong back.

Mariah clasped her hands behind her and rocked on her heels, trying to force the lustful thoughts out of her head. She knew she should turn around and walk away, yet she couldn't resist being near him.

"I'm glad I found you," she said, keeping her tone brisk and businesslike.

Jake eyed her skeptically. "I would have thought after last night you'd be carrying that shotgun to protect yourself from me."

Mariah felt herself blush. "I can't blame you for my behavior. I let myself get carried away. But I understand now that those—urges—can be difficult to control. They tend to make one behave irrationally."

"Thanks for the explanation, Doctor." With a disgruntled frown, Jake began to pull on his stockings.

Mariah ignored his sarcasm. "The reason I wanted to speak with you is that I talked to Luther about the explosion. I thought you might want to know what I learned."

He paused to gaze at her. "Go on."

"Luther denied ever having seen or spoken to Willy that day. In fact, Luther said he wasn't at the quarry when the blast occurred. But he once showed me scars on his hand that he said he'd gotten from the explosion."

Jake finished lacing his shoes and stood. "It's probably nothing more than a mix-up on Luther's part, but I'll ask Dan if he saw him before the blast."

"Thank you. I'd appreciate that."

He folded his arms across his chest, drawing her gaze there. "Is that all you wanted?" he asked, his voice dropping to a sensual growl.

Was that all she wanted? Not in the least. Mariah's gaze moved from his chest down to his flat belly—and lower. What she wanted at that moment she was too scandalized to admit.

Chapter 25

"There was one other thing I've been meaning to discuss with you," Mariah said hastily. She clasped her hands tightly behind her back, squeezing her fingers until they hurt. She had to stave off those dangerous urges.

With his smoldering gaze fixed on her face, Jake started toward her, making Mariah's heart pound in anticipation.

"And what was that, Mariah?" he asked huskily.

Her tension increased as he closed the gap between them. *Think, Mariah. Behave as a doctor, for heaven's sake.* She took a deep breath and released it, feeling a measure of control return.

"When Luther injured his arm," she began, "he told me he'd reached up to grab hold of the rope. But Luther is right-handed. Wouldn't it seem most probable that he'd use his right hand to reach for the rope?"

Jake stopped inches away, frowning, as though talking about Luther was the last thing he wanted to do. "That would be the hand I'd use."

"Yet it was his left arm that got hurt. And the gash looked too cleanly cut to have been made with a rope."

"What are you saying?"

"He did it intentionally, most likely with a knife."

Jake rubbed his jaw, looking perplexed. "Why would Luther cut his own arm?"

"Why would he lie about being at the quarry at the time of the explosion? Why would he lie about talking to Willy?"

"Maybe he just didn't remember."

"What if it's more than that, Jake? What if Luther is responsible for the explosion?"

"That's an awfully big leap you're making."

Mariah scowled in frustration. To go from suspecting that Luther had cut himself to thinking he might have purposely killed his own coworkers *was* a huge jump, yet her instincts were usually right.

Jake gently turned her chin with his finger. "What are you thinking?"

"I know it seems implausible, but I truly believe I'm onto something. I just need more information."

"I'll take it from here, Mariah. If there is something to all this speculation, I don't want you placing yourself in any danger."

Mariah pressed her lips together and said nothing.

"I want your word you'll stay out of it," he insisted.

"But what if—"

"No what ifs. Stay out of it."

"But—"

"Mariah, don't you understand? If something happened to you, I'd never forgive myself."

Jake's expression was so earnest, his gaze so unexpectedly open, that Mariah was stunned by what he revealed—love!

Her throat tightened as her own buried emotions shoved their way to the surface. There was no mistaking what she felt.

Mariah felt a sudden rush of relief. She'd never been able to admit it before, but she had to now, if only to herself. She loved him. Dear God, with all her heart, she loved him.

But that left her with a terrible dilemma. Because of Ben's death, she'd vowed she'd never love Jake. Yet she'd never truly stopped loving him. How could she resolve it?

"I want your word, Mariah, that you'll let me handle this."

Mariah gave a quick nod, so overwhelmed by her newfound love that she was barely aware of what she was consenting to do.

"I also want to clear the air about last night," Jake said. "You weren't behaving irrationally." His voice grew huskier and his eyes darkened to midnight blue as he lowered his head. "You were simply behaving like a woman."

Mariah closed her eyes as Jake's lips captured hers. All the passion she'd tried to lock away pulsed through her veins. All the need she'd held in check clamored to be sated. All her reasoning evaporated under the onslaught of his kisses. Her only thought was that she loved him.

Jake lowered her to the leaf-strewn ground, nibbling her lips, her chin, her throat, ravishing her with his kisses. Mariah reveled in the feel of his bare skin beneath her fingers. She stroked his sun-warmed back and ran her hands across his smooth shoulders, drawing circles with her palms on the light mat of curly hair on his chest.

Jake lifted his head to gaze down at her, then kissed her again as he opened the buttons of her white blouse. He parted the material, exposing her neck and bosom, then cupped one breast in his hand, stroking one taut nipple with his tongue.

"You're so sweet, Mariah," he whispered against her skin. "Sweet and desirable."

Mariah sighed in ecstasy. How on earth could she curb those urges when Jake was so skillful at driving them forward?

As he continued his sensual onslaught on her breasts, she felt his hand slip beneath her skirts, skimming upward along her bloomers until he reached the waistband. He pulled the ties and eased his hand inside, stroking down the sensitive skin of her belly, sending a jolt of electricity through her when he touched the triangle of curls between her legs.

She reached for his hand but stopped with a gasp as he stroked between the petal-soft folds, circling the very core of her femininity, bringing on a rise of desire so strong she clutched his shoulders and cried out.

Jake quieted her with a kiss while his touch pushed her deeper and deeper into a swirling tide of passion until she was blind to everything except the building tension inside her. She arched against his hand, gasping as he stroked harder. "Jake," she cried breathlessly.

He bunched her skirts around her waist and lowered her bloomers over her hips, then followed with hot kisses pressed on the sensitive skin of her belly even as his fingers continued their maddening, sensuous rhythm. As his kisses moved lower, he inched the bloomers further down, exposing the golden triangle of curls, the soft ivory flesh of her thighs.

She inhaled sharply when his tongue flicked the tiny, swollen bud of her passion, then cried out as he stroked it with both fingers and tongue. When Mariah thought she could bear the tension no longer, Jake opened his trousers and knelt between her legs. Bracing himself on his arms, he pushed against the dewy folds and slowly slid his engorged manhood inside her, gently easing her open, the strain of holding back evident on his face.

Mariah gasped at the sudden sharp intrusion of

his flesh, but as he rocked against her, going deeper and deeper, she welcomed him, falling into the rhythm just as the first wave of deliverance washed over her. She cried out in abandon, nearly sobbing from the relief, as Jake groaned and collapsed against her.

Slowly, Mariah became conscious of leaves rustling, of birds singing in the trees. Every sound seemed to be magnified, every smell in the breeze more intense, as she regained awareness of her surroundings.

This was the passion she had dreamed about. She'd never imagined the profound feelings of love it engendered. With a sigh of contentment, she ran her fingers through Jake's hair and down the hard planes of his face, stroking over the scar on his cheek, tracing the lines of his mouth, delighting in every detail of him.

Jake raised his head and gazed at her, his eyes speaking volumes. He gently kissed her cheek, then both eyes, and finally pressed a long, lingering kiss on her lips, before he stood to fasten his pants.

Perhaps there was hope for them after all.

After Mariah had gone, Jake sat down on the rock and stared at the bed of leaves where he and Mariah had just made love. His emotions were so jumbled he could barely make sense of them.

Mariah was the most exciting female he'd ever met. Just the thought of her lush body aroused him again. Yet it hadn't been lust that had overwhelmed him; it had been love, sweeping him along on a tide of emotion so strong he'd been powerless to stop it.

Yet Mariah had been a virgin, and the full implication of what they'd done made him feel a scoundrel. If word were to get out, it'd be Mariah's reputation that would be ruined, not his. The only way he could protect her was to marry her—but Jake held little hope she'd accept his proposal.

Still, he couldn't help but recall the tender way Mariah had gazed at him after they'd made love. There had been no recrimination in those green eyes, no regret, no blame. Maybe the past was finally behind them.

Wrapped in a cocoon of happiness, Mariah fairly floated home. She put Lazarus in the backyard, then stopped at the dispensary to let Annie know she had returned.

"A telegram arrived from Eliza," Annie told her, "and Emeline sent an urgent message asking you to please call on her as soon as possible."

Mariah said distractedly, "I'll take care of everything in a short while."

Ignoring Annie's puzzled glance, Mariah locked the connecting door behind her, put water on to boil for tea, and sat down at her kitchen table to reflect on what had happened. She felt completely changed inside. She was in love with Jake Sullivan. And the most surprising aspect was that the guilt she should have felt was gone.

Later, as she tied on her apron in the supply

room, Annie studied her quizzically. "Are you feeling all right? You look flushed."

Mariah felt a hot blush color her cheeks. "I'm fine, really. Don't worry."

Still eyeing her skeptically, Annie said, "Here's the message from Emeline and the telegram from your sister."

Mariah opened her sister's telegram first.

HELLO SIS STOP WILL ARRIVE NOON SUNDAY STOP
SINCERELY ELIZA STOP

How good it would be to hear her sister's cheerful voice again, Mariah thought, handing the wire to Annie to read. Eliza could always be counted on to liven things up.

She broke the fancy wax seal on Emeline's stationery and read the note that asked her to please stop by as soon as possible for an important discussion.

"I'd better go see her now," she told Annie. "Jake's worried she won't go through with the wedding."

Mariah picked up her bag and opened the dispensary door, nearly running headlong into Luther.

"Hello, Dr. Lowe. I'm glad I caught you. Mama's having a real bad day. Can you come by?"

With his pleading gaze and his hands nervously squeezing his tweed cap, Luther looked so completely harmless that Mariah couldn't help but question her suspicions about him. Still, her instincts warned her not to trust appearances.

The problem was, she'd given Jake her word that she'd let him handle Luther. Mariah frowned thoughtfully. That didn't necessarily mean she couldn't *help* Jake.

"I have a call to make first, then I'll be there," she told Luther.

"I'll tell her. Thanks, Dr. Lowe."

Mariah watched him turn and saunter down the street, nodding cheerily at the townsfolk he passed as though he hadn't a care in the world. There wasn't another person in town who thought Luther capable of setting off that explosion.

Why, then, did she?

Mariah arrived at the Sullivan house to find Emeline pacing rapidly across the porch, her full, blue silk skirt sweeping the wooden planks. "Thank goodness you've come, Mariah," she exclaimed, hurrying toward her, a waft of rose-scented toilet water following in her wake.

"Has something happened?"

"I can't tell you here." Emeline took her by the wrist and led her into a cozy back parlor off the kitchen. Closing the door, Emeline swung to face her. "I need to ask you an enormous favor, Mariah. I swear it will be the last favor I ever ask of you."

Mariah seriously doubted that. "What is it?"

"Jake is going to be furious with me for asking— you know how private he is—but will you please help Owen?"

"Help him how?"

"Make him give up drinking."

Mariah shook her head dubiously. "That's a tall order."

Emeline began to wring her hands. "Oh, Mariah, he's going to ruin my wedding! He's drunk nearly every night now. He makes a terrible scene at the dinner table, then he passes out cold. My nerves are strained as it is." She grabbed Mariah's hands. "Please say you'll try to help him. Please?"

Mariah sighed. "All I can do is talk to him."

"Would you? Now? We won't be sitting down for supper for another two hours. That will be enough time, won't it?"

Two hours to convince a man to quit drinking? She shook her head. "Where is he?"

"I heard him come in a short time ago. He's probably in the den. He always goes there before supper for a glass of scotch."

Emeline took her to the room where she had treated Jake's burn but stepped back out of sight as Mariah tapped lightly, then opened the door.

Owen had been standing at the window, sipping from a short glass as he gazed out into the back-yard. Hearing her, he turned in surprise, his glance moving from her face to her black bag.

"M-Mariah! I mean, Dr. Lowe. Jake isn't here."

"You can call me Mariah. I came to see *you*, Owen."

"Me?" He seemed to suddenly realize he was holding a glass and quickly set it down on the desk. "Why?"

"Are you having some health problems?"

"Just a few aches now and then. Nothing serious."

"Would you mind if I examined you?"

His hand shook as he brushed back a lock of hair. "I told you, it's nothing serious."

Mariah walked toward him. "That's not how your sister feels. I'll warrant that's not how Jake feels, either. And I'll wager you know exactly what the problem is."

Owen eyed the glass on the desk longingly but didn't reach for it. "What's wrong with having a drink?"

"Nothing as long as it doesn't affect your health or your family. But it's affecting both, isn't it? You have stomachaches all the time, you embarrass your brother at the mill, and your sister is frightened to death that you'll ruin her wedding. Is that fair to them?"

"What's fair in this life? You of all people know the answer to that," Owen said bitterly, reaching for his glass.

"So because life isn't fair, you've decided to drink yourself to death."

He gulped the beverage and set the glass down with a hard thunk. "Why not? I wasn't lucky enough to drown like Ben."

Mariah wanted to slap him for his cruel remark. "Do you think Ben was lucky? Can he wake up and listen to the birds singing outside his window? Can he smell an apple pie cooling on the sill? Can he hold a loved one in his arms? I don't feel

sorry for you, Owen, though you certainly feel
sorry for yourself. And to make sure everyone else
knows how sorry you feel, you're trying to ruin
their lives, too."

Owen's chin quivered with emotion. "That's not
true."

"Then tell me the truth. Tell me why you drink."

Tears leaked from his eyes. "To forget."

"Forget what?"

"Your brother's death," he whispered hoarsely.

A sharp pang tore through Mariah's heart. She
turned away, pressing her hand against her chest,
afraid to take the subject further, afraid of the terrible pain of remembrance.

Yet she had an obligation to help him. She took
steadying breaths, focusing on Owen's pain
instead of her own. Steeling herself, she swung to
face him. "Has it worked, Owen? Have you forgotten Ben's death?"

He shook his head. "I relive it every day, like it
just happened. Jake, Ben, me, sitting outside the
cave, passing around a bottle of rye until we were
drunker than—"

"Stop." Mariah glared at him until he dropped
his gaze. "Ben didn't drink. He never drank, so
don't ever say such a thing again. He knew how
our father felt about alcohol."

"I'm sorry, Mariah," Owen said, hanging his
head. "I thought Jake had told you—I thought you
knew."

"What I know is that Ben didn't drink. The alcohol is obviously fogging your memory."

As Owen stared at her in dismay, Mariah said, "Your sister is getting married in two days. I want your word as Ben's friend that you'll stay off the liquor until after Emeline is safely wed and gone."

"Two days?" Owen swallowed hard, as though already feeling the dryness of his throat. Slowly, he turned and gazed out the window as Mariah waited impatiently, tapping her foot against the carpet.

Finally, he drew a deep, shuddering breath. "All right. For Ben. You have my word."

Mariah spun around and marched out. How dared Owen make such accusations about Ben! To claim he'd gotten drunk was simply ludicrous. That was more like something Jake would have done.

She breezed past Emeline, who'd been standing just outside the door, no doubt eavesdropping.

"Mariah," Emeline whispered, hurrying after her. "Are you all right? You're as white as a ghost."

Mariah paused briefly at the front door, too upset by Owen's outrageous claim to address Emeline's concern. "Your brother promised he wouldn't drink until after your wedding. I hope that helps."

"Thank you, Mariah. I can't tell you how much I—"

Mariah didn't stay to hear the rest. Instead, she hurried down the porch steps and headed for home. She felt dazed and angered by what Owen had said. It just couldn't be true. Ben would never have disobeyed their father.

He lied about his intention to become a doctor.

But that was different from getting drunk. Ben simply hadn't had the courage to face their father. He would never have behaved as recklessly as Owen had suggested.

Jake stood in the arched doorway of the long stone building that housed the horses, watching silently as Luther rubbed down one of the sturdy mares. He'd thought about Mariah's accusation long after they had parted, but he wasn't sure what to do about it. The sheriff hadn't found any evidence of foul play, nor did Mariah have anything concrete to link Luther to the blast, only supposition and a boy's vague memory of a voice. Given what Jake knew about Luther, it was nearly impossible to believe he could be capable of such a criminal act.

But what if Mariah was right? There was no way in hell Jake was going to let anything happen to her.

Luther rubbed the mare's coat vigorously, seemingly unaware of Jake's presence. Yet suddenly he said, "Something you needed, Jake?"

"How's that arm healing?" Jake asked, sauntering toward him.

Luther gave him a curious glance. "It's doing fine."

"Tell me how it happened again."

"I reached for the derrick rope to trim the end and it snapped up."

"You reached with your left arm?"

Luther shrugged. "Just my luck I had a knife in my right hand at the time. It was one of those stupid things that happen sometimes."

"You seem to have had your share lately. Dan said you got your hand pretty cut up in the explosion, too."

"Aw, that healed a long time ago. It wasn't bad at all."

Jake leaned against the stall door. "I'm trying to find the man who spoke to Willy Burton out at the quarry early on the morning of the explosion before the other men arrived."

"Golly, I don't know who it was, Jake, except that it couldn't have been me. I wasn't out there early." Luther slid past him to fill the feedbags with oats. "You can even ask Dan. He'll tell you I got there the same time everyone else did."

Jake watched Luther for a few moments more, then left the building. He knew Mariah wouldn't be pleased, but all of Luther's answers seemed reasonable. All he could do was talk to Dan and see if the story checked out.

Luther walked over to one of the windows and watched Jake head for the quarry.

Go ahead, bastard. Go find Dan and ask if I was there early. You think you're smarter than I am, don't you? But you're wrong.

Luther knew exactly who was behind Jake's sudden interest in his whereabouts that morning: Mariah.

It looked like he wasn't going to be able to wait

for her to get on that train after all. He had to get rid of her now. But how?

A wagon pulled to a stop outside the cutting mill. It was loaded with tables and chairs and a green and white striped canvas. Luther left the stable and ambled over to the wagon driver.

"Looking for someone in particular?" Luther asked amiably.

"Jake Sullivan. I've got a delivery for him."

"He just left for the quarry, but I can catch him. What kind of delivery?"

"It's for a wedding. He told me to stop here and he'd direct me to his house."

"I'll get him for you." Luther walked away, whistling. He'd forgotten about the Sullivan bitch's fancy wedding. Most everyone in town would be there.

It was amazing how some things just fell into place.

Chapter 26

"Say, Doc," the barber called, stepping out of his shop. "I was hoping to catch you."

Stewing over Owen's absurd story, Mariah stopped and turned around. "Did you say something, Mr. Barrow?"

The barber scratched behind one ear and gave her a quizzical look. "Yes, ma'am, I did. I wanted to tell you about a strange thing that happened with Oscar yesterday."

Mariah moved closer. "What was it?"

"He was out here washing my window when all of a sudden he started yelling, 'mad dog,' over and over. When I ran outside, he was pointing at Luther Sinton."

"What did Luther say?"

"He just took off a-runnin' down the street. Didn't say nothin'. Poor ol' Oscar was so shook up

I had someone take him home. I haven't seen him around today, so I thought maybe you'd want to check on him."

It wasn't the first time in Mariah's memory that Luther had upset Oscar—not to mention how he had scared Willy. She was beginning to see a pattern in Luther's behavior.

"Thank you, Mr. Barrow. I'll go see Oscar right now."

"Mrs. Drubb?" Mariah knocked on the door of the small house and waited. In a few moments, the door opened.

"Come in, Dr. Lowe," Oscar's mother said. "How kind of you to stop by. Did Mr. Barrow send you?"

"Yes, he did. Is Oscar all right?"

"He's frightened. He hasn't left his room since he came home yesterday."

"Why didn't you send for me?"

Mrs. Drubb sighed sadly. "What good would it do? No one believes me when I say Luther's trying to frighten my son. But I tell you, there's something wrong with Luther Sinton."

"You and I may be the only ones who think so, Mrs. Drubb."

Oscar's mother led Mariah down a short hallway and opened a door. Mariah stepped into a tiny, cheerful room that held a narrow bed covered by a patchwork quilt, a pine dresser, a rocking chair, and several rag rugs. Oscar had pulled the chair to the window and was staring outside, rocking slowly.

"Oscar, the doctor is here," his mother called.

Mariah set her bag down, walked over to his chair, and knelt beside it. "Hello, Oscar. How are you today?"

He continued to stare out the window.

"It's a beautiful day outside. Wouldn't you like to get some fresh air?"

She saw his lips move, but the words were unintelligible.

"Oscar, Mr. Barrow said something happened yesterday at the barber shop. Did Luther frighten you?"

Oscar began to rock faster, muttering louder, clearly agitated by her question. His mother stood at his other side, her hand on his shoulder to calm him. "The doctor wants to help you, dear."

"I won't let Luther hurt you," Mariah promised. "You're safe here. You can tell us what happened."

His muttering grew louder and more distinct: "Mad dog, mad dog, mad dog."

"Is that what Luther said to you?" Mariah asked.

He nodded.

"Why did he say that? Do those words mean something to you?"

"Oscar, please tell the doctor," his mother urged.

The chair creaked as he rocked it faster and faster. "Mad dog bites. Mad dog send her bad. Bad people."

Mariah glanced at his mother. "I don't understand what he's saying."

"Mad dog send her bad *people*," Oscar insisted, banging the arm of the chair with one hand.

Mariah tried again. "The mad dog is a bad person? Is Luther the mad dog?"

"Mad dog *send her* bad people," he said.

"How do you know he's bad?"

"Oscar heard 'em," he said.

"You heard *them?*" Mariah was puzzled. "What did they say?"

"Have to kill whats."

Mariah was growing more confused. "Whats?"

Oscar stopped rocking and put his fingers in his ears. "Kill whats. Owwwww! Oscar's ears hurt. Bad sound. Owwwww!"

"He's talking about the explosion," Mrs. Drubb whispered. "He calls it the bad sound."

"Kill whats?" Mariah repeated. At once, an idea occurred to her. "Do you mean Watts?"

"Watts, Watts. Kill Watts. Bad people. Owwwww!" With his hands clamped over his ears, he began rocking again, muttering to himself.

"He must be referring to Edmund Watts," Mariah said. "He's connecting Luther to Watts's death."

Mrs. Drubb stroked her son's head soothingly. "It's all right, Oscar. The bad sound is gone." She turned to give Mariah an imploring glance. "You won't put my boy in any danger, will you?"

Mariah rose and picked up her bag. "I won't tell anyone what Oscar said until I know it's safe to do so." She patted Oscar's arm. "You've been a big help, Oscar. It's going to be all right now. No more bad sounds or bad people."

Mariah's mind swam with puzzling bits and pieces of information as she headed for Luther's house. "Have to kill Watts," she said aloud. That much she understood. "Mad dog send her bad people." What did that mean? If mad dog was Luther, had he sent someone—a woman—to kill Watts? Clearly Oscar was speaking of more than one person. The only thing she couldn't figure out was where Hugh Coffman fit into the picture.

Mariah felt a sudden prickling on the nape of her neck. She swung around, frightening a pair of ladies walking behind her. With a hasty apology, Mariah glanced around but saw nothing to cause alarm. She tightened her grip on the handle of her bag and continued down the street.

But the feeling wouldn't go away. Someone was watching her.

As she came to the milliner's shop, Mariah paused as though to gaze at a hat in the window. Through the reflection, she watched several people pass on the sidewalk behind her, but none paid her the least bit of notice. As a wagon rumbled by, Mariah started to turn away, then suddenly caught a glimpse of a man standing in the shadowy recess of a doorway on the opposite side of the street. He quickly ducked out of sight.

Mariah's heart thudded heavily against her ribs as she continued down the street. She paused at the tobacconist's shop and again searched the reflection in the glass. This time she saw his face.

Luther! Mariah's trepidation turned to anger. She whirled around and headed straight for him. He might be able to intimidate Oscar and Willy, but she wasn't about to let him do it to her.

"Dr. Lowe, I thought that was you," Luther called jovially, sauntering toward her. "I had to stop for some soda water for my mama." He held up a glass bottle. "Are you on your way to see her?"

"Yes, I am." She heard the tension in her voice and quickly cleared her throat. She wouldn't get any answers from him if he sensed her vexation. "You're going home early today, aren't you?"

"I can leave whenever I need to," Luther boasted. "Jake understands how it is with my mama's health."

"The other men aren't jealous?"

"Nah. The others, they know the senator's a friend of mine."

Something about the way he said *senator* brought Oscar's cryptic words to mind: *Mad dog send her bad people.*

Send her—senator. That's what Oscar had been trying to say!

Mariah chose her next words carefully. "How lucky you are to have such a powerful friend. You mentioned the senator gave you a job at the quarry when you were fourteen. You must feel very indebted to him."

"He's a great man," Luther said reverently.

"You'd do anything for him, wouldn't you?"

A sly grin crept across his face. "Why do you think that?"

Mariah had the distinct feeling Luther was wise to her strategy. Cautiously, she said, "The senator seems to have a lot of confidence in you."

"Sure he does. He trusts me." Luther paused, and then, as if he couldn't help himself, he added, "I know things none of the others at the quarry know."

"Really?" Mariah raised her eyebrows as though impressed.

"Sure I do—like what's going to happen to the company in a couple of weeks."

Mariah bit back the urge to question him further. Knowing how much he liked to boast, she stayed quiet and hoped he'd offer the information.

Her plan worked. As they turned onto the narrow road where he lived, Luther glanced over his shoulder, then said quietly, "The deal's made. As soon as the road is finished, the senator and Jake are turning the company over to Bernhardt, the new owner. They're going to make a fortune, and I'm getting a cut."

Mariah eyed him skeptically. "Jake doesn't want to sell the company."

"There's a lot you don't know about Jake," Luther said, with an uncharacteristic sneer. "He's got everyone fooled into believing he's trying to save the company. But it's all about money to him."

"I don't believe you."

Luther snickered. "Your daddy worked hard for

the stone men all his life, and now you're doing it, too. Do you really think Jake would tell you he was going to sell out to get rich?"

Mariah didn't reply. It was obvious Luther was lying, but why?

As though he sensed her doubt, Luther said, "You don't have to take my word for it. Ask Dan. He was there when Bernhardt's men came to look over the mill."

"I might do just that."

Luther merely shrugged, as though it made no difference to him.

When they reached his doorstep, Luther leaned close to whisper in her ear, "What I told you is just between you and me, Doc. Just between *you* and *me*."

Mariah suppressed a shudder as Luther opened the door, his gaze fixed on her face, a cunning smile on his lips.

"Luther, is that you?" his mother called out.

His voice became boyish again. "Yes, Mama, it's me. I've brought the doctor."

Mariah sat down at her desk that evening to record everything she knew about the explosion, determined to find answers for the townspeople. She'd begun to understand her father's passionate involvement in their problems.

She turned to glance at his notebooks in the bookcase. On impulse, she pulled out a volume and paged through it.

It was all there—his concerns about his patients,

records of their health problems, and even their family trees. Mixed in were notations about his own children's lives—their accomplishments, joys, and sorrows—anecdote after anecdote about Mariah, Ben, and Eliza.

Growing more curious, Mariah checked the last row of books and found the year she had gone away to medical school. She leafed through the pages until she found the September day when Annie, Eliza, and her father had taken her to the train station. Mariah scanned the heavy black scrawl, touched by what he had recorded: his pride in her, his hope that she would return someday to join him in his practice, his fear that she would never come back to mend her heart.

His last words leaped out at her: *mend her heart.* He must have been referring to her grief over Ben's death. She remembered again the outlandish account Owen had given her and instantly grew angry. Why would Owen make up such lies about Ben?

Exasperated that she had gotten sidetracked, Mariah put the book away and went back to her original task. As she recorded her suspicions about Luther, her thoughts turned to their recent conversation. It sickened her to think of the quarry being sold, yet she didn't doubt that Coffman would do it. Jake had warned her of that himself. Still, she refused to believe Jake had a hand in it. He wouldn't lie to her. And he cared too much about his men.

But hadn't he forced them to work ungodly

hours with dangerous equipment? Hadn't he readily dismissed the explosion as an accident? Hadn't
he repeatedly downplayed her concerns?

A hard rap on the door jolted Mariah from her
thoughts.

"Who's there?"

"Jake."

She rose reluctantly. Now that the initial rapture
of their lovemaking had faded and she'd had time
to ponder her behavior, she felt ashamed and
embarrassed. She'd thrown caution to the wind,
giving herself to Jake with abandon, assuring herself that the love she felt for him was all that mattered. But that simply wasn't true. How could she
look him in the eye now?

She drew a deep breath and opened the door.

As Jake stepped inside, he noted instantly the
change in her. Mariah's arms were folded across
her chest almost protectively, and she didn't want
to meet his gaze. "Is everything all right?"

"I've been very busy." As though to prove her
point, Mariah went to her desk and began to
straighten papers.

Jake put his hands on her shoulders and ran
them down her arms. "I've missed you." He
pressed his lips against the nape of her neck as his
arms encircled her waist.

Mariah seemed to stiffen at his touch. "Why did
you come?"

He didn't know what to make of her behavior,
but he knew the timing was wrong for a proposal
of marriage. "I—just thought you'd want to know

that I talked to Luther about what he was doing the morning of the explosion; then I spoke with Dan to verify his story."

She turned to face him. "What did you find out?"

"Their stories match. Dan confirmed that Luther arrived with the rest of the men."

"But Willy recognized his voice," she insisted.

"Willy could have been mistaken. He did suffer a head injury."

"He could also be right."

"I can't accuse Luther of lying without anything to prove it."

"So you'll just live with the lie and hope Luther doesn't do it again?"

"I need proof," he repeated firmly.

"Then I'll get you proof."

"No, Mariah. I told you I'd handle it."

"By waiting for it to fall into your lap?" she exclaimed.

"I won't let you put yourself at risk."

"You won't *let* me?" Indignation glittered in her green eyes. She walked to the door and opened it. "Good night, Jake."

She couldn't look at him as he walked out. She shut the door and locked it, then marched to her bedroom, where she pulled her traveling bag from beneath the bed and began to pack. Jake had no business giving her orders; he had no claim on her.

She needed to get away, to distance herself from Jake. It was the perfect time to go see Willy.

She woke Annie before dawn and gave her

instructions for her patients, with a specific direction to say nothing to Luther about where she had gone. By six o'clock that morning, Mariah was at the depot buying her ticket. By seven, she was on her way to Fort Wayne. She had two days in which to make the trip and get back in time for Emeline's wedding.

Luther waited all through the noon hour, but Mariah didn't come. He seethed with fury until his belly burned from the heat of it.

"Luther," his mother barked from her bedroom, "you lied to me again, didn't you?"

"No, Mama, I wouldn't lie to you. Besides, you heard the doc yourself. She said she'd come at noon today."

"Well, then, where is she?"

"Maybe she got called out for an emergency or something. I'll go down and check for you right now."

"You're a worthless son, Luther. Do you hear me? A worthless son!"

Luther eased the door shut so as not to anger her further, then started toward the dispensary. He wasn't a worthless son. His mama knew that. She just liked to tease him; she had a wicked sense of humor. *Wicked*. The word echoed in his brain.

" 'Afternoon, Luther," someone called.

He lifted his hand, forcing a smile, though his nerves felt stretched to the point of breaking. Why hadn't Mariah come? She'd always kept her word before. He opened the door to the dispensary and flinched at the sound of the bell overhead. He hated that happy tinkling sound.

" 'Afternoon, Miss Annie," he said, trying to be his usual cheerful self. Luther glanced at the door to the surgery and saw that it stood open.

"What is it you need, Luther?"

"Doc told me she would come check on Mama today, but I see she's not in." He paused, and when Annie didn't volunteer any information, he said, "She must be out seeing patients, huh?"

"Is there something your mother needs, Luther? Maybe I can help her."

"No," he snapped, then instantly regretted his sharp tone. Now Annie was peering at him suspiciously, just like his mother always did. He tried to smile, but one corner of his mouth kept twitching.

"The doctor has a full schedule today, Luther. She did tell me your mother should keep taking her pills."

Annie was deliberately avoiding telling him where Mariah was. Luther tightened his grip on the knife in his pocket until the edges bit into his palm. *Keep your secrets, old hag. I don't need your help.*

"Well, that's great," he said, forcing enthusiasm. "Maybe she'll be kind enough to look in on Mama sometime soon."

"I'll tell her you were here."

The bell tinkled as someone came in. Luther turned, nodded to the lady behind him, and stepped outside into the glaring sunlight.

Now he had to tell his mama that Mariah wasn't coming to see her today. She wouldn't be happy about that at all. But she'd have to get used to it. In two more days, Mariah would be dead.

Chapter 27

Mariah hired a buggy to go to the Burtons' farmstead. She drove down narrow, rutted lanes through acres of corn and wheat, coming at last to a rambling white house in need of a paint job. A yellow hound sprawled lazily on the front porch beside Sophie Burton, who sat at a butter churn, working industriously.

When she saw Mariah step down from the buggy, Sophie mopped her face with the hem of her apron and rose. "My, this is a surprise. There's nothing's wrong, is there?"

"Not at all. I had to take a trip," Mariah explained, stretching the truth a bit, "so thought I'd stop by to see Willy."

"Come on inside and have something cool to drink. Willy's weeding the onion patch with my son Noah." Sophie opened the door and stood back to let Mariah pass.

"Is he doing all right?" Mariah asked.

"He's fine. We're still strangers to him, but he's getting used to us." She showed Mariah into a spacious sitting room just off the front door and left to get Willy.

A late afternoon breeze billowed the plain white curtains at the windows, bringing with it the pungent smell of farm animals mixing with the delicious aroma of roasting meat emanating from the kitchen. In the middle of the room stood a black woodstove. The furnishings were sparse but comfortable—several upholstered chairs in a faded tan print, a worn brown horsehair sofa, and side tables crowded with books and bric-a-brac. A threadbare rug that might have once been colorful covered a wooden floor scuffed and scarred from decades of wear. All told, it seemed a homey place, a good house in which to raise an active boy.

Mariah settled onto the sofa and waited. In a few moments Willy came running into the room and flew straight into her arms. "You came, just like you said."

Mariah hugged him against her. He wore only a pair of overalls. His arms and feet were bare. He smelled of the soil, and she could see by the smudges on his face that he'd been working outside.

"Of course I came. And Aunt Annie and Aunt Gertrude both send their love."

He lifted his head and gazed at her with hopeful brown eyes. "Can I go back with you?"

A lump rose in Mariah's throat as she smoothed his unruly hair. "No, Willy, this is your home now. But we'll come to see you from time to time, and I know Aunt Annie and Aunt Gertrude will be writing to you. Maybe sometime soon you can come back to Coffee Creek for a visit."

Willy looked down. "Oh."

"Here's a glass of lemonade," Sophie offered, bustling over to the sofa. "The men will be coming in from the fields soon for the evening meal. I hope you'll stay."

"Thank you. I'd like that."

Sophie glanced from Mariah to Willy. As though she sensed Mariah's desire to speak to the child in private, she said, "Well, then, I'll just leave you to visit with Willy," and backed out of the room.

Mariah encouraged Willy to tell her about his new family. He showed her the second-floor bedroom he shared with his cousin, then he took her out to the vegetable garden in the backyard, proudly pointing out where he'd hoed.

As they walked around to the front of the house to sit on the shady front porch, Mariah carefully brought up Luther. "Do you remember what you told me before you left Coffee Creek?"

Willy was sitting cross-legged beside the old hound dog, scratching it behind the ears. For a moment he didn't respond, then he muttered, "I remember."

"You said you recognized Luther's voice. Do you remember what he said to you?"

Willy nodded slowly. "He said, 'I should kill you right now, you stinkin' brat.'"

"Why would he want to kill you, Willy?"

"'Cause I wasn't supposed to be there, I guess."

"Maybe he was just angry. Are you sure he said those exact words?"

Willy nodded again, this time with a violent shudder. "He had a knife."

"Did he threaten you with the knife?"

"He—" Willy swallowed hard. "He put it to my throat and pretended like he was drawing a line across it. He said if I told anyone I saw him there, he'd kill me that easily, and it wouldn't bother him at all, cause mad dogs liked to kill."

Mariah went cold inside. *Mad dog.* Oscar's exact words.

Dear God. Her instinct had been right.

Jake ate supper alone, which suited his brooding mood. Emeline was in a flurry of last-minute preparations, and Owen hadn't made an appearance all day. Just as well, Jake thought. He had little appetite for food and even less for conversation.

All he could think about was Mariah. Irritated, he shoved back his chair and went outside. He wandered out to the gazebo, expecting to find Owen in a drunken slumber. Instead, his brother was sitting on the steps, his head in his hands.

At his approach, Owen looked up. His eyes

were bloodshot, his skin was pale and blotchy, and his white shirt was soaked with perspiration.

Jake propped one boot on the step and gazed down at him with a scowl. "How much did you drink tonight?"

Owen gave a harsh laugh. "Would you believe me if I told you nothing?"

Jake sat down beside him. "No."

"Isn't that ironic. I've gone through twenty-four hours of hell, and I look more like a drunkard than ever." He pressed trembling hands against his temples. "I don't think I can take this, Jake. I ache everywhere, even in my teeth. My skin is on fire. My eyes burn. And I can't stop shaking."

Jake studied him closely. "You really haven't had anything to drink?"

"Not unless you count coffee."

"What brought this on?"

"Mariah, of course."

"Mariah?"

Owen lifted his head to gaze at Jake through bleary eyes. "You didn't send her? Well, what do you know. It was devious little Emie."

"What did Mariah say, Owen?" Jake asked impatiently.

"Do you want the whole painful tale or just the gist of it?" At Jake's scowl, he said, "She asked me to stop drinking until the wedding was over—for Ben's sake."

"You discussed Ben?"

Owen let out his breath. "There's no discussing

Ben with Mariah. She's placed him on a pedestal."
He hung his head. "She didn't know we got drunk
that day."

"What in blue blazes made you tell her, then?"

"It doesn't matter. She didn't believe me."

"Damn it, Owen, she didn't need to know that."

"Still playing the martyr, aren't you, Jake?"

Jake froze.

"Why shouldn't she know, Jake? Why should
she still blame you for everything? I was the one
who brought the rye, and Ben drank just as much
as we did."

"I'd rather she blame me than have her memory
of Ben ruined. I've got to talk to her." He started
off, then swung to face his brother. "Don't tell her
anything else, do you understand?"

Jake went straight to Mariah's house, but the
house was dark and no one answered his knock.
He tried Annie's house next. "It's Jake Sullivan,"
he called.

Annie opened the door, a surprised look on her
face. "What is it, Jake? Is someone ill?"

"Where's Mariah?"

Annie glanced up and down the street. "You'd
better come inside."

Luther watched from his hiding place across the
street as Annie let Jake into her house. Luther had
been waiting for Mariah since early afternoon, but
she hadn't come home. He'd already checked at
the livery stable, but she hadn't hired a buggy,

either. Luther had begun to suspect she'd gone somewhere with Jake, but as he just saw, Jake was looking for her, too.

Luther settled more comfortably in the tall grass and waited for Mariah to return. He'd wait all night if he had to. If she hadn't come home by morning, he'd hie down to the train station and ask a few questions. Ol' Tom Hodges, the station master, was dumber than a sack of potatoes. It'd be easy enough to get Tom to tell him where Mariah had gone—and more importantly, when she'd be back. Luther didn't think she'd miss that wedding, but he wasn't taking any chances.

"Mariah went to Fort Wayne," Annie explained to Jake. "I was surprised she decided to go so soon, but she said she had new information she had to check out. She woke me this morning before the sun was up. Had her bag packed and instructions for me all ready. She must have been up half the night preparing."

"Did she tell you what this new information was?"

"It's a long story, but what it boils down to is that Oscar heard Luther say he was going to kill Edmund Watts."

Jake gave a sharp sigh of frustration. "Oscar isn't a reliable source."

"Mariah was quite sure about this, Jake."

"Did she tell the sheriff?"

"She wanted to talk to Willy first."

"I told her to stay out of it," he muttered angrily.

"I wish she'd taken your advice. I'm fearful for her. If what Oscar heard is true, then Luther is a dangerous man."

"Oscar could very well have gotten it all twisted around," Jake reminded her.

"Luther still worries me. He's been coming around here nearly every day, making Mariah very uneasy. He came looking for her today, too, but I wouldn't tell him where she'd gone. He was none too pleased about it, either. And then there's the mysterious letter. Did she tell you about it?" Annie asked him.

"What letter?"

"She found it on her pillow one day. I don't remember what it said, but she was frightened. It disappeared a few hours later. She probably didn't tell you about someone rifling through her desk, either."

Jake frowned, remembering Mariah's feeling of being watched and then finding the rat at her door. Clearly, someone was trying to scare her. He just didn't see a connection to Luther. "When is Mariah coming home?"

"Tomorrow morning."

Jake rose and walked to the door. "I'll meet her train."

As the noisy locomotive pulled into the station at Coffee Creek, Mariah checked her watch. One hour until Eliza arrived. She had just enough time to get home, change out of her sooty clothing, check in with Annie, and return to the station to meet her sister.

Mariah picked up her bag and headed toward the front of the car. She now knew enough about Luther to realize how dangerous he was. How much peril she was in depended upon how threatened Luther felt. Hopefully, he didn't have any idea how much she knew.

But she still needed Luther to admit the identity of his accomplice. She knew she stood a better chance of coaxing him to reveal the senator's part in it than either Jake or the sheriff. Luther liked to boast, and she knew best how to get him to do it.

Mariah glanced through the window and saw Jake leaning against a post, watching the people getting off the train. Just the sight of him made her heart ache. She'd tried her best to erase him from her thoughts, but Jake was in her blood, in her dreams, in her soul. She didn't know how to eradicate him; she only knew she had to try.

When Mariah stepped down from the train, Jake pushed away from the post and strode toward her, that customary emotionless look on his face.

Peeved, Mariah tilted her head to gaze up at him from beneath the brim of her traveling hat. "What are you doing here?"

"I came to meet your train." His tone was so matter-of-fact she was at a momentary loss for words. It was as if nothing had happened between them. He held out his hand. "I'll carry your bag."

Not wanting to make a scene, Mariah handed the bag to Jake and let him guide her across the platform and down the four steps to the street.

"How's Willy?" he asked, as several ladies passed by, giving them friendly nods.

"He's fine. How did you know where I was?"

"From Annie." He waited until they were away from the station to say, "She told me about Oscar."

"Naturally, you don't believe him."

"Did you learn anything more from Willy?"

"Does it matter?" Mariah held out her hand. "I'll take my bag now."

"I'll carry it."

"I can look out for myself, Jake."

He guided her around the corner away from the dispensary. "I'm taking you to see the sheriff."

Mariah bristled at his imperious tone. "I can do that myself, too."

"You can, but you won't. I know you too well, Mariah—you think you can handle this on your own. I want to make sure you talk to him."

Mariah came to an abrupt stop. "Give me my bag." She glared at him and waited, her toe tapping against the sidewalk. Jake's jaw worked as though he wanted to say something, but in the end, he simply handed her the traveling case.

"Thank you." Mariah spun around and marched toward home. There would be time to see the sheriff after the wedding.

Jake stood in the middle of the sidewalk and scowled at Mariah's back. Stubborn female. He turned and stalked toward the sheriff's office. If Mariah wouldn't make a report, then at least he could put Logan on alert.

Caleb Carter, a retired deputy, dozed contentedly in the sheriff's chair, his feet on top of the desk, his head lolling to one side. At the sound of the door shutting, Caleb gave a snort, swung his legs down, and sat up. "Well, say there, Jake. How're ya doing?"

"Hello, Caleb. Is Logan in?"

"Nope. He and his missus are getting ready for your sister's wedding. I'm just filling in for him." Caleb flipped open his pocket watch and checked the time. "Hadn't you oughta be getting ready yourself, Jake?"

"I suppose. If Logan stops by, tell him I'm looking for him."

Chapter 28

〜〜〜◦○○◦〜〜〜

Mariah, Annie, and Lazarus waited eagerly on the platform in the hot noonday sun as the big locomotive came to a stop, brakes screeching and black smoke huffing from the stack. In a few moments, the passengers began disembarking.

"There she is!" Annie cried excitedly, waving. "Eliza! Over here, honey."

Juggling more traveling bags and hatboxes than she could possibly need in one weekend, Mariah's sister started toward them. She would have looked every inch a city girl in her smart traveling outfit of black alpaca with white piping if her black Marlboro-style hat, ornately decorated with large red roses and white ostrich feathers, hadn't slipped its pins. The hat leaned precariously to the left while one glossy black curl hung over her right eye. Eliza

343

blew it out of the way and smiled, nearly stumbling over Lazarus, who had gone to meet her.

"Well, hello, big fellow!" she said, stopping to regain control of her bundles.

As Mariah and Annie reached her, Eliza let everything fall to her feet and with a whoop of joy, threw her arms around them.

"It's so good to see you," Mariah said, laughing. "It feels like ages."

"It has been ages," Eliza replied. "At least a month."

"Honey, you look prettier than ever," Annie exclaimed, beaming as Eliza kissed her soundly on the cheek.

"And you're younger than ever, you adorable dumpling," Eliza proclaimed. She released them and stepped back, frowning as she studied Mariah. "It appears you and I have lots to talk about, don't we, Sis?"

"And very little time, if we intend to make it to the wedding," Mariah reminded them, glancing at her watch.

"Isn't that just like my big sister?" Eliza said to Annie as she began piling hatboxes in Mariah's arms. "An incurable unromantic." She crouched down and held out her arms. "Come here, Laz, and give me a big kiss."

The dog happily complied, and her sister laughed in delight, nearly tipping over. Eliza was just the tonic Mariah needed.

* * *

Emeline's ceremony was held in the white gazebo behind the Sullivan house. The day was sunny, but the breeze carried the smell of a brewing storm. The extensive green lawn had been neatly clipped and the gazebo festooned with ribbons of pink and yellow satin. Clay pots overflowing with fragrant pink petunias and yellow chrysanthemums edged the steps of the trellised structure on all five sides, and rows of wooden chairs encircled it.

Mariah, Eliza, and Annie sat in the fourth row. Mariah glanced at her sister, who looked stunning in her garden-party toilette of off-white silk with an aqua-colored lace jabot and waistband, voluminous leg-of-mutton sleeves, and a matching ruffled parasol. Annie was more sedate in a dark teal shirtwaist dress, its blouse decorated with embroidered braid.

Mariah smoothed the skirt of her own gown, a Chicago purchase in peach satin with cream lace frills at the shoulders that crossed at her bosom and draped in long tails down each hip. The short, puffed leg-of-mutton sleeves contrasted with her long cream gloves. Dainty cream-colored slippers and a cream straw hat trimmed with peach ribbons completed her toilette.

Mariah glanced around at the other guests, all dressed in their finery. Not a single seat remained empty, and a few people even stood at the rear. Everyone rose as Emeline came out of the house and started across the lawn, looking radiant in her satin and lace gown with its ten-foot train. Instantly, the four fiddlers seated at the rear struck up a wedding march.

"What a lovely bride," Annie whispered, as Emeline walked up a rose-petal-carpeted aisle.

"She doesn't look a bit nervous," Eliza commented.

Mariah barely noticed. Her eye was on Emeline's escort.

Jake walked tall and proud beside his sister, making Mariah's heart swell with longing. He wore a black swallowtail suit with a single-breasted gray vest over a white shirt, and a white and gray striped ascot. He looked so handsome she couldn't pull her gaze away.

"Eliza, I'm sorry your friend Eileen didn't make it," Annie remarked quietly.

"So am I. She didn't even reply to Emie's invitation."

Mariah barely heard a word of their conversation. She watched as Jake handed his sister to Percy, then walked back to his seat in the front row beside Owen. Just before he sat down, his gaze locked with Mariah's. Her heart skidded to a stop. For a brief moment, it was as if no one else existed.

Jake sat rigidly in his chair, staring unseeingly at his sister. His thoughts focused solely on Mariah. He'd been concerned that she wouldn't come. But now, as the wedding vows were spoken, he almost wished she'd stayed home. All he could picture was himself standing beside Mariah repeating those same words.

After the ceremony, he and Owen joined the newlyweds as they greeted their guests, who lined up in the aisle to pay their respects. Jake forced a smile and shook hands, but his gaze was on Mariah.

There was a joyous reunion between Eliza and Emeline, the two friends squealing and hugging and laughing like schoolgirls. As Mariah waited her turn, Jake moved up beside her.

"I have to talk to you later."

"We have nothing to talk about," she whispered, barely turning her head.

"Mariah!" the new bride cried happily, oblivious to their brief exchange. Emeline gave Mariah a hug. "I'm so glad you came. Eliza, your sister is a wonder. She's the reason I'm here today, you know."

"She's a wonder, all right." Eliza gave Mariah a mischievous smile. Then her gaze moved to the man standing beside Mariah and back to her sister, and a speculative look crossed her face. "Hello, Jake."

"Eliza," Jake replied with a nod. "Good to see you again."

Mariah hooked her arm through Eliza's. "Shall we let other guests pay their respects?" She quickly shepherded her sister and Annie through the crowd.

"What was that about?" Eliza asked.

"It was about moving out of everyone's way."

"I'll wager it was more about getting out of Jake's way. Am I right, Annie?"

"Now, you girls know I don't mix in your squabbles."

The fiddlers played a merry tune while the guests lined up to help themselves to a banquet laid out on a long table near the rear of the house. Annie and Eliza chattered happily as they loaded their plates with the delectable food, but Mariah kept her eye on Jake, who stood at the end of the banquet table, greeting guests as they came by.

As she moved past him, Jake gave her a meaningful glance. Mariah quickly averted her gaze and walked away. Whatever he had to say, she didn't want to hear it.

After they'd seated themselves at one of the smaller tables, Eliza said quietly, "If you don't tell me what's going on between you two, Mariah, I swear I'll burst with curiosity."

"If there was anything to tell, I would."

"Well, I'll be!" Eliza exclaimed with a laugh. "You still get that little twitch in the corner of your mouth when you're not telling the truth. Come on, Sis, fess up."

"We can talk this evening before bed."

They were soon joined by Annie and Gertrude, who insisted on hearing all about Willy. As they were eating, Annie leaned over and whispered, "I see Sheriff Logan and his wife sitting at the table to our far right. You be sure to see him after the reception, like you promised."

When the tables had been cleared, the dancing began, starting with a dance to honor the bride and groom. As the fiddlers struck up a waltz, others joined in. Eliza was swarmed by hopeful young men, and even Annie accepted an invitation. Gertrude turned to talk to someone at the table behind her, and Mariah suddenly found herself facing a black suit coat and gray vest.

With a pounding heart, she raised her eyes and met Jake's intense gaze.

"May I have this dance?"

His husky voice sent shivers deep into Mariah's belly, a bittersweet reminder of the passion they had shared. She was about to decline when Gertrude nudged her arm. "You'd better hurry. The dance has started."

Mariah reluctantly rose and put her hand through Jake's arm. Leading her into the circle of dancers, Jake turned to face her, taking Mariah's hand in his and placing his other hand on the small of her back.

"I'm glad you came," he said. "I wanted to talk to you about what Owen said the other day."

Mariah tensed. "Please, Jake, not now."

"Just let me say this, Mariah: Ben was a good person."

"Of course he was. Why would I think otherwise?"

Jake's brows drew together. "After what Owen told you—"

"You think I'd believe such an outlandish tale?"

There was an immediate look of relief on Jake's

face. They danced in silence for a moment, then he said softly, "You look lovely, Mariah."

At his tenderly spoken words, she blushed. "Thank you."

He gently squeezed her hand. "As I watched Emie and Percy say their vows, I couldn't help thinking it should be us up there." He paused, as though to gauge her feelings, then he blurted, "I want you to marry me."

Surprised, Mariah glanced up, her heart turning over as she gazed into his earnest blue eyes. She couldn't deny that she loved Jake, but was that enough to overcome their differences?

As though he sensed her hesitance, he added, "I want to do right by you, Mariah."

"Do right by me?" she repeated.

He seemed flustered. "Protect you. After all, there may be a child to consider, and I don't want your reputation tarnished. I'd certainly want it to have my name."

It? Suddenly, the reason for Jake's proposal became clear: he feared she was carrying his child. Mariah came to an abrupt stop and yanked her hand out of his grasp. "When I marry, Jake, it won't be out of obligation. And if there is a child, I can take care of *it* myself!"

She suddenly became aware of people staring at her and Jake with wide-eyed curiosity. Oh, no— how many had heard? How many now knew she and Jake had been intimate?

Red with humiliation, Mariah began to weave through the dancers, hearing their whispers as she passed by. She held her head high as she moved rapidly across the lawn and circled to the front of the house.

"Mariah!"

Fearing Jake would follow her all the way home, she swung around, only to find Owen, not Jake, calling to her. In her agitated state she didn't want to talk to Owen, but as he approached, Mariah saw with dismay that he held a drink in his hand.

"It's water," he assured her, holding up the glass, guessing her thoughts. "May I talk to you?"

Mariah glanced nervously over her shoulder to see if Jake had followed. "I can't stay, Owen. I have to go home."

"I'll walk a short piece with you, then," he said, seemingly oblivious to her agitation. He fell into step beside her, saying nothing until they reached the road. "It's been a hellish two days, Mariah, but I kept my word—for Ben."

Mariah took a closer look at him, noting the bags beneath his eyes and his pallor. He did indeed look like he'd suffered. "You should be proud of what you're doing, Owen."

"Before I swell up with pride," he said dryly, "I'll wait to see if I can last the week."

"I truly hope you can."

Owen glanced at her sheepishly. "I want to apologize for shocking you the other day. Jake took a bite out of me for telling you about the drinking."

Mariah held up a gloved hand to stop him. "I've had a very bad day, Owen. I'd rather not discuss it, if you don't mind."

"Please, Mariah, listen to me. Jake has shouldered the blame for Ben's death for ten years. It's time for that to stop. We were all to blame."

Mariah felt a sudden sting of tears behind her eyelids. "You can't make me believe my brother chose to jump in that lake. Ben was afraid of water."

"We were all drunk. He wanted to prove he wasn't afraid. Jake tried to save Ben and nearly drowned himself. That's how he got the scar on his face."

Mariah walked faster, brushing away the tears that slipped from her eyes. "I don't believe you."

"You father knew the truth. He didn't blame Jake."

"Then why didn't he tell me?"

"Maybe he didn't want you to think badly of Ben."

Mariah tried to remember what her father had said that day, but it was a blur of pain. *It will be in his notebooks*, a little voice inside her head whispered.

Owen came to a stop. "I'm sorry, Mariah," he called as she continued on. "I truly am. But don't blame Jake—he's suffered as much as you have."

Mariah hurried up Center Street, wanting only to lock herself in the safety of her home and sort out her thoughts. She breathed a sigh of relief when the dispensary came into view.

As Mariah unlocked her front door, she heard Lazarus barking in the backyard. She shut the door, removed her gloves and hat, and set them aside. For a long moment, she stood perfectly still, staring at the shelves of black notebooks, a feeling of dread in her stomach.

Your father knew the truth.

Mariah closed her eyes and took a deep breath. She had to know, too.

Her eyes swept across the row of books, searching the dates on the spines until she found the year of Ben's death. Her hand shook as she pulled the dusty volume from the shelf and took it to her desk. She sat down and turned the pages until she found the one dated June 25, 1888.

Her heart ached as she read her father's despondent words.

My beautiful, beloved only son drowned today, taking a part of my heart with him. He was here such a brief moment in time. How do I go on? How do I accept that I will never, in this lifetime, see him again? He had such promise, such grand dreams, such high hopes. A bright light snuffed out by the lure of drink, by the thrill of youthful rebellion.

Tears rolled down Mariah's cheeks. Her father had known. Why hadn't he told her? Why had he let her blame Jake?

And how my heart grieves for my daughters, most especially Mariah, who thought the sun rose and set in her brother. Mariah cannot abide an ill word spoken about Ben. Instead, she closets her emotions and forges ahead with a brave front. I fear she will never be able to mend her heart unless she can bring herself to face the truth. How I wish her mother were here to talk to her. God forgive me for not having the courage to tell her myself, but I just can't add to her grief.

Mariah stared at the words until they ran together. Was that why her father had wanted her to come home? Because he knew she'd never learn the truth unless she did?

Owen's words echoed in the silence. *Jake has shouldered the blame for Ben's death for ten years. It's time for that to stop.*

"Jake," she whispered raggedly, pressing fingers to her trembling lips. He'd accepted the blame so readily, letting her think the worst of him. He'd protected her brother's reputation, just as he'd offered to protect hers. That wasn't the act of a self-centered man.

She turned ahead to the date of her brother's funeral, but there were only two lines written on it, blurred in spots by what she guessed were tears.

Our beautiful son is with you now, my darling Jennie, my dearest wife. Take care of each other until we all meet again.

Her throat tight with emotion, Mariah turned to the next page, where she saw with little surprise that her father had resumed his duties as town doctor. One notation near the bottom caught her eye.

Jake Sullivan left town today. He has assumed full responsibility for the accident. But I fear it was Mariah's blame, and not his own, that drove him away.

Stunned, Mariah closed the notebook and sat with it in her lap, staring blindly at the floor. She'd been wrong about Jake all these years. Her grief, her stubbornness, her blindness to the truth, together with his own sense of responsibility, had driven him away.

She knew now she could never marry Jake. He deserved a wife who was fair and just, not one who was self-righteous and judgmental. Mariah had always prided herself on her clear, logical thinking—but what a tragic muddle she had made of this. Ten years of hiding from the truth. Ten long years of misplaced blame. How Jake must have suffered.

With a sorrowful heart, Mariah put the notebook on the shelf and went to the kitchen to make coffee. As she pumped water into the pot, she suddenly realized she hadn't heard Lazarus barking for some time. She opened the back door and looked out, but he was nowhere to be seen, yet the back gate was closed.

Mariah's stomach churned as she walked toward his doghouse. Something was very wrong. "Laz," she called. "Here, boy."

Then she saw it: a piece of paper tacked to the roof. Mariah's heart pounded as she yanked it loose.

Be at Devil's Cave at five o'clock. Come alone.

She read the message twice, her hands shaking so hard she could barely focus on the words. She'd be a fool to go. Yet she dared not ignore the note, either. She couldn't risk Lazarus's life.

Mariah checked her watch. It was four forty-five. There was no time to go for help.

Chapter 29

Eliza wove her way back to the table where Annie sat talking to Gertrude. "Annie, have you seen Mariah?"

"Not for a while, honey."

"I saw her," Gertrude piped up. "She and Jake were dancing, then all of a sudden she rushed away. She headed around the front of the house."

"I was just handed this," Eliza said, holding out a sealed envelope. "A boy gave it to me. He said it was for Doc Lowe."

"Someone must be ill." Annie took it and rose. "I'll go find Mariah. You stay and enjoy yourself."

Jake paced the den, cursing the day Mariah returned to Coffee Creek, then cursing his own folly for loving her.

"Jake?"

He swung around as Owen came into the room.

"Did you and Mariah have a falling out?"

Jake sighed heavily. "You could say that."

"So that's why she seemed so upset."

"You saw her?"

"Just a short while ago, as she was leaving."

Jake eyed him skeptically. "You didn't say anything to her, did you?"

"I—I did speak to her briefly." Owen gave his brother an embarrassed look. "I apologized for hurting her the other day."

Jake sank down in his chair and dropped his head into his hands. "I told you not to talk to her about that."

"The thing is, Jake, that she thought her father was unaware of the circumstances of Ben's death. I thought she should know."

Jake banged his fist on the desk. "What in blazes made you think that? Are you trying to hurt her?"

"Why do you insist on carrying the blame for everyone, Jake?"

"I don't insist—"

"Yes, you do. You've blamed yourself for my drinking all these years, giving me the perfect excuse to keep at it. 'I can't help myself. Jake pushed me to it. It's all Jake's fault.' " Owen held out trembling hands imploringly. "Why can't you just step back and let me take responsibility for my own behavior?"

Jake stared at him, stung by his reproach.

"I know what I have to do, Jake. What about you? You love Mariah, but she'll never be able to return your love until she can stop blaming you for Ben's death. She can't do that unless you let her know the truth, yet you refuse to tell her. Why? Is it just to protect her memories of Ben? Or are you afraid she'll hurt you again?"

Jake had no answer. He stood helplessly in front of Owen, feeling as though he'd just been turned inside out and revealed a fraud.

Owen sighed wearily. "If it will put your mind at ease, all I told Mariah was that her father knew the true story."

Jake dropped his head and shut his eyes. All these years, he'd told himself he had to protect Mariah from the truth. But Owen was right: as long as he continued to do that, she couldn't love him. Was that what he wanted?

He had to see her.

Mariah dashed into the dispensary and propped the letter on Annie's desk, then hurried back to get the shotgun hanging over the mantelpiece. But as she started for the door, she thought better of it. Whoever was waiting at the cave certainly wouldn't show himself if he saw the weapon.

She ran to her room and dug in her bureau drawer until she found the derringer. Tucking it in her medical bag, she hurried out the back door.

Charcoal gray clouds had rolled in, blotting out the sun. Thunder rumbled in the distance, and the wind had kicked up, swirling leaves on the path as Mariah hurried along. She was hindered by her full-skirted dress with its layers of petticoats and by the thin satin slippers, which gave no protection from the sharp stones underfoot.

As she approached the cave, Mariah prayed that Lazarus hadn't been harmed. Whoever had taken him before had obviously come back. Why?

Mariah stopped in the shelter of the trees and stared at the wide entrance to Devil's Cave. The hair on the nape of her neck prickled ominously, sending slivers of fear up her spine. Cautiously, she began to circle around the hill.

Footsteps crunched behind her, and Mariah swung around, her heart hammering against her ribs. No one was there. She waited a few moments, then moved on.

A twig snapped to her right. Mariah gasped, but it was only a squirrel. She wiped a perspiring palm on her skirt, shifted her bag, and wiped the other. Tightening her grip on the handle, she continued on until she'd completed her circuit of the hill. But she saw no sign of either her dog or his kidnapper.

Her watch read two minutes after five o'clock. She stared at the opening, uncertain of her next move. Finally, Mariah called softly, "Here, Laz."

She heard a whimper from inside the cave and called again. Why didn't he come? Was he hurt?

Sharp talons of fear gripped her heart as Mariah slowly approached the cavern's mouth. She squinted into the dim interior but could only see a few yards inside.

"Laz?" Another whimper. Mariah frantically

searched her memory. Where were the emergency candles and matches she and Ben had stashed in the cave?

Taking a breath, she stepped inside and waited for her eyes to adjust. She shivered at the cold clamminess, remembering each detail of the cave, even to the smell of the damp air.

At its center the main cavern was one story tall, with smooth, slippery limestone walls and a floor strewn with layers of dead leaves. At the back was a smaller opening to a narrow, twisted passage that led deep inside the hill, winding, dipping, then forking into two paths, both leading to a deep underground lake.

As her vision adjusted, Mariah went quickly to the right side and knelt down, feeling along the rocks until she found the emergency tin. She pried it open with shaking fingers, removed a candle and match, and lit it.

Holding the candle, she moved deeper into the cavern, quickly scanning the area. She heard Lazarus whimper again and saw him tied to an iron ring near the back. He was muzzled but seemed unharmed.

Mariah felt the prickling again, but when she looked around, the cave was empty. Clutching her bag in trembling hands, she spoke, trying to keep her voice steady. "It's five o'clock, just as the note said."

She waited, but there was no answer. Her nerves felt ready to snap as she moved cautiously toward

Laz, who whimpered and watched her with frightened eyes.

"It's okay, Laz. I'm here." Mariah knelt down beside him, wedged the candle between two rocks, found the scalpel in her bag, and sawed at the thick rope.

"Don't do that, Mariah," a voice hissed.

With a gasp, Mariah jerked around. In the opening, a dark shape stood silhouetted against the light.

Mariah quickly doused the candle and pushed it behind the rock. In the next instant, a match was struck and then, by the flickering light of a lantern, she saw Luther's face, a mask of malevolence that made her shrink back in terror.

"It *is* all right if I call you Mariah, isn't it?"

She swallowed hard, trying to keep her voice from shaking. "What do you want?"

"What do you want, *Luther*," he corrected. "Say it, Mariah. Say my name."

"Wh-what do you want, Luther?"

"Much better. But shouldn't I be asking that question?" Luther moved toward her. "What do *you* want? Do you want your dog back? Do you want the truth about the explosion? Or do you want one last wish before you die?"

Mariah shifted her body to hide her bag. She had to get him to talk, to divert his attention so that she could reach her gun. "I'd like the truth—if you know it."

"Sure I know it. Who do you think planned that explosion?" Luther set the lantern on the ground between them, then crouched down to face her. "Who, Mariah?"

"You."

"That's right, me," he said, thumping his chest. "I know all about dynamite—like how it behaves when it gets old." He laughed harshly. "No one thought to check the holes before they dropped in the uncapped sticks."

"Why did you kill your friends at the quarry?"

He shrugged. "It had to be done."

"Just so the senator could win his election?"

Luther's eyes grew flat and cold. "He has to win. It means everything to him."

Behind her back, Mariah slipped her hand into the bag. Her fingers moved over the objects until she found the derringer. "So his selfishness justifies murder? What a sterling trait for our noble senator."

Luther leaned toward her, his eyes snapping with outrage. "Don't say that, Mariah. The senator is a good man. He deserves to win."

"He deserves to go to prison." Quickly, Mariah jumped to her feet, aiming the gun directly at him. "And so do you."

Shock flickered briefly in Luther's eyes, then, with a sly grin, he stood up. "You won't shoot me. You're a doctor."

"Don't tempt me." Keeping the gun pointed at him, Mariah knelt beside Lazarus and picked up the scalpel in her left hand. Awkwardly, she tried to cut the rope, but made little progress on the thick hemp.

"Why don't you use this?" Luther flicked open a switchblade and gave her a chilling smile. "It works real well. Let me show you."

Lazarus growled, straining against his tether. But his muzzle gave him no chance to protect either himself or Mariah.

"You tried to kill Laz, didn't you?" she cried.

"I tried to frighten you off, but you just wouldn't go."

"Stop, Luther," she ordered, as he advanced on her. "I swear I'll shoot you."

He halted directly in front of Lazarus. As though the dog sensed his peril, Laz backed to the end of the short rope. Mariah began to tremble so hard that she had to drop the scalpel to hold her gun hand steady. She was not going to let Luther kill her dog.

"Don't touch him, Luther," she commanded, through chattering teeth. "This is your last warning."

He laughed. "Go ahead, Doc. Shoot me."

As he raised the blade above Laz's head, Mariah fired, the bullet missing Luther by several feet.

"You bitch!" he cried, falling back on his elbows.

Mariah's heart slammed against her ribs as Luther sprang toward her. Only one bullet remained.

She pointed the gun at his head, shut her eyes, and fired. When she opened her eyes, Luther was staring at his left shoulder. But it was only a flesh wound—not enough to stop him.

He began to laugh, an insane sound that sent

chills up her spine. "Good try, Doc. Too bad you're out of bullets."

Flinging the gun at his head, Mariah grabbed the lantern and fled through the narrow opening in the back wall. Without light, Luther wouldn't be able to see. He would either have to leave the cave or follow her. Either way, Laz would be spared.

She heard the crunch of leaves behind her and knew he was on her trail. Now she was running for her life.

Chapter 30

~~~⌒⌒~~~

With the letters clutched in her hand, Annie rushed up the deserted street, her heart beating so fast she thought she'd faint. She had to find help.

Ahead, she spotted Jake coming toward her. "Oh, Jake, thank heavens!"

"What happened?"

Annie thrust the two notes at him. "This came for Mariah at the reception, and I found this note on my desk. Mariah must have gone to the cave. I've looked everywhere for her."

Jake's heart lurched as he read the messages. The first asked her to come to the dispensary for an emergency. There was no signature on it. The second was the one that truly frightened him. But why would Mariah take such a risk? She had to know the danger she'd be in.

"Take this note to the sheriff," he instructed. "I'll head for the cave."

Lightning crackled across the sky as Jake tore through the woods. His feet felt weighed down, as though he was running through mud. What if he was too late to help her?

When he finally emerged from the trees, Jake stopped short. Devil's Cave yawned before him like a giant toothless mouth, waiting to swallow him alive. Squeezing his hands into fists, he gulped air, fighting the nauseating panic that threatened to cripple him.

"Mariah," he called hoarsely.

He heard a dog's whimper and briefly thought he'd imagined it. But then he heard it again. "Lazarus," he called, and again heard an answering whimper.

Mariah had to be nearby. Why hadn't she answered?

Jake's legs felt like blocks of wood as he took a step forward and then another. Sweat dotted his forehead as he peered inside.

The whimpering grew louder and more frantic, but Jake couldn't bring himself to go further. Flashes of memory sent violent shudders through him. He saw himself walking out of that gaping mouth with his best friend's lifeless body in his arms.

Jake wiped sweat from his eyes. He had failed Ben. He couldn't fail Mariah.

Dragging deep breaths into his lungs, he stepped several feet into the darkness and crouched down, feeling along the bottom edge of one wall for the tin. To his surprise, it was open. Mariah must have used one of the candles.

Jake lit another and stood, carefully scanning the area. As his sight adjusted to the gloom, he saw Lazarus tied at the back with Mariah's black bag nearby.

"It's all right, Laz," he soothed as he knelt beside the dog. Jake spotted the scalpel and guessed Mariah had tried to cut the rope. Something or someone had stopped her. He glanced up at the small opening that led to the underground lake, fighting a fresh wave of panic. Mariah must have fled through it.

Lazarus tugged frantically on his tether, but Jake feared untying him. The dog would undoubtedly charge in after Mariah, barking furiously. Until Jake knew what her circumstances were, he couldn't take the chance.

"You'll have to stay here, boy."

Wiping his forehead with his sleeve, Jake rose and started for the tunnel.

"Bitch!" Luther roared. "You won't get away from me. You can't hide in there forever."

Mariah heard his raspy breathing as he followed her. She had to duck her head as the tunnel got smaller. The walls were damp and slick, and a thin stream of water ran down the middle of the stone floor, making the footing treacherous.

The path turned sharply and then split. Mariah

took the right fork, then immediately doused the lantern. She hadn't been through the maze since she was a child, but her memory was as keen as if it had been only yesterday.

"Dang it!" she heard Luther shout as the tunnel went black.

Mariah knew there was nothing more disorienting than pervasive darkness. Now she had the advantage.

The path began a steep climb and then turned to the left. At the turn she stopped to tuck the hem of her skirt into her waistband, then hurried on.

Finally, Mariah emerged onto a narrow ledge that surrounded the deep underground lake where her brother had drowned. Hoping she had lost Luther in the dark maze, she stopped to light the lantern. She dared not proceed along the slippery path without light.

The ledge encircled the lake only three feet above the water, with another opening at the opposite side leading to a passageway back to the outside. Mariah edged along the rim, her back against the cold limestone. She spied an iron peg in the wall a foot above her head and hooked the handle of the lantern on it so she could move more quickly.

"You think you're smarter than me, don't you?"

Mariah turned with a gasp to see Luther standing on the ledge behind her, his features deformed by madness.

Mariah inched backward. "I *am* smarter than you, Luther," she said with false bravado. "Do you think I'd come out here without letting the sheriff know?"

"Let the bastard come. He'll find you dead, floating in the lake." Luther flicked open his knife and started toward her.

Mariah backed up, shaking so violently she feared she would slip over the side. She gulped back a sob of terror. Luther was just a few feet away. Her only hope for escape was to jump into the lake and swim across. But what if Luther circled around faster than she was able to swim?

A movement several yards behind him caught her eye—a hunched form that crept from the opening onto the ledge and slowly straightened. For a moment, Mariah was too stunned to react, then tears of relief sprang to her eyes.

Jake had come to save her.

Jake kept his gaze fixed on Mariah, afraid that if he glanced at the water he'd be paralyzed. Her fancy gown was muddy and torn. Her hair had come loose from its pins, and her face was smudged with dirt. And the look of terror on her face tore through his gut.

He pressed one finger to his lips to warn Mariah not to give him away. At once, she began to talk to Luther, keeping her back flat against the wall. "I knew y-you were lying about Jake s-selling out," she said in a shaking voice. "Jake would n-never put his men's jobs in j-jeopardy."

Luther snorted contemptuously. "He's a weakling. Why do you think the senator had to go behind his back?"

"H-how much did the senator p-pay you for setting the explosion?"

Jake was within reaching distance when Luther suddenly swung around, his knife clutched in his hand. "Bastard! You think I didn't know you were there? Come on, Jake," he said, motioning him closer. "Come get me."

Jake's fists came up, his fury so strong that he knew he could easily kill Luther with his bare hands. Luther feigned a lunge and Jake dodged it, but as he swayed back, he made the mistake of glancing down at the lake.

"Jake!" Mariah cried in alarm, as he fought for balance.

Quickly, Luther pivoted and grabbed Mariah's left forearm, dragging her in front of him and pressing his knife to her throat. Mariah gasped as he inched her toward the water.

"You can't outsmart me, Jake," Luther shouted, his voice ricocheting off the walls like bullets. "No one can outsmart me."

Jake clenched his fists as sweat trickled down his forehead. "I'll tear you apart if you harm her."

"That's brave talk for a man with no weapon. Look at him, Mariah. The mighty Jake Sullivan is sweating. Are you scared, Jake? Sure you are. You're wondering if you can stop me from killing her. Well, you can't, so which way should Mariah die? I can cut her throat and end her misery quickly, or I can slice her belly, push her into the lake, and let her drown. You decide."

Jake's heart seemed to skid to a stop. If he made a move, Luther would cut her throat, and Mariah would die regardless of what he did to save her.

"What do you want, Luther? Money?"

Luther's insane laughter echoed through the chamber. "Money. Isn't that just like him, Mariah? He thinks money will solve everything."

"Isn't th-that why you killed those men?" Mariah rasped.

"I told you I did that for the senator, Mariah. Money doesn't mean as much to me as it does to Jake. Say, Jake, do you want to buy Mariah? How much is she worth?"

"Name your price."

"How about your life for hers?"

"It's a deal. Let her go."

Luther's face stiffened. "You still think you can outsmart me, don't you?" He pressed the knife point into Mariah's neck. "Which way will she die, Jake? Decide, or I'll do it for you."

Jake's gaze shifted to Mariah's terrified green eyes. He blinked hard as sweat blurred his vision. He'd tried to save Ben, but he hadn't been quick or strong enough.

He couldn't fail again. There was no way in hell he'd let Mariah die.

He forced a mocking smile, forced his hands to uncurl and his shoulders to relax, assuming a casual stance. "Coffman was right about you after all."

Luther's eyes narrowed. "What are you talking about?"

"He said you were a coward."

"The senator wouldn't say that. He's like a father to me. He trusts me."

"That's not what he told me."

"You're a liar!"

"Then why are you still working in the stables? Why hasn't he made you a partner? He would have made his son a partner," Jake scoffed. "You *are* a coward, Luther, hiding behind a woman's skirts with a knife in your hand. You can't come face-to-face with a man, can you, *boy*?"

Insanity glittered in Luther's eyes as he slowly lowered the knife and let it clatter to the ground. Jake let his breath out. Now to get Mariah out of harm's way.

Suddenly, Luther gave Mariah a hard shove, sending her flying out over the water. For a moment she seemed to hang suspended in the air, her face registering shock, then she dropped into the blackness.

Luther swung to face Jake, his fists raised, evil radiating from his body. "Now it's your turn."

Time halted for Jake as the ripples closed around Mariah. All he could see was Ben's face as he disappeared beneath the inky surface.

It was happening again.

Fighting the heavy layers of skirts, Mariah kicked her way to the top and greedily gulped air, shoving sodden locks of hair out of her eyes.

Above her, she saw the panic on Jake's face as he scanned the water, oblivious to the man who stood ready to kill him.

"I can swim, Jake," she cried, her voice ringing off the limestone walls. "I'm all right."

His expression turned to blind rage, and he swung around to square off with Luther.

In that instant, Mariah realized what her father and Owen had been trying to tell her: Jake hadn't caused her brother's death. He would have done everything in his power to save Ben. He had taken the blame needlessly—to protect her.

She stared, astounded, as Jake grabbed the smaller man and lifted him over his head. With his teeth clenched and the veins in his neck straining from the effort, he heaved Luther out into the lake with a roar of fury.

Mariah swam toward the ledge. "Jake," she cried, "help me up!"

As though her voice finally penetrated the red veil of rage over his eyes, Jake glanced down at her, then dropped to his knees to grab her hand. He pulled Mariah into his arms, hugging her tightly to his chest.

"Mariah," he said in a ragged voice, "I don't know what I would have done if I'd lost you."

"Jake," she gasped breathlessly, taking his face between her hands, "I love you."

"I love you, too, Mariah. Dear God, how I love you!"

At that moment, Luther surfaced, beating the

water with his hands and gasping for air. "Help! I can't swim," he cried, sinking once again.

Jake swung around to stare at the water, yet he made no move to save Luther. For an instant, Mariah wondered if he intended to let him drown. But then Jake jumped to his feet, kicked off his shoes, and dove into the chill water.

Suddenly, shouts echoed through the tunnel. Mariah ran to the opening and saw a distant glow. "We're here," she called. "Hurry!"

A few moments later, Sheriff Logan appeared, followed by several deputies. They watched anxiously as Jake tried to help the struggling, terrified man.

The sheriff tossed down a noosed rope. "Here, Jake, grab hold."

Jake swam to the rope and grabbed the end, then looped it under Luther's arms. He trod water as the men hauled Luther up, then he grabbed the rope again and let them pull him up.

Mariah wrapped her arms around Jake's waist and gazed up at him, her heart swelling with love. "I knew you wouldn't let Luther drown."

"There's been enough death in our lives," he said, stroking her wet hair.

As soon as they reached the outside, Annie and Eliza came running up with blankets and nonstop questions. Luther was handcuffed and led away, while Jake talked to the sheriff. Mariah hastily recounted her story to Annie and her sister, then glanced over at Jake, her heart overflowing with emotion. "I'll be home soon," she said. "I have to talk to Jake."

She waited quietly beside Jake as the sheriff finished writing his notes.

"I'd say Senator Coffman is in for a big loss this year," Logan commented dryly. "Wonder how he'll take to a bench in a jail cell instead of a seat in Congress?" He closed his small notebook. "What's this going to do to the quarry, Jake?"

"Save it. Now I can run it my way."

Mariah waited until everyone had gone, then she turned to Jake, taking his hands in hers. "I need to talk to you."

"Every time you say that, I get a lecture."

"Not this time."

"Tell me something first," Jake said, raising her hands to his lips. "Did you mean what you said in there?"

"Every word of it. You're a good man, Jake. And I know you tried to save Ben. All these years I blamed you for Ben's death, when it seems I was the only one who didn't know—and didn't want to know—the truth. But please don't be angry with Owen. The whole account was recorded in one of my father's notebooks. I'd just never looked."

The weight of the world seemed to be lifted from Jake's shoulders. He closed his eyes and let out his breath, feeling born anew. Then he drew her hands to his lips and kissed them, gazing down into the eyes of the woman he adored.

Mariah smiled and wrapped her arms around

his neck. "I love you, Jake Sullivan, with all my heart."

He kissed her lightly, then with building passion, until she gasped for breath.

"I love you, Mariah," he said, kissing her eyelids, her nose, her temples, her chin. "I've loved you forever, and I'll love you always." His arms tightened around her. "You're the best thing that ever happened to me. When I came back to Coffee Creek and found you gone, I thought my life was over. And when you returned, I was afraid to let myself hope that there could ever be anything between us again."

Mariah laughed and cried at the same time. "I felt the same way."

He kissed her again. "Let's go home and change and then see if we can drag the preacher away from the food at the reception."

She gave him a coy glance. "Why would you want to do that?"

"To make you the happiest woman in the world."

Mariah gasped in mock outrage. "You beast!"

"Brat," he laughed.

"Kiss me again," she demanded, leaning into him.

"Not until you say 'I do.' "

"I *do* want you to kiss me again—and I *do* want to marry you."

Jake picked her up, ignoring her cries of protest as he carried her away. "Time's a-wasting, Dr. Sullivan."

**Take a break from the holiday hustle
and bustle with Avon Romance.
Two fantastic love stories . . . by two
unforgettable authors.**

She's the Rita Award-winning author who is
also known as Ruth Wind . . .

Don't miss **Barbara Samuel's**

NIGHT OF FIRE

Imagine Cassandra St. Ives' surprise when she discovers her secret admirer is no proper gentleman . . . but a virile stranger who knows her heart's desires.

She's been called "a superior writer" by
Romantic Times . . .

Don't miss **Margaret Evans Porter's**

IMPROPER ADVANCES

Darius thinks the stunning widow Oriana Julian is a scheming adventuress . . . but she stirs in him an undeniable passion he is powerless to resist.